TWISTED

Nick Stryker Series,

Book Two

The Shallow End Gals

TERESA DUNCAN

VICKI GRAYBOSCH

LINDA MCGREGOR

KIMBERLY TROUTMAN

Copyright, 2015 Vicki Graybosch & Teresa Duncan & Linda McGregor & Kimberly Troutman
All rights reserved
Printed in the United States of America
Copyrighted Material
ISBN: 1511452870
ISBN 13: 9781511452878
Library of Congress Control Number: 2015904834
CreateSpace Independent Publishing Platform
North Charleston, South Carolina
Edited by Erika Canter
Cover Photography by Kamber Lee Hadley

Books by The Shallow End Gals
Alcohol Was Not Involved,
Book One of Trilogy
Extreme Heat Warning,
Book Two of Trilogy
Silent Crickets,
Book Three of Trilogy
Catahoula, Book four of Series

The Nick Stryker Series
Cusp of Crazy, Book One

Twisted, Book Two

A very special thank you to:

Sheryl Noland

Michael Sutherland

List of Characters at the End
of the Book

CHAPTER 1

Monday 6:45 p.m.

A key scratched in the lock. He quickly tightened the blanket around his shoulders and faced the wall in a fetal position. He willed his breathing to slow and prayed they would think he was sleeping. He heard heavy footsteps. Someone had walked toward the cot and stopped. A large finger pried his eyelid open. He forced his eyes to look back into his head and not stare at his captor. The finger released his lid and a rush of cold air replaced the warmth of the blanket. His veins surrendered to the icy burn of the drug as it pulled him into total darkness and back to the edge of hell.

* * *

54 Dalton Street, Chicago

Karen Lomas had grudgingly planned tonight's surprise birthday party for her husband, Reggie. His parents had flown into Chicago expecting her to have something special planned. Few people on this earth were more miserly, narrow minded and unlikable than Reggie. His parents were among them. Karen was financially trapped in a loveless, mind numbing existence until she completed her online courses next fall. With a well-paying job already secured and waiting, she took some comfort that this would be the last birthday of Reggie's she had to endure.

Karen threatened two of his coworkers into attending and Reggie's only friend had brought the cake. That was good; she had forgotten a cake. Karen had grabbed a couple of ties from Reggie's closet and wrapped them as his gift. He'd never know the difference. She wasn't about to spend money from her meager household account on him.

Reggie's parents had arrived early with one of his childhood photos blown up and framed as his gift. She wondered how they had ever gotten it on the plane. It was a 24 by 24, ten year old toothless Reggie, in his undersized baseball uniform. Karen left for the kitchen when Reggie's mom began walking around the living room with a hammer and nail.

Karen took a swig from a vodka bottle, replaced the cap, and gasped as it burned its way down her throat. She wasn't a drinker, yet. She heard the kids laughing at grandpa's tired magic tricks. She cringed at the sound of the hammer banging on her newly patched plaster walls. The living room crowd clapped. The picture was hung; the deed was done.

Reggie's mom screeched from the living room, "It's almost seven, Karen! You better get in here! We're turning the lights out now."

Karen snatched a piece of cheese from the snack tray and glanced up at the clock. Six fifty nine. She still had six minutes. The one thing she could give Reggie credit for was predictability. He always arrived home at precisely five minutes past seven. Karen glanced at her reflection in the microwave door. She was still pretty. There was still time. She walked to stand in the doorway between the kitchen and living room. That awful picture now glared at her from over her fireplace. Chips of plaster were scattered across the hearth.

Everyone stood silent in the dark. Reggie's mom stood to the side of the door with one hand on the light switch and the other hand up to her mouth signaling quiet.

Reggie walked up the front steps, disappointed that the house was dark. He would have thought that Karen might have at least fixed him a dinner on his birthday. He turned the doorknob and pushed open the door.

The living room light came on and a crowd shouted "Surprise!" at the very instant his head exploded from a sniper's bullet.

* * *

Attorney James Baxter's cell phone rang as he pulled into his brownstone's garage. The caller ID was blocked or the caller was using a burner phone. "Yes?"

Alexia Cummings' voice screeched from the other end. "Do you know what time it is?"

James had arranged for Alexia's husband to be shot when he arrived home at precisely seven this evening. Alexia had paid 50 grand for this divorce alternative. James looked at his watch: 7:30 p.m. "Is there a problem?"

Alexia paused before answering curtly, "You could say that. I never received that package you promised would be delivered tonight." Even though she was on a disposable cell, Alexia wanted to be careful of what she said. It was well known that Attorney James Baxter represented the mob. She was already nervous doing business with him.

James exited his BMW. The lock chirped on his car as he walked to the door. "Something must have happened. I'll get back to you." He disconnected the call and punched in Frankie's number.

Eventually Frankie answered, "Yeah."

James tried to control his anger. Using Frankie for these hits was risky. If the mob found out they were contracting jobs on the side, they were both dead. At one time, Frankie was the best hit man the Chicago crew ever had. He was still trusted and, in theory, enjoying his retirement.

"I've got an unhappy customer at 45 Dalton Street." James waited for Frankie's excuse.

Frankie frantically pulled a slip of paper from his shirt pocket. Did James just say 45 Dalton Street? He had written down 54 Dalton Street. Frankie's hands began to shake. He willed them to stop and answered, "I had a problem. There were too many people around. Tell her I'll do it tomorrow."

James detected nervousness in Frankie's voice. "Are you okay? You're starting to worry me. If we mess up and Dom finds out, we're dead. This bitch is 50 grand pissed."

Frankie steadied his voice even though his mind was swirling. "I told you I'd take care of it."

Frankie glanced at his rifle case resting on the couch and slowly hung his jacket in the closet. He slid the gun case under his bed, walked back to the kitchen and poured himself two fingers of scotch. The booze burned his throat. He noticed that he had left the milk out on the counter. He could have sworn he had put it away.

A rush of fear swept through Frankie's mind. What had he done? This was a serious mistake. How could he fix this? Frankie forced his mind to focus. The newspaper will report the shooting at 54 Dalton Street. James will figure out he had hit the wrong address. James will distance himself from Frankie, and then set him up. That's how it works. The bitch at 45 Dalton Street might figure this out, too. Frankie's arthritis was gnawing at his knees. Damn it. He didn't have a choice. He had two more kills to do tonight.

Frankie layered up in his heavy, brown cardigan and long coat. He checked his pistol, dropped it into his pocket and descended down the steps to the sidewalk. As he walked toward the bus stop, he remembered when he had to disguise himself as an old man for a hit. There was spring crispness to the night air and the sidewalks glistened from a recent brief shower. Frankie's allergies relaxed in the clean air.

Frankie rang the doorbell at 45 Dalton Street. He briefly wondered who he had shot less than an hour earlier just a block away. Alexia opened the door and Frankie shot her between the eyes. The quiet 'pop' was barely audible. As she slid down the doorframe, Frankie picked up the newspaper from the stoop and slowly walked back toward the bus stop. He still had to visit James.

On the small front lawn at 54 Dalton Street, patrol officers struggled to keep the victim's mother under control. The wife, Karen, was squatting down, her arms embracing her two children. Nick Stryker, Homicide Detective, and Jen Taylor, Nick's partner, stood in the center of the living room. The coroner and Crime Scene Unit were preparing the body of Reggie Lomas for transport to the morgue.

One of the CSU agents walked over. "We're done here. Looks like everything happened right at the door like they said. Single bullet, a .300 Winchester Magnum, or something like it based on the damage. We'll know more after we get him on the table."

Nick tilted his head for Jen to walk away from the crowd with him. "What's your take on the wife?"

Jen shrugged. "I'm sure she's upset for the kids, but I haven't seen a tear yet."

Nick respected Jen's instincts. Jen wasn't sold on the wife's innocence.

Nick glanced out the front door. "This was a sniper shot. Got that little park across the street; I'm going to check it out. See if you can't get a list of family friends, business associates, anything."

Jen kept her voice soft and answered, "Not that many people here for a surprise party. Could be there aren't many friends." Jen noted the oversized picture of a young Reggie over the fireplace and plaster chips on the hearth. The furnishings were what her mom would call 'thrift store treasures'. It was a pricey neighborhood. Jen was surprised at how austere the interior was furnished. Her mom would call it 'shabby sad'.

Jen added, "I'll see if she won't come in for an interview in the morning, and I'll have her sign a release for bank and phone records now."

Nick pressured the Crime Scene Unit to work through the crime scene quickly. He wanted to be able to release it back to the family as soon as possible. It was always hard when family members witnessed the murder of a loved one, especially children. Nick's five years in homicide hadn't made dealing with grieving family members any easier.

Nick walked to the small park across the street and walked around a six foot tall memorial wall. The wall would have provided cover for the shooter. Scrape marks on the concrete walk confirmed that the iron park bench had been slid to rest against the back of the wall. It made a perfect step ladder.

Nick whistled for a CSU agent to join him. "Our shooter stood here. Check the bench and the top of that wall for prints." Nick knew they wouldn't find any. He glanced behind him again. A row of shrubs across from the walk would have offered perfect cover. The sidewalk circled back toward the street from each side of the memorial wall. The neighboring building was windowless on the side facing the park. Everything pointed to a professional job.

Sticky, wet dogwood blossoms carpeted the sidewalk and grass along the walk. Tonight, the tiny neighborhood park was both a beautiful, green oasis blanketed in dogwood blossoms and the chosen spot of a killer.

Nick's phone buzzed. He listened to dispatch announce another shooting victim one block away. He lifted the crime scene tape, crossed the street and touched the coroner's shoulder. "You're going to get a call to head down the block. 45 Dalton. We'll meet you there."

Jen also received a call on the second shooting and met Nick at their car. "I guess we can come back later to canvas the neighborhood."

Nick grinned as he pulled their car into traffic. "Livin' the dream."

Jen smiled, "You better call Lacey. You're going to miss that awards dinner tonight."

Nick cursed. "I forgot all about that, thanks."

Jen listened to Nick make his apologies as they sped down the block. She was convinced he couldn't handle a real relationship without her help. He was so single-minded when on a case that he had left her at crime scenes.

Nick glanced over, "Once again, you saved my butt."

Jen shook her head. "It's purely selfish. If I marry you off, I don't have to watch over you anymore."

* * *

Attorney James Baxter stood at his back door as his wife's Pekinese sniffed the bushes and grass for the perfect spot to do her duty. She had scratched a circle in at least three spots before deciding they were unworthy of her droppings. The dog never noticed him stumble forward from the steps and fold down onto the lawn, his lifeless form only feet from the orb of the back door's light. Frankie considered taking the dog. Cute little bugger. He decided he didn't want the bother. He'd probably just kill it after a few days anyway.

He was tired and Dom had called a meeting for the morning. It wasn't that often he was included in mob business these days. Something special was on the agenda. He needed to be fresh and alert, especially now that he had just shot Dom's attorney.

* * *

45 Dalton Street, Chicago

The Coroner whispered to Nick, "This is going to get messy."

"How so?"

"Do you know who that guy is?" The coroner pointed to the grieving husband.

Nick glanced over his shoulder and back to the coroner. Jen leaned in closer to hear.

The coroner said, "Travis Cummings, investment banker for the mob."

Jen moaned, "Great."

Nick looked at the wound between Alexia's eyes. "This wasn't a case of mistaken identity. This was up close and personal. If he tests clean for gunshot residue, this might have been a warning shot."

Jen added, "From very bad people."

Nick leaned against the trunk of his car as he jotted notes from the street scene. The amber street lights cast eerie shadows down the long sidewalks. The brownstone adjacent to the Cummings' residence did not have a front light on. Nick walked to stand at the edge of the darkness. In his peripheral vision, he saw something lodged at the edge of the sidewalk in the wet grass. He bent down; it was a dogwood blossom. Neither he nor Jen had walked that far from the crime scene.

Nick bagged the blossom and asked each of the responders if they had walked on that part of the sidewalk. None of them had been more than fifty feet from the crime scene. Jen joined Nick outdoors and raised her eyebrows at the sight of his plastic evidence bag, "We have something?"

Nick smiled as he handed Jen the baggie. "No dogwoods on this block." He winked. "But there are plenty in the park across from 54 Dalton."

CHAPTER 2

Tuesday 8:00 a.m.

*H*e forced his mind to focus on his body. He practiced moving his fingers and toes, and did some deep breathing exercises. He sat upright on the cot and dangled his legs over the side. The small room began to spin, but he hung on to the edge of the mattress. His hearing seemed impaired. Noises outside the room sounded as if they were underwater or miles away.

There was a very small window secured with iron bars up near the ceiling. Bright rays of daylight streamed to the corner of his cot. He held his hand in the beam and gasped at the purple bruises and dehydrated skin. How long had he been here? He tried to remember where he was, who he was; before they came back.

* * *

Mitch had a small computer station set up behind the sandwich case of 'Momma's Corner'. He and his mother owned the sandwich/ newspaper shop, and the morning rush had just ended. Momma had excused herself to freshen up and Mitch had decided to work on some of the charity brochures for Joseph's homeless community in the tunnels.

The bells at the door jingled and announced the arrival of a well-dressed elderly man. Mitch rose to wait on him.

The elderly man removed his hat and said, "Good morning, young man. I have an appointment with Momma, but I see I'm a little early. Would you be so kind as to inform her that Artie is here?"

Mitch opened his mouth to answer just as Momma whipped through the curtain door from the back and squealed. "As I live and breathe! Artie my love. Give Momma a big smooch!"

Artie wrapped Momma in his arms and planted a kiss on her cheek. He pulled back and studied her face. "How did you manage to become even more beautiful after 25 years?"

Momma giggled, squeezed Artie's waist and turned to look at Mitch. "I've been waitin' on that kiss for 25 years." Momma's face erupted into a toothy smile and Artie kissed her cheek again.

Mitch stammered and walked over to shake Artie's hand. "Obviously you're a good friend of Momma's. I'm Mitch, her son."

Artie smiled and clasped both his hands around Mitch's. He turned to look at Momma. Artie raised one eyebrow and Momma nodded. Artie smiled at

Mitch and said, "You are a fine looking gentleman. Momma did well. We need a proper introduction. My name is Artie Corsone. I have loved your mother for 40 years. Sadly, she didn't love me back." Artie's eyes twinkled. "I am honored that she considers me her good friend."

Momma gestured for Artie and Mitch to sit at the small café table by the window. She served them each a cup of tea and said, "Artie saved us from the cruelty of your father. You could say he's been our guardian angel. He made sure we had everything we needed all of these years. He even paid for most of your college." Momma brushed a tear from her cheek. "This is the first I've seen him in 25 years." Momma reached across the table and squeezed Artie's hand. He raised her hand to his lips and gave her a soft kiss.

Mitch looked at Artie, "Thank you. I...I'm not sure what to say. Where have you been for 25 years?"

Momma answered, "He's the best forger the mob ever had. He's been in prison until this morning."

Artie corrected her. "Actually, I prefer the title 'document man', or artist. Pick which one you like best." He shrugged and smiled.

Mitch's jaw dropped as Momma giggled again and kissed Artie's cheek.

* * *

Nick arrived at the 107th Precinct to find Jen already busy at her computer. They had gone home for a few hours of sleep after canvassing both blocks of Dalton Street last night. Much of the information they needed now would come from bank records and CSU reports. Detective Wayne Dunfee was napping in his chair.

Jen whispered, "Lacey forgive you last night?"

Nick's boyish grin spread across his face as his eyes twinkled. "I gave her my most heartfelt apology."

Jen mumbled, "I just bet you did," and looked back to her computer.

Nick sat at his desk and pulled up the reports for the morning. Jen had already done much of the work on the reports for their two homicides. Nick noticed Wayne had pulled a homicide last night, too, Attorney James Baxter.

Nick whispered over to Jen, "Why do I know that name: Attorney James Baxter?"

Wayne opened his eyes, "Big mob lawyer."

Jen and Nick exchanged glances.

Nick walked over to Wayne's desk. "Let's play poker. I call ya. I've got a mob banker's wife, and I'll raise you a dogwood blossom." Nick dropped the baggie on Wayne's desk.

Wayne yawned and stretched his arms to the ceiling. "Crap."

* * *

Six men sat at the round table in the back of an obscure bar. The lights were dim and the air hung heavy with the stench of stale whiskey and cigars. Two large men flanked the group and stood to face anyone foolish enough to approach.

Frankie hadn't slept well. He was nervous. His whole life had been tied to Dom's crew. He had survived because he didn't make mistakes. Now he was making mistakes. His aging mind was playing tricks on him, setting him up. He had to focus and be extra careful, extra sure about everything he did and said.

The crew had made sure that he had a free place to live, a generous monthly stipend, and a few jobs to keep him loyal. He had earned his position with Dom. He was one of a handful of men Dom trusted.

Obviously the meeting had started long before Frankie had been told to arrive. Newspapers were thrown on the floor and Dom's face was flushed in anger. He had been shouting. Frankie could tell from the facial expressions of the other men: this was not a pleasant meeting.

Dom gestured for Frankie to sit. "You know four of our boys got out of prison this week?" Dom pointed to the newspapers on the floor. "Carson got popped two blocks from the prison after he got released yesterday. Two blocks!" Dom slammed his fist on the table. "I'm gonna find out who did this!" Dom's eyes had narrowed. Frankie felt the effect of lasers shooting toward him. He hadn't seen Dom this animated in years.

Frankie flinched as Dom suddenly leaned forward and pointed at him.

"Our banker's wife and our lawyer got popped last night, too. Somebody's lookin' to make a statement." Dom leaned his chair back and took a slow drag on his cigar. "I got ears and eyes on this already. Could be the Feds, could be the heroin boys lookin' to expand business." Dom focused on Frankie and whispered, "When I get a name, I want you to take care of it. We understand each other?"

Frankie twisted in his chair. It was bad enough he had shot Dom's lawyer, he didn't know he had shot Dom's banker's wife. He prayed he had covered his tracks well enough that Dom would finger someone else. Dom was the boss for the Westside crew. Frankie tried to sound stern. "Got it."

Dom nodded approval. "In the meantime, we look out for our own. Until we line up a place for Artie, he stays with you. Shouldn't be more than a few days. We've got FBI up our shorts just waitin' for us to make a mistake."

Dom waved his hand to shoo Frankie away. "Make Artie feel welcome, but keep your business to yourself. He's always been a weak link. Too soft. If it wasn't for his father's memory, I'd pop him myself. You're retired, understand? The heat will be watchin' him close; that's why I want him with you. You know how to keep yourself clean."

Frankie stood to leave, "I understand."

Outside the bar, Frankie hailed a cab and cursed under his breath. He not only had to keep his continued active employment with the mob secret from Artie and the FBI, he had to hide his 'side jobs' from everybody. If Dom ever found out he was supplementing his income and risking the crew, he'd be the next prone, bloody body circled by cops and photographers. Artie would arrive at Frankie's apartment sometime this afternoon. Frankie exhaled; the first thing he had to do was get that head out of his freezer.

* * *

Mitch took care of the morning customers as Momma and Artie caught up at the corner table. Each time the store was empty of customers they broke into animated conversation. Mitch tried hard not to listen in, but it was so darn interesting. Artie had the inside scoop on everything in and out of prison. Artie was quite the charmer and Mitch was mesmerized.

Artie glanced over and saw that Mitch was staring at them, his wiping rag frozen on the glass case and his jaw dropped. Artie tried to remember the last thing he had just said.

Artie smiled at Mitch. "What I meant to say was the guy was a great swimmer! Not that he was swimmin' with the fishes." Artie and Momma laughed. Mitch nodded his head quickly and resumed his work. Holy Jesus.

The door chimes jingled and Mitch's friend Eli entered the store. Mitch enthusiastically greeted him. "Eli!"

Eli glanced around and saw Momma and a man at the corner table. The rest of the store was empty. Eli shrugged. "Hey, I'm going to be a no show for darts tonight. Sis's car finally died. Her neighbor gave her a lift to work, but I've got to pick her up."

Momma walked over. "You talkin' about Renee? If she needs a car for a bit, she can use mine. You and Mitch check it out; make sure there's gas an' all. Heck, it ain't been out of the garage since last fall; not like I'm gonna miss it."

Artie stood. "I'm so sorry to interrupt, but I just noticed the time. I must take care of some business." He kissed Momma's hand again and asked, "After I get settled in, may I stop back later to visit more?"

Momma smiled. "Seein's you ain't worked for 25 years, why don't you help me at five so Mitch can help Eli deliver my car?" Artie chuckled, pointed to his watch and turned for the door. Momma watched him leave, glided to the back of the store and disappeared behind the curtain.

Mitch hissed at Eli. "That dude just got out of prison! He works for the mob! And he's in love with Momma!"

Eli could see that Mitch was excited, but he was more interested in Momma's car. It would be great not to drive his sister all over Chicago. Eli asked, "If I stop here at four when I get off work, can we take Momma's car?"

Mitch frowned at Eli. "Did you even hear what I said? That friend of Momma's is in the mob."

Eli raised an eyebrow and said, "What part of that surprises you? Momma knows everybody in this town. Word on the street has always been to leave Momma be."

Mitch raised his hands, palms up and said, "I've never heard any 'word on the street'."

Eli chuckled as he grabbed a muffin from under a glass dome. "That's 'cuz you ain't never on the 'street'."

Frankie dumped the last of the ice into the cooler on top of the head. Just as he secured the lid, his front door rattled with pounding. He hefted the cooler and rushed it into his bedroom. His bed was already heaped with items he had gathered that needed to be hidden from Artie. The pounding started again. Where the heck was the key to lock his bedroom door? He couldn't think with that racket going on.

Frankie slid the bolt to the side and opened the apartment door. He recognized Artie from his pictures. Artie was dressed in a suit and had two leather bags resting next to him. Frankie smelled aftershave. Way too much aftershave. He could feel his sinuses preparing a pounding.

"Man! You stink. First thing you got to do is shower and don't put that junk back on!" Frankie backed up so Artie could enter.

Artie smiled and grabbed his bags. Obviously Frankie wasn't going to volunteer to help him. "I assume you are Frankie Mullen? You were notified of my arrival?"

Frankie shook his head and backed further into the room. "I'm serious about that smell. Smells make me sick."

Artie nodded, "Just point me to the shower and my room and I shall remedy this unfortunate turn of events."

Frankie pointed down the hall as he continued backing up. "Last door at the end of the hall is your room. Don't touch that first door. That's my room."

Frankie opened the window over the kitchen sink and waved the fresh air into the room. He opened the freezer door of his refrigerator and inhaled deep breaths of the icy air until the pressure in his head receded. The sound of Artie's shower starting was little comfort that this living arrangement was going to work out.

Frankie made three trips from his room to the parking garage two flights below to move his stuff to his car. He was exhausted. Before he left with the last gun case, he left a note on the counter with a key. "I'll be back. Don't shut the window until the stink is gone. Make yourself at home. There's no food."

Frankie sat in his car trying to decide where to take his things. He knew a friend of the crew that had a few storage units about twenty blocks away. It should be safe for the few days Frankie would need it. He'd have to replace the ice in the cooler daily. He rubbed his wrinkled hands over his face and moaned. He had forgotten to pack the pistol hidden under the couch cushion. His knees already screamed with pain. He walked back up the two flights of stairs to get the pistol.

Kevin Brown, street name 'Mo', and Dan Summers, street name 'Flash', had slid down in the front seat of their Jeep to smoke dope in the dark parking garage. They had watched Frankie carry what looked like gun cases to his car and place them in the trunk. As soon as Frankie left the fourth time, Mo said, "That's good shit, man. Looks like gun cases. Let's get that shit."

Flash nodded his approval and the two of them raced over to Frankie's car, popped the trunk lid, emptied the contents to their Jeep and slammed the trunk lid shut. They slid back down in the Jeep's front seat to watch as Frankie returned, slid behind the steering wheel and eventually drove away.

Mo and Flash fist bumped and started up the Jeep. They got about three blocks from the garage when Mo said, "Pop open that cooler and see if we got us some booze."

Flash opened the cooler and peeled away the layers of plastic wrap. "Ain't no booze; some kind of meat or somethin'." Flash jumped back and screamed. "It's a head! A real, frozen head!"

Mo pulled the Jeep over and looked for himself. The mass inside the plastic wrap was dark with freezer burn and the frosted surface was melting on what was definitely a human head. "This ain't good, man. That there is big trouble." Mo pressed the lid back on the cooler and pushed it away.

Flash sputtered, "Big trouble, like the mob?" They stared at each other in horror.

* * *

Frankie paid for a month on the storage unit and purchased a new lock set from the man behind the counter. He would replace it with a better lock later. He backed his car into the unit, lowered the overhead door and opened his trunk. His knees buckled and he felt a flash of heat rise up his neck. His trunk was empty.

CHAPTER 3

Tuesday 9:00 a.m.

*H*e woke to the clanging of a metal cart slamming to a stop outside of his room. The door opened and he decided to sit up and face his captor. A young man in blue scrubs put his finger over his lips to signal quiet as he closed the door behind him. He quickly walked closer and said, "I'm going to help you get out of here, but you have to trust me."

He realized that he was nodding his head in agreement. The man looked somewhat familiar. Who was he? Why was he dressed like that? Was this a hospital? He watched as the man removed a small bundle from his shirt pocket and pushed it toward him.

"Eat this. You need food. I emptied your shot in the potted tree again. I'm probably going to kill it." His captor snickered and then glanced nervously at the door. "Hurry up. If they find out I'm helping you, we're both dead."

There was something about the man's mannerisms that was very unsettling. His unkempt appearance and the intensity of his icy blue eyes added to the bizarre nature of his visit. His left cheek rose quickly to meet his left eye in a nervous tick. He suddenly glared, "If someone else comes in here, pretend you're drugged out. Do you understand?"

Once again, he nodded his head. He knew better than to ask any questions. Not yet.

The first rays of spring sunshine burst through the blinds of the homicide wing of the precinct building. The blast was blinding to anyone glancing east. Instead of closing the blinds, computer monitors were shifted and chairs rolled away from the intrusion. The sunlight highlighted the dust in the air and gave life to great swirls that traveled along the floor with each passing of shoes. The standing joke was that the dirt and dust was what held the old building together.

Jen returned to her desk after interviewing Karen Lomas. Nick had just finished reviewing the medical examiner's findings and the CSU reports from both 45 Dalton Street and 54 Dalton Street. The fourth member of the detective squad, Sam, had just reported to work from a week's medical leave.

Jen greeted Sam, "Hey! How's the leg?"

Sam grinned as he pushed his chair up to his desk. "Leg's been fine since day one. Thank God that punk only had a 22. He was so damn far away the bullet barely broke through the skin." Sam had been shot in the thigh chasing down a murder witness. "I've been catching up on darts. Figured I might join that team of Wayne's and show 'em how it's supposed to be done."

Wayne glanced over and scowled. "Since you're all perky again, why don't you jump in and help with some detecting? We picked up three new ones last night. Two are mob related."

Sam got up and adjusted the blinds, rolled his neck and moaned, "I knew I should have asked for another week."

Wayne walked over and dropped a stack of papers in front of Sam. "Known associates, Attorney James Baxter, deceased."

Sam whistled. "Who's number two?"

Nick answered, "Alexia Cummings, wife of Travis Cummings, mob banker." Nick held up his bag with the dogwood blossom. "Also picked up a Reggie Lomas, who may or may not be connected to the other two by this flower."

Sam shook his head. "I'm not takin' the bait, Stryker. You say the flower is important, it's important. Whatever makes you happy."

Jen stretched her arms above her head and twisted her desk chair to face Nick. "Karen Lomas is taking a poly right now. She has no clue why someone would kill her husband. She's just glad they did. I believe her."

Nick pointed to a short stack of papers on the corner of his desk. "That's the Lomas pile. There's nothing interesting in her phone or bank records, but she'll get over a million in life insurance."

Jen smiled. "I'm glad. According to Karen, Reggie Lomas was a tight fisted S.O.B. and proud of it. She earned every penny. I'll start working his co-workers."

Nick glanced back at his computer screen. Bank of America had sent him an email with an attachment. "I asked for a copy of one of Cummings' checks from Bank of America because of its size. I have a check for 50 grand clearing the Cummings' checking account last week." Nick leaned closer to the screen. "Well, I didn't expect this." He hit print and yelled over to Wayne. "Do you have the bank records for Attorney Baxter yet?"

Wayne changed screens on his computer. "Looks like they came over 20 minutes ago. What am I looking for?"

"A 50 thousand dollar check deposited last week."

"Got it."

Nick rubbed the back of his neck and spoke to no one in particular. "I was hoping this would lead to something. The check was made out to Attorney Baxter, but signed by Alexia Cummings." Nick smiled at Jen. "I guess it would have been too easy to have Cummings pay his lawyer for a hit on his wife. Too bad she signed the check."

Jen offered, "Could be a fee for a divorce. Maybe our investment banker got wind she was going to divorce him and decided to speed up the process."

Wayne added, "Looks like Attorney Baxter withdrew half of it the same day he got it. In cash." Wayne snapped his finger, "Hey, looks like he had a 50 thousand dollar deposit last month, too." Wayne cursed. "Jen, show me how to find this deposit document on this darn thing. I want to see who wrote this check."

Jen walked over, highlighted the deposit date and clicked on a tab that said 'document'. "How do you guys function?"

Wayne whistled. "We might have stepped into something. Last month he got a check for 50 grand from Kerry Starke." Wayne looked over at Nick. "Starke, our dead IRS dude."

Nick grabbed a file from the bottom of his stack. "I asked her about that check. She said they had paid for some legal fees." Nick waved the file in the air. "You know how many people wanted this dude dead? IRS agents make lousy homicide files."

Wayne scrolled further on the screen. "And here's our 25 thousand cash withdrawal same day. Why is this guy splittin' big fees and paying with cash?"

Wayne and Nick just stared at each other. It meant something. What?

Nick frowned. "Let's go back at least a year on Baxter and see how many of these we have. What if our mob attorney was a middle man for hits? Wait, Alexia Cummings signed the check; she wouldn't have paid for a hit on herself." Nick started clicking his pen again until Jen frowned at him to stop.

Nick's phone rang. He listened for a moment, said thanks, and hung up. He turned to face the others. "Ballistics confirmed Baxter and Cummings were shot with the same gun."

Sam leaned back in his chair and asked, "What about your flower? Maybe it's not so special after all?"

Nick smiled, "My flower was a sniper shot. I knew it would be different."

Nick leaned his chair forward. "Something else is bothering me. Isn't it weird that the addresses on Dalton Street are reversed? What if someone transposed the numbers by mistake? That's a good neighborhood. What are the odds of two murders in that neighborhood on the same night?" Nick smiled, "Just suppose that Lomas was a mistake. Alexia Cummings is the only one that paid our attorney. What if the killer went to the wrong house first?"

Jen rolled her eyes. "And also killed a man by mistake instead of a woman? And then decided to kill his meal ticket attorney friend? Gettin' out there, Stryker."

Nick leaned forward, "Stay with me a minute. Let's say 45 Dalton Street was a mistake. 54 Dalton Street gets upset because the paid for hit that didn't happen. It would explain Alexia writing the check if Travis was the target."

Wayne rolled his chair closer. "54 Dalton lady calls lawyer to complain; lawyer calls hit man."

Nick smiled, "Hit man kills the two people that know he made a mistake before the first murder is reported. Problem solved and reputation still intact."

Jen asked, "Who cares that much about reputation?"

Wayne and Nick both answered, "The mob."

Nick pointed at Jen. "Or…maybe we have scenario number two. Mob banker is being pressured by somebody that kills his wife as a warning to play ball. This person might have a problem with the mob in general. Maybe they decide to really send a message by killing the mob's attorney on the same night."

Jen asked, "What about Reggie Lomas? How does he fit into this scenario number two?"

Wayne answered, "He doesn't. You said he wasn't very likeable. His hit was a sniper shot, different from the other two. His hit could be totally unrelated. In spite of Nick's flower."

Nick stood, "I think I want to hear Dom's take on this."

Jen asked, "Dom who?"

"Guioni." Nick smiled at Jen's expression. Dom was known to be the Westside mob boss.

"I was afraid that's who you meant."

Nick's phone rang again; he answered, listened and then said, "Yes, sir."

Nick looked at Jen, "Chief says someone from Special Cases is here to have a chat."

* * *

Mo whispered, "Wait, no need to panic. Why don't we just dump the head and sell the guns?"

Flash pointed at the blue cooler in the backseat. "Man, I don't care, as long as we get rid of that."

Mo turned the car around.

Sirus Corn watched two young men in a Jeep pull up near the fence at Sumac Park on East 42nd Street. The passenger got out and put a perfectly good cooler in the dumpster. Sirus rubbed his chin and watched the boys drive away. Sirus knew Maude would be turning the corner any minute to search the dumpsters. If he was going to get that cooler, he'd better hurry.

Sirus gave his overfilled cart a push forward and lifted the lid on the dumpster. There it sat, just as pretty as you please. He grabbed an armload of treasures from his cart and placed them on a nearby bench. He hefted the cooler. It was heavy. He shoved the cooler as far down as he could in his shopping cart and replaced his other treasures on top. He could barely see over the pile.

Maude's hunched over frame struggled to push her already overloaded shopping cart. She cleared the line of shrubs at the corner and headed quickly towards Sirus. Maude screeched, "You best get away from here. This is my street, Mr. Sirus Corn!"

"You pay as much in property taxes as I do you ol' bitch. You don't own no street." Sirus sounded brave, but he turned his cart and quickly headed away from Maude. She was known to carry a big knife and wasn't afraid to use it. Sirus just wanted to put as much distance as he could between them. Tonight he would go back to the little 'apartment' he shared with his friend, Daryl, in the tunnel community. He was safe there from people like Maude.

* * *

Frankie tried to figure out how to dial his apartment manager on his new phone. He hated this phone. It was one more inconvenience of having to babysit Artie. He didn't want Artie hearing messages from his jobs on the apartment line. Frankie had several sources that used his skills and had given all of them his new number this morning. He was going to have to figure out the stupid phone sooner rather than later. He finally reached the apartment manager and told him he would be there shortly and wanted to see today's surveillance camera feed from the parking garage.

Frankie went to his favorite gun shop and purchased new guns to replace his stolen guns from the 'special' selection room of the store. He drove back to the storage unit and locked them inside. He kept his pistol in his coat. Artie would expect him to carry something for personal protection.

Back at the apartment building, Frankie and the manager watched two punks empty Frankie's trunk and drive away after Frankie left. Frankie's heart clenched as he watch the punk heft the cooler from his trunk and throw it into the Jeep. That was his most prized trophy. He had kept it safe for decades.

The manager was shocked. "Well I'll be. Didn't take 'em but five minutes to clean you out. Don't recognize them boys as belongin' around here."

Frankie pointed to the screen. "Back this up and zoom in on that plate. I'll know who they are soon enough."

Frankie sat in his car in the garage as he called a mob friendly officer at the Chicago PD. "Hey. Got a plate number I need you to run." Two minutes later Frankie was writing down the address for Mo.

* * *

Travis Cummings had spent two hours being questioned by Nick. His answers to Nick's questions never wavered. No, he had no idea who would want to kill his wife. Yes, his marriage sucked, didn't they all? No, he hadn't used Attorney Baxter for anything lately. He had no idea why his wife paid Baxter 50 grand. No, there was not a divorce being planned that he knew of. Yes, he was aware that the majority of his clients were thought to be tied to the mob. No, he wouldn't discuss any of his clients. Finally, Travis suggested they give him a polygraph test so he could resume his life. He passed.

Instead of returning home, Travis drove to the Westside, where he purchased a prepaid phone, dialed Dom, and asked for a meeting. Dom refused and pointed out that the cops would be watching

Travis closely even though he passed his poly. Dom assured Travis that Alexia's death was not mob ordered and that he personally would see to it that whoever was responsible would pay.

Travis tossed the phone into the nearest trash receptacle when the conversation was over. He didn't feel any better after talking to Dom. In fact, he felt worse. He was a month late posting the contract fee from the hospital. Dom's cut of the fee, the skim, could not be late. He couldn't post what hadn't been sent. But how could Dom know already? The statement wasn't due to be sent out until next week. Travis knew that Dom had eyes and ears everywhere. He had to assume Dom knew there was a problem. It was Travis's job to make sure the skim came in uninterrupted. No excuses.

Travis had called Dr. Elmhurst and told him to pay up. Elmhurst had said something about budget problems with the State. Travis had warned Elmhurst that it was a big mistake to disappoint Dom. Elmhurst had screamed at him to back off. Could Elmhurst have ordered Alexia killed as a warning?

Travis had a chilling thought: could Dom think he had kept the money? Travis glanced around his surroundings looking for people that might not fit in. Everyone looked suspicious. Stryker had mentioned that Attorney Baxter had been shot last night too. Why had Alexia paid Baxter 50 grand? None of this made sense. He was in the middle of a nightmare.

Travis walked into a Starbucks and ordered a coffee. He wasn't sure what to do next. It hit him that he hadn't told Alexia's family she was dead. He was so tired and scared after the police left last night that he drank half a bottle of scotch and passed out.

A young gal next to him turned and smiled. She was beautiful. Travis smiled back realizing for the first time that not everything was wrong today.

CHAPTER 4

He finished the sandwich and stuffed the paper wrapper under the mattress. His mind was starting to connect thoughts. He looked at his arms and saw a tattoo of a staff and a single serpent wrapped around it. He ran his finger slowly over the tattoo. It was Asclepius, the Greek symbol of healing. The realization that he knew what it meant caused a tear to roll down his cheek. "I'm a doctor."

* * *

Nick gave a quick rap to the Chief's door and walked in. Seated inside were his Chief, Detective Bud Holmes, and a man Nick didn't know. The Chief stood and made introductions. "Nick, I believe you know Bud from Special Cases and this is their FBI liaison, Agent Steven Phillips."

Nick shook hands with both of the men, took a seat and returned his gaze to the Chief.

Chief Dawson asked Nick, "Exactly what do we have so far on the homicides of Alexia Cummings and James Baxter?"

Nick recapped the connections they had made through bank records and his theory about Alexia's shooting being a warning to Cummings. Nick noticed Agent Phillips lean back when he mentioned his second theory that Baxter was acting as a middle man on hits. Nick stated he planned on speaking to Dominick Guioni today for his take on the events. Nick noticed Phillips glance quickly at Detective Holmes.

Holmes spoke to Chief Dawson as if Nick was not in the room. "This is precisely why we should take over the case." Detective Holmes looked at Nick, "This is no reflection on you Nick. Hell, I know you were a Navy SEAL and all. Nobody questions your integrity or ability. Phillips and I inherited an investigation that started 25 years ago. We're so close to the end of it that we can taste it. The Westside crew, Dom Guioni in particular, is this close to finally going down." He had his index finger and thumb pressed together for effect.

Agent Phillips said, "This week four of the old Chicago crew were released from prison for their 1990 indictments. Carson was shot practically on the courthouse steps; Artie Corsone, Tommy Albergo and Anthony Jarrett are still alive, but maybe not for long. We didn't get everyone we wanted in 1990, but we might get them soon. Thanks to info from the Family Secrets trial and ongoing FBI investigations, all that's left is crossing the T's and dottin' the I's. Our problem is that these new murders don't fit with what we know. Until we figure this out, we can't spook Dom."

Detective Holmes added, "We also have some prison chatter that suggests one of these four men plan to take down Dom. That mutiny info is on top of what we've been working on, but with all of the same players. You can see that a lot is happening all of a sudden. The last thing we want Dom thinking about right now is the name Stryker."

Nick's mind swirled. What the hell? He'd never had anything to do with the mob. Nick leaned back, "I think there's some kind of mistake. The mob can't have a problem with me. I've never worked a mob case and I've never spoken to Dom."

Agent Phillips leaned forward. "You work Chicago homicide. You've never been given a mob case before. You think that's a coincidence? We're referring to your mom, Sophia. We can't risk Dom putting two and two together."

Nothing Agent Phillips said was making sense. Nick hadn't seen his mom in 25 years. She had left him and his dad and never looked back. Agent Phillips stared at Nick's face. "You don't know, do you?"

"Know what?" Nick was angry that he seemed to be the only one not privy to some secret about his mom.

Agent Phillips handed Nick a card. "Talk to your dad and then call me. We'll go from there."

* * *

Jen could tell immediately that Nick was upset. His posture was stiff, his jaw set and he had that deep brooding look he got when he was angry. She wanted to ask what happened in the Chief's office, but she knew Nick would tell her when he was ready.

Nick sat heavily in his chair, glanced at his computer and then abruptly stood. He rubbed the back of his neck as he rolled his head from side to side. "Can you work with Wayne on Baxter's bank records for a couple of hours? I want to know how long this pattern of 50 grand checks has been going on." Nick leaned over and lowered his voice, "I've got a problem downtown I have to straighten out."

Jen nodded. "Sure. We've got plenty to do; take your time."

Jen watched as Nick left the room, his cell phone to his ear.

Wayne cleared his throat, "Everything okay?"

"Oh, yeah." Jen knew everything was not okay. Even she couldn't explain her loyalty to Nick. She instinctively knew something was very wrong. Nick would talk about it when he was ready. It had taken years for their trust to develop, yet there were times she felt she knew nothing about him.

Nick placed a call to his father, Martin Stryker, who was a professor at the University of Chicago in the Liberal Arts Department. Martin told Nick he had a lecture class starting shortly that would run a couple of hours and then they could meet. Nick felt as if he was going to explode. He had twenty 25 years of unasked questions about his mother assaulting his mind. He decided to go to the downtown shooting range and blow off steam. The University was nearby and he needed the practice time anyway.

Mo pulled the car over to the side of the road and put it in park. They were back in their own neighborhood and had to decide what to do with the stolen guns. Flash started to light a joint. Mo smacked the lighter from his hands. "What's wrong with you? All we need is to give the cops a reason to stop and find these guns!"

Flash shrugged. "Sorry, man, I ain't thinkin'. I'm still screwed up over that head. Who we know might buy these guns?"

Mo tried to think as he watched all of his mirrors for cop cars. "Hell, I try to stay away from the dudes with the guns. I ain't got any ideas. You?"

Flash stuffed the joint into an empty cigarette box and shrugged. Just then a rap on his window made him jump and grab his chest. A neighborhood kid, Joey, had rolled up on his bicycle. Flash lowered his window. "What the hell you want?" Flash enjoyed acting street smart to a kid.

Joey pointed down the street. "Thought you might wanna know some ol' dude's been parked down from your house for a bit. Got binoculars and everythin' watchin' yo' house." Flash peeled off a dollar bill and handed it to Joey. Joey frowned. "A lousy buck?" Flash peeled off a five and told Joey to get lost.

Mo and Flash stared at each other in silence. Finally Mo said, "Let's roll around the back and check this out."

Flash sat up straight and nodded. "Don't get too close, man."

Mo turned the corner and pulled into a vacant lot down the street from his house. In the driveway of a boarded up house sat the same car they had robbed in the parking garage.

Mo threw the Jeep in reverse and sped away from the neighborhood as fast as he could. Flash was rocking in his seat as if to help propel the car forward faster. He finally looked over and screamed above the roar of the Jeep's motor. "Dude knows where you live!"

* * *

Nick had been at the firing range for over an hour. He had a pile of weapons next to him and a three inch thick carpet of brass at his feet. He was in the zone. It felt good to focus on the targets and forget the other issues on his mind.

His case load was ridiculous. The city was manipulating crime statistics to make it look like crime was down. The Mayor had just ordered reducing the number of homicide detectives just to prove his point. In reality, they would just be transferred to other precincts temporarily and then quietly moved back. All that would accomplish would be assigning personnel to unfamiliar neighborhoods where they had no street informants. One of Nick's current homicide cases had just been reclassified a vehicle accident on the monthly statistics report. The medical examiner had changed the cause of death to 'undetermined'. Nick took aim and destroyed the center of his target. The guy wouldn't have run his car into a brick wall if he hadn't been shot in the head first.

Nick knew his precinct captain was fighting to keep Jen and him at the 107th. Captain Swartz had a unique advantage in the political hierarchy of the Chicago PD. His brother was the Commissioner and the Chief wasn't afraid to say and do what he thought was right. Nick respected him for that. He had witnessed the Chief place his own job on the line when fighting for his officers.

Now Nick had two, maybe three mob cases to add to his pile. Nick waited for his targets to be replaced. Someone tapped his shoulder and he turned. The duty sergeant motioned for Nick to follow him out of the indoor range area. Once through the heavy steel doors the duty sergeant said, "Terry is asking for help at Ohio and Michigan. Bank robbery at Chase. SWAT is too far away. They're outgunned, that's all I know."

"I'm taking your best gear." Nick remembered he had his Harley. "And I need a car."

The duty sergeant took a deep breath and then threw a set of keys at Nick. "Everything here is crap. Take mine. Blue GTO all souped up. Lights and sirens added by yours truly. That baby is a tank."

Nick could tell the sergeant was proud of his car. Nick winced; he knew his track record of destroying vehicles. Nick strapped his vest on and grabbed a high capacity magazine clip. "You might want to rethink this."

"What the hell. Even if you total it, it's insured to the hilt and I can say it died for Stryker. I've got another one at home I like better. Go!"

Nick nodded. He loaded two impact concussion grenades into his equipment belt, located the GTO in the lot, and apologized to it as he turned on lights and sirens, and stomped on the accelerator. The firing range was very close to where the robbery was taking place. Nick had placed his phone number on the available for emergency list for just this sort of call.

The GTO was outfitted with the latest on dash computer and Nick signed into the city's live feed camera of the robbery scene. Chicago was known as the City of Cameras thanks to Mayor Emanuel. At least a two block stretch of Michigan Street was engaged in the shootout. It looked like the robbers had two heavily reinforced vans in a 'V' pattern in the center of the street. Bodies were scattered over sidewalks, in the street, and from open patrol unit doors. The cops were seriously outgunned. Nick counted four shooters. Utility construction obstructed the ability of the police to gain good vantage points behind the shooters. The alley in the center of the block was the only way in, but provided no cover and was the obvious escape route.

Nick dialed Control Central, identified himself and asked to be patched to the senior officer at the scene. A moment passed, Nick heard the voice of Special Teams Leader, Terry Mann. "Nick, thank God. Where are you?"

"I'm crossing the bridge right now. Clear the area around the gate next to Newman's. I think I can get in there and bust a hole in their cover. ETA three minutes. Get our guys away from that alley."

The static from the phone made it almost impossible for Nick to hear. He assumed Terry had heard him. Nick nudged a cab out of his way and nearly sent it into the Chicago River. The GTO was just warming up. The sergeant had been modest when he said the car had been souped up. Nick patted the dash when he saw the back side of the alley to his left. "Sorry, old girl. It's for a good cause."

Nick twisted the steering wheel a hard left and floored the GTO down the long alley. He blasted through the black iron gate and aimed the GTO directly at the van on the left, smashing the rear quarter panel. Nick rolled out of the GTO just before impact. He opened fire on the back door lock of the van on the right until it was nearly missing, swung it open and jumped inside.

A shooter was firing at officers using the driver's door for cover. Nick shot him squarely in the back of his head, slipped into the driver's seat and threw the van into drive. He yanked the steering wheel to the right sending the van up over the curb and onto the sidewalk and opening the area the shooters were using for cover. Two of the three remaining shooters turned to face Nick and opened fire. Nick's vest took a bullet, but he was able to toss one of the grenades directly between the shooters. It was designed to have a limited, but lethal, radius of destruction. The explosion rocked the area and sent the bodies of the robbers flying. The last robber was stunned by the explosion and standing with no cover. He was quickly shot by remaining officers.

The order to cease fire echoed through the chaos. Officers rushed to the aid of their fallen partners. EMT sirens blasted from all directions and officers struggled to keep panicked shoppers from exiting the stores.

Nick was trained in emergency medicine and tore his sleeve as tourniquet for an officer's leg wound. He applied pressure while he waited for the EMT's and scanned the area. He looked over to a panicked crowd on the sidewalk and saw one man in dark slacks and a buttoned down blue shirt standing perfectly still, staring at him. Nick's blood turned cold. The man smiled. The EMT van pulled up next to Nick. Nick sprinted around it and crossed the street to the crowd. The scene was surreal. The man had vanished. Nick's mind swarmed with memories from five years ago. Jake Billow, cop killer. It couldn't be. Billow had been sentenced to prison for nine life terms.

Jake Billow's lungs wheezed from running the entire length of the alley. He was out of shape. The ambulance that had pulled between him and Stryker had bought him just enough time to get out of Nick's sight. He dashed inside a bookstore and hid behind a rack of books as the other shoppers watched the chaos on the street. He heard them whispering that something awful had happened only a block away.

His breathing finally returned to normal and he realized that he felt giddy. The look on Stryker's face had been electrifying. His mind flashed back to the day Nick had finally caught him. Nick had pushed him against the slimy wall of the alley and told him to prepare to rot in hell. Jake had thought about Nick for five long years. Now he knew Stryker was still in Chicago. He decided it must be fate that their paths crossed again today. Who was he to question fate?

* * *

Dominick Guioni hung up from his call with Travis Cummings. The 'Dom' had survived decades in his position because his instincts about people were seldom wrong. Travis was more than worried, he was guilty of something. Guilt that fueled a fear he had lost favor with the crew. Dom dialed his number two banker. "Find a way to check Cummings' books now. Something's not right."

Dom ended the call and slipped on his overcoat. His bodyguards surrounded him as he walked out to the curb and waited for his car. Those who knew him well could read the determination on his face. There was new trouble on the Westside.

CHAPTER 5

Tuesday 4:00 p.m.

*T*he metal cot was surprisingly light as he dragged it across the room to rest under the high barred window. His strength was starting to come back and he had spent most of the day doing exercises. He used his fingertips in the cracks of the cement block wall to pull himself up and peek out the window. The sunlight blinded him. Precious moments were wasted waiting for his eyes to adjust.

The grounds appeared manicured and vast. He could see several large buildings and a winding service road that connected them all. In the far distance a huge concrete wall went on forever. The sun blasted from its razor wire topping. He would have thought it was a prison if it weren't for the many people casually walking the grounds and gathering at small tables in conversation and laughter.

A few people were in wheelchairs being pushed by people in scrubs. Where in the world was he?

His door flew open and his captor stood facing him. His face was red with anger. "What are you doing?" He walked over and grabbed the corner of the cot. "Help me move this back!"

When the cot was returned to its spot, his captor frowned at him. "You leave me no choice. You're going to ruin everything."

He injected him with a full syringe. His veins screamed in pain as he felt his tongue being injected, too. His visitor scolded him, "I can't have you talking."

* * *

Martin Stryker found it difficult to concentrate on his lecture class. There was a tone in Nick's voice that Martin couldn't identify. Whatever was on Nick's mind was important. Martin had just called him and told him he was available. Nick said he was nearly there.

A student from Martin's film class poked his head into Martin's office. "Got a minute?"

Martin nodded. He encouraged his students to stop by whenever they needed. Martin gestured for the student to take a seat. "Chad, right?"

The young man beamed. He couldn't believe Professor Stryker actually remembered his name. "The documentary assignment you gave us last week? I'm stuck. I was hoping you could give me some ideas."

Martin pushed his chair away from his desk so he could lean back. "What do you care about? What do you think is right about this world? Wrong? What do you think people need to be told?"

Chad stared back. "Everything! Nothing. I don't think people care anymore."

Martin stood when he saw Nick waiting in the hall. Martin said, "You can partner with another student for inspiration on this. If you believe people don't care anymore, then there is your motivation. Make them care."

Chad left the room smiling and Nick took his seat after closing the door. Nick looked at his dad. "I need to know about Mom."

Martin knew this day would come. "Your mother made me promise to keep everything about her secret until you came to me and asked. She also made me promise to tell you nothing but the truth."

Nick cleared his throat. "All you ever said was that mom didn't leave, she couldn't stay. It never made sense to me, but I accepted it. Now I need to know more."

Martin sighed, "I'm going to give you the short version for now, we can talk later if you'd like. I have another class soon and I think you will need some time to digest this." Nick waited for his dad to continue.

"You were ten years old when your mom was asked to testify for the FBI in a huge mob case. It was the right thing to do. The FBI needed her. She was the witness that made their whole case. The

FBI won the case, four long time mobsters went to prison, and your mom went into witness protection. She went alone because she had no confidence the FBI could really protect anyone from the mob. She didn't want you or I involved in any way."

"She was right of course, about the mob. They located her, killed two FBI agents and shot her four times. They believe she died. She didn't. She vowed to finish the job and get rid of any players in the crew she considered to be a threat to our family. My understanding is the FBI helped her change her identity, trained her and has used her for the last twenty five years."

Nick swallowed, "Have you talked to her, seen her?" He wanted to ask if she had asked about him.

Martin smiled, "A few times over the years I thought maybe I saw her sitting in the back of some of my lectures." Martin tried to keep his voice from cracking. "Your mother is a force to contend with. She believes she must stay away from us to protect us. I know in my heart she will succeed and come back. Taking down Dominick Guioni is no small assignment. The guys she put away just got out of jail this week. Maybe we're getting close."

Nick stood. His knees felt weak and he struggled to speak. "Thank you, dad, for being honest. I still don't understand how she could just leave us for all of these years."

Martin stood and put his hand on Nick's shoulder. "She didn't leave. She couldn't stay."

* * *

Eli walked into Momma's sandwich shop and waited for Mitch to ring up his last sale. "You almost ready?"

Mitch scowled, "Almost. Momma said her friend, Artie, is going to come by to help her."

As if on cue, the door to the street opened and Artie stood smiling under the jingling bells. "Reporting for work, Mitch. Where's the boss?"

Momma walked through the curtained door with a crockpot of meatballs. "Get over here Artie and take this thing, darlin'. It weighs a ton."

Mitch smiled, "See? It doesn't take long for Momma to start bossin'."

Momma reached into her apron pocket and tossed a set of keys at Eli. "You tell Renee I ain't in no hurry. She needs to be able to get to work and save up for a reliable car."

Eli and Mitch took turns giving Momma hugs and left out the back door to Momma's small garage. The structure had originally been a large back porch for deliveries. When the city closed the alley to trucks, Momma had the structure enclosed as a garage. Eli unlocked and lifted the overhead door and marveled at how clean the car looked. Mitch held out his hand for the car keys. "I'll drive this and follow you. Where're we goin'?"

"Brookfield Place, out past the airport."

Mitch dropped the car keys. "The *psycho* prison?"

* * *

Jen and Wayne stopped what they were doing to stare at Sam. He was yelling into his phone and slapping his desk with his palm. "You're shittin' me! A grenade? How many down?"

Sam glanced over at Jen and asked, "Is Stryker okay?"

Jen's heart stopped. Wayne walked over to Sam's desk. Sam shook his head and said to his caller, "Let us know if you need us for anything. Damn. Unfreakin' believable." Sam hung up and retold the story about the bank robbery downtown.

"Stryker blasts a GTO into the center of the shoot-out and takes out the bad guys with a grenade!" If it had been anyone else, they wouldn't have believed it. Nick had a way of ending up in the middle of everything.

Jen asked, "Is he okay?"

Nick answered from the doorway. "I'm fine, but I'm starving. How about we grab a sandwich somewhere?"

Jen grinned, "No offense, but I'm driving."

* * *

Mo and Flash stopped the car and decided to have Joey tell the old man that Mo didn't live there anymore. After following several kids on bikes they finally found Joey and pulled him over. Mo asked, "Think you could chum up to that old man and convince him I don't live there anymore?"

Joey put his index finger to his chin. "That sounds like some expensive acting you're wantin' me to do."

Flash yelled across the seat, "How much?"

"Fifty dollars."

Mo slammed his fist on the steering wheel. "Twenty. You report right back to us when you're done. We'll be right here."

Joey peddled away and Mo ran his hands over his face. "We're so screwed. I can't even go home."

Flash shrugged, "You can stay at my place."

Mo couldn't think of another place to go. "Thanks, man. I'm thinkin' we best swap out this Jeep, too."

Ten minutes passed and they saw Joey heading toward the Jeep. Mo rolled down the window.

Joey was animated and sweating from his ride. "Ol' dude got a gun on the seat of his car, man. I asked if he be lost and he asked about your house. Said he was wantin' to buy property or some shit."

Joey took a deep breath. "I told him you were in jail and didn't know when you'd be gettin' out. He asked about your Jeep and I said I thought it got stole."

Flash and Mo were mesmerized by Joey's account of the conversation. Mo asked, "Then what?"

"Then he drove away. Didn't look none too happy though."

Flash and Mo fist bumped and Mo gave Joey 20 bucks. "Good job, little dude."

* * *

Frankie parked his car in the apartment building garage and slowly made his way up the two flights to his apartment door. It was a relief that Artie wasn't there stinking up the place. Frankie hung his coat in the closet and walked over to the kitchen. Fatigue washed over him as the pressure in his head began to throb. He opened the kitchen window and opened the door to the freezer. It looked so empty without the head. What was he going to do? He had to get it back. If that Jeep was stolen, it meant that anyone in the city could have robbed him.

Frankie grabbed a bag of frozen peas from the freezer door and pressed it to his head. His back and neck screamed in pain from having sat in his car for so long. The cream his doctor gave him for his arthritis stunk. There was no way he could use it. He opened the refrigerator to get a bottle of water. Artie must have purchased groceries. Frankie made a bologna sandwich and walked to his bedroom. He locked the bedroom door and ate the sandwich as he sat on the edge of the bed.

His whole world had crashed today and all he had was a bologna sandwich and a bag of frozen peas. He needed a nap. Then he would get an idea. He would get his head back. Frankie moaned as he hefted his body to rest on the lumpy mattress. He slapped the bag of peas on his forehead and slipped into a restless sleep.

* * *

Nick and Jen sat at the bar at Cubby's and waited for their burgers. Nick held up his mug of ice tea. "I wish this was a beer."

Jen smiled, she knew Nick was getting ready to talk to her about something important. Nick's expression was hard for her to read. He almost looked sad. It took all of her control not to just ask him what was wrong.

Nick signaled the bartender to bring him another tea. He turned to Jen and said, "I want to tell you something personal."

Jen nodded. Nick told her about his mom.

Nick and Jen sat in silence while they ate their burgers. Jen could only imagine the range of emotions Nick was feeling. Nick finished his burger and said, "That's not all. You remember Jake Billow?"

Jen was surprised at the conversation turn. "My first case with you. Cop killer. Loony tunes."

Nick frowned, "I'm either going loony tunes, too, or I saw him today at the robbery scene."

Jen didn't know what to say. It was impossible that Nick saw Jake Billow. Jen rubbed her temples. "Tell you what, I'm going to research the system and see where Mr. Billow is supposed to be."

Nick laughed out loud and squeezed her shoulder as he threw his money on the bar. "Now that's a great partner. No matter how crazy something sounds, you're going to follow up."

"Nick, I feel honored you shared all of this with me. Just keep me posted on what you decide to do on the case."

Nick raised an eyebrow. "Oh, that's decided. We're not only on the case, Dominick Guioni is about to experience another Stryker."

CHAPTER 6

*R*yan stood looking at the man on the cot. He didn't look good. Had he given him too much of the drug? He gingerly placed his fingers on the man's neck in search of a pulse. He couldn't find one. Panic seized him. Now what? He ran into the hall in search of a real nurse. Maybe they could give him something to bring him back.

The door to Dr. Elmhurst's office was open and Ryan screamed, "Room 47, I think I killed him!"

Dr. Elmhurst pushed a button on his desk that started a siren. He grabbed the PA and ordered the nursing staff to Room 47. That's the last thing he needed right now. Another death. He pushed his way past the curious patients and headed for the now crowded doorway of Room 47. Ryan handed Renee the lithium vial the last injection had come from. Renee looked at Ryan, "How much did you give him?"

*Ryan answered, "I guess 5 CC's, the whole syringe."
Renee panicked; where was Dr. Elmhurst? What had Ryan
been thinking?*

*Renee pulled the cap from a hypodermic needle with
her teeth and injected the patient with Naloxone, a stabi-
lizer drug. She prayed she was giving the proper dosage.
She only had minutes, maybe less. Anxious staff stood staring, watching for signs of life. The patient gasped. Vomit
erupted from his mouth and Renee rolled him to his side.
She shook her head as she instructed Ryan to sit with the
patient until he was coherent.*

*Renee locked eyes with Dr. Elmhurst. He had been
watching from outside the room. He muttered, "Nice job,"
turned and walked away.*

*Renee rested against the hallway wall, her heart pound-
ing. She had been told there were no patients in this wing.*

* * *

The sign announced Brookfield Place / Restricted
Facility. Eli's car turned into the densely wooded lane
and Mitch followed in Momma's car. It seemed as if
they drove a few miles before reaching an iron gate.
The gate was attached to a tall concrete wall topped
with razor wire. Eli had stopped his car and was talking to a uniformed guard that had appeared from a
small brick building. The guard kept glancing back at
Mitch. Mitch waved each time. Mitch couldn't believe
that Renee worked at this place. A psycho prison?

Eli pulled his car over to park in front of the small brick building and walked back to Mitch's car. "Guard says the only cars that can go in have to be on his register list. He says we can drive Momma's car in for Renee, but we have to either have the campus cops drive us back or walk."

Mitch frowned, "Campus cops? Does he think this is a college or something?"

Eli shrugged. "He told me they try to maintain a casual living environment for the patients."

Mitch frowned as he pulled the car through the tall iron gate. "You mean prisoners, don't you? This place is creepy. Seemed pretty damn easy to get past that guard; you'd think it would be harder to get in this place."

Eli chuckled, "I think the trick is getting out."

The drive ahead made a big circle to the right and Eli pointed, "Guard says we have to look for Building D. He says it's way to the back. That's where all the really bad patients are." Eli was looking out his window at the people walking around or just standing still looking at the ground. "I can't believe my sister works here."

"I can't believe you talked me into coming here with you." Suddenly a man jumped out from some bushes directly in front of the car and started waving his arms for them to stop.

Eli and Mitch looked at each other. Mitch stopped and rolled down his window. The man had putrid breath and only a few teeth. He stuck his head too far into Mitch's window and Mitch leaned toward Eli.

"You got cigarettes? Booze? You need cigarettes to move on." The man was making grabbing motions with his hands. Eli took a candy bar out of his pocket and tossed it to the man who ran away giggling.

Mitch sighed as he moved the car forward again. "Where are these cops that are supposed to get us out of here?" They turned a bend in the road and an old man in a wheelchair sat motionless at the curb. Mitch slowed to almost a stop. The old man's chin rested in the center of his chest. Mitch looked at Eli, "I think that dude is dead."

Eli motioned Mitch to move on. "Remind me to tell Renee."

It seemed as though they would never get to Building D. Eli read off the letters on the other buildings as they passed them.

Mitch looked over, "I can read."

"Sorry. This place just creeps me out. It's startin' to get dark out and there ain't no way I want to walk all the way back to that guardhouse."

Finally Building D loomed in front of them. It looked different from the other buildings. It almost looked like some kind of large castle. Mitch parked in the employee parking space in front of the massive door. "I'll wait for you here."

"Like hell you say. I ain't goin' in there alone." Mitch was afraid Eli would say that.

They both walked slowly to the front door. No one seemed to bother them or even care that they were there. When they entered the foyer a large man stood with his arms crossed at his chest. He put one ham sized hand up and asked, "Where do you gentlemen need to go?"

Eli cleared his throat and said, "I need to see a nurse here named Renee Johnson."

The big man nodded his head and turned, "Follow me."

Mitch elbowed Eli at the sight of a woman picking the leaves off a potted tree and eating them. Eli raised his eyebrows and quickened his pace to be closer to their escort. The big man pointed down a hall. "Don't be goin' down that way. Got a whole bunch of them down there that won't take any meds. Some ain't so bad, but most will hurt ya just for fun."

Mitch was now even with Eli, the two of them practically on the heels of the big man. He continued his tour advice. "See them double doors down there? That's where the dining room is. If we can't find Ms. Johnson, she might be in there. Don't want you two in there though. They always think new people are there to steal their food. Gets *real nasty* mighty fast with them all havin' knives and such."

Eli had no doubt the first chance he got he was going to talk Renee into getting a new job. Just then Renee came from around the corner. She put her hands on her hips and shouted for someone named Ryan. Ryan ran from around the corner and quickly tackled the big man and cuffed his wrists with zip ties.

"How the hell did you get out this time?" Another orderly showed up and helped escort the laughing man down the long hall.

Renee smiled at Eli. "You just let a serial killer give you a tour of the facility."

Eli nearly fainted. Mitch grabbed the wall for security. "How do you work here?"

Renee's expression got very serious. "It isn't easy."

Eli remembered the man in a wheelchair. "It looks like some old dead guy in a wheelchair out by the road."

Renee sighed, "He's probably been over medicated is all. I'll have someone check on him."

Mitch handed her the car keys. "We parked out front. Momma said not to rush about getting it back to her. She knows you have to save up for a new one." Renee looked like she was going to cry.

She kissed Mitch's cheek. "You give that to Momma for me."

Eli asked, "Can you call the campus cops to take us back to the gate?"

Renee shook her head, "I will if you want, but it will take them at least an hour to get here. They don't like Building D."

Mitch watched the woman eat more leaves from the tree and then looked at Eli. "I ain't waitin' no hour. Let's just go."

Eli and Mitch headed back toward the gate at a quick walking pace. Soon there were three men walking behind them. Eli and Mitch increased their speed to a moderate jog. Now there were five men jogging behind them; one of them pushing the old dead man in the wheelchair. Soon more men jumped from the bushes and joined the group. Eli and Mitch poured on the steam to stay ahead of the growing mob. Mitch started screaming in a high pitch and the mob mimicked him. Mitch and Eli hit the gate at a flat out run, shaking the iron bars and screaming for the guard.

* * *

It had been a heavy dinner rush at Momma's. Everyone knew that Tuesdays were meatball sub day. Artie caught on quickly and before long he was singing out the orders to Momma like he had worked there all of his life. When the last customer left, Artie leaned against the cash register and whistled. "Woman, you can surely work the pants off a fella."

Momma leaned over and kissed Artie's cheek. "Soon as the boys get back from deliverin' that car we got another job to do."

Artie wiped his brow in an exaggerated movement. "And just what new hell do you have planned for me?"

Momma smiled, "I was hopin' you would help me take some meatballs to the community."

"What community?"

"Mitch calls them the tunnel people. We discovered a passageway to the tunnels from my basement last year and found a whole 'nother city down there."

Artie had heard rumors about people living in the tunnels under the city. He had to admit that it fascinated him. "It would be my pleasure, darlin'."

* * *

Mo drove the Jeep to the house owned by Flash's mom. He parked in the driveway and noticed a man across the street waxing a Camry that had a for sale sign on the windshield. Mo asked Flash, "How much you think he wants for that car?"

"Too much, knowing him. It's been for sale since last fall."

Mo got an idea. "Maybe he'd be ready to deal? Let's say this Jeep and some mighty fine guns for that car."

Flash shook his head. "I think them guns alone worth more than that car."

Mo's eyes got big, "Not to me they ain't. I want them gone."

"Good point."

Mo and Flash walked across the street and found out that Gus wanted five thousand dollars for his nine year old Camry. Mo proposed his deal and the three of them walked across the street to look at the guns. Mo could tell that Gus loved the guns, but was trying to play it cool.

"Lookey here where the numbers was scratched off. Who these guns belong to?"

Mo answered, "I ain't gonna lie to ya. We don't know nothin' 'bout the history of these guns. We kind of just ended up with them this mornin'. Here's the deal, the guns and the Jeep for your car."

Gus held up the long gun. "This here is old school. Favorite rifle for mob hits in the old days."

Gus stared through the scope and pretended to shoot. "Sniper shot, that was."

Flash and Mo glanced at each other.

Gus turned to Mo. "That Jeep got a title or did it just show up this mornin', too?"

Half an hour later, Flash and Mo were cruising through the hood in their new Camry looking to score some weed. Life was good again.

Mitch and Eli arrived back at Momma's just before closing. After listening to their account of their horror trip, Momma talked them into helping her carry the two crock pots of meatballs down to the tunnel. Artie carried a large bag of sub sandwich buns and Momma had a sack of apples and oranges. Artie was amazed at the tunnel entrance in Momma's basement.

"I could have sure used this in my younger days. What a great escape route from the coppers." Artie ran his hands over the large wheel lock door to the entrance. "They don't make stuff like this anymore."

Once through the opening, Artie's jaw dropped at the sheer expanse of the room they were in. Eli explained to him that the city's main water system line used to be housed there. Dozens of tunnels shot off from all sides.

Artie asked, "You guys explore all of these tunnels?"

Momma answered, "Joseph said most of them are blocked off and sometimes the bad people hide there."

Artie frowned, "Who is Joseph?"

Mitch pointed to a large man walking toward them out of the steam vent tunnel. "Him."

Joseph walked over and gave Momma a hug and kiss, shook hands with Mitch and Eli and introduced himself to Artie. "They call me the Mayor of this little community. My name is Joseph."

* * *

Jen walked into the homicide room and sat at her desk. Wayne looked up from his computer. "Nick okay?"

"Yeah, I had to drop him off downtown so he could get his bike. He tried to lend it to Jim to use until the insurance company paid up on the car Nick trashed."

Sam stood and put his jacket on to go home. "Not just any car. A GTO." Sam shook his head and started laughing. "I can't get that image out of my head. A friggin' grenade!"

Jen started a list of places she could call to follow up on Jake Billow. It didn't take her long to discover that the prison system as it relates to the mental health system in general was in crisis and that the mental health system within the Department of Corrections was pure chaos. Legislation in Illinois since 2011 made it clear that the state wanted out of the business of mental health. The industry, including prisoner housing, had been privatized with little funding allocated for monitoring. Jen got a chill. It didn't take much imagination to see the risks of these new policies. Nick may be right. Billow may be out.

Wayne was still reviewing the bank records search on Attorney Baxter. Nick walked in and plopped in his chair.

Wayne looked up and smiled. "Are we a little tired?"

Nick grinned back. "No. We're a lot tired. I say we work 'til seven and call it a night."

Jen smiled, "No argument from me. John thinks I deserted him!" She immediately regretted saying that. She hoped it didn't make Nick think of his mom. If it did, he didn't show it and Jen relaxed. She was going to have to be more careful.

Nick asked Wayne, "How many suspicious transactions have you found on Baxter?"

Wayne walked over with a fistful of papers. "You're going to love this. Ten 50 thousand dollar deposits this year, followed by cash withdrawals of 25 grand each time. Each deposit was by check and each person that wrote him a check had a spouse meeting an untimely death shortly after."

Nick sat back, "Every one of them?"

Jen smiled, "Every one of them."

* * *

Joseph helped Momma set up the crock pots on a table, and Momma, Artie, Mitch and Eli all began to serve the meatball sandwiches. Suddenly a blood curdling scream filled the air and Joseph took off running into the tunnel. Momma, Artie, Mitch and Eli followed at a distance. A crowd of people were standing around a blue cooler. One of the men in the crowd began praying. Several people cried and crossed themselves.

Joseph looked at Sirus Corn who was holding the lid of the cooler and shaking.

Joseph grabbed Sirus' shoulders. "What's wrong?"

Sirus pointed to the cooler. "I found it in a dumpster, I swear. That's a head. A frozen head."

Joseph bent down to get a closer look. Artie leaned in close, too. Momma, Eli and Mitch backed up.

Joseph looked at Artie. "I don't know what to do. We don't want police down here."

Artie took the lid from Sirus and pressed it tight on the cooler. "Might I suggest that I properly dispose of this without involving the community?"

Joseph stood and shook Artie's hand. "We would be forever grateful."

Artie looked at Momma, "Due to this new twist of events, I'm hopeful you will excuse me from meatball duty." Artie hefted up the cooler for effect.

Momma wrung her hands. "Oh Lordy, what is this world comin' to? You go do what you got to do and just make sure you lock up my shop tight when you leave."

Mitch and Eli watched as Artie crawled back through the tunnel entrance to Momma's shop and disappeared with the blue cooler.

Eli looked at Mitch, "You don't see that every day."

CHAPTER 7

Tuesday 8:00 p.m.

Ryan quietly slipped out the door of Room 47. He double checked the lock and headed down the hall toward the exit. As he passed through the double doors to the foyer, he saw Renee unlocking a car door out front. He waited inside. As much as he wanted to breathe the fresh air outdoors, he didn't want to answer any of Renee's questions. He couldn't trust himself to give the right answers. Renee was smart. She was going to be trouble.

* * *

Nick had called Agent Phillips and asked to meet with him at Cubby's. The clacking of the balls on the pool table and muffled spurts of laughter had always defined Cubby's as a safe neighborhood bar. It was perfect for cops that just wanted to relax and not be bothered. Wayne was a member of a dart team at Cubby's. His nickname was 'Oink' and Nick smiled when he saw it at the top of the Darts Honor Board.

Nick had just been served his second beer when Agent Phillips walked in. Phillips walked to the end of the bar, took a stool next to Nick and signaled a beer from the bartender. He looked around and smiled, "You've been coming in here since you were ten years old. Used to sit in that corner and watch your dad hustle pool after work. Then your dad started classes at the University and had Mitch's mom hire you to work at the sandwich shop."

Nick smiled and glanced around to make sure they were out of earshot of anyone. "You've done your homework. I suspect dad came here to vent his frustration. Never drank. He used to have the bartender order him Vernor's Ginger Ale from Michigan." Nick pushed his beer away. "I want to thank you for agreeing to meet with me."

"No problem. I assume you spoke to your dad?"

Nick exhaled, "Yeah. Quite a story. You were right, I didn't know."

Agent Phillips put a ten dollar bill on the bar and took a gulp of his beer. "What else do you want to know?"

Nick thought for a moment. "How active is mom? Do you talk to her?"

Agent Phillips shook his head. "I don't know who her handler is. I never have known. All I know is she is one of our 'ghosts'. Sophia's invisible, master of disguise and good. Almost every piece of intel on the Westside crew has come from her." Agent Phillips saw the pain in Nick's eyes. "I don't know how to contact her. There is an internal agency web site that I update with reports. Where it goes from there is above my grade level."

He knew he wasn't saying what Nick needed to hear. He couldn't. "Twenty five years is a long time. Sophia is relentlessly driven. I can't think of anyone else that could have accomplished what she has. The scope of the case she has built for us is mind blowing."

Nick felt a sense of pride in what he was hearing. At the same time, his heart ached from deep wounds. Nick looked at Agent Phillips, "I don't want to be pulled from this case. If we play this right I can cause people to make mistakes." Nick didn't have to wait long for a reply.

"I've been thinking the same thing."

Nick lowered his voice, "I'd like to meet with Dom. Maybe suggest he's lost control of his crew."

Agent Phillips laughed, "I'd love to be there for that! Fair warning, there will be backlash. Be careful, stick to the files on your desk when you talk to Dom. We'll take this one step at a time."

* * *

Travis Cummings arrived home about seven thirty and noticed that Rosa, his cleaning lady, had managed to remove Alexia's blood from the front door and foyer. Travis hung his coat, poured himself a scotch and walked around the quiet townhouse. It was wonderfully silent. He sat at his desk in his study and logged into his bank account. If he used his own money to cover the missing funds from Brookfield Place, he would be broke in two months. The skim was 70 grand per month. He turned in his office chair in thought. He did have a decent amount of insurance money coming from Alexia's death, but it wasn't safe to wait three weeks for the insurance money to come. Somehow he had to get Brookfield Place to pay up.

Travis swallowed the last of the scotch and dialed Alexia's mother. While the phone rang he wondered how to tell her that Alexia had been murdered last night. When she answered, he decided to just blurt it out.

After a full five minutes of wailing, Alexia's mother got silent. "It took you 24 hours to tell me my daughter had been murdered? It was you. You had her killed!"

Travis smiled, "Actually, the cops have proof that I didn't. I passed a polygraph, Marie. But it's real nice of you to think of me. Let me know when you have completed arrangements, of course I'll pay for them." Travis hung up and smiled. He wasn't going to miss Alexia or her mother.

His thoughts returned to his problem at Brookfield Place. It might be best to visit in person. Time was running out, he'd have to go in the morning. Dr. Elmhurst had to understand that paying the skim was not optional. Travis wasn't going to leave without that money.

He noticed the message light on his landline blinking. He listened as his secretary informed him the computer man had come today and made the updates he had requested. Travis felt a chill race up his spine. He hadn't ordered any computer updates. Someone was searching his records. He could only think of one person that would be that bold: Dominick.

Dr. Elmhurst made sure his ID badge was clearly visible on his lapel. He didn't want that stupid guard giving him the third degree again. He carried a stuffed pillowcase to his trunk. It was pitch black outside. He preferred to leave work earlier, but he needed the cover of dark tonight. The pharmacy delivery of narcotics had barely fit in the pillowcase. He figured Alex would pay close to three hundred grand for what he had tonight. The street value had to be at least four times that. This was so easy. He would requisition more from the state in the morning. It would be a year, if ever, before anyone noticed all of his duplicate orders. In 30 days, he'd be long gone and living in Belize.

He honked loudly at the iron gate. The guard walked over and pointed his flashlight into the back seat and then waved him through. He chuckled to himself that the state couldn't have designed a more screwed up prison system if that had been their intention. Nobody knew who was in charge of what and when it came to the mental prisoners, nobody wanted to know. As long as he was head administrator for Building D, everyone let him be.

He drove five miles and pulled into the commuter 'Ride Share' parking lot. He parked next to a blue van, made sure there were no people near and hit the button to unlock his trunk. Jake Billow crawled out of the trunk and walked to the driver's window. Elmhurst pointed to the pillowcase Jake carried and said, "We should get at least 300 grand for that. I'll get my half in the morning when I pick you up here."

Jake smiled, unlocked the blue van driver's door, got in and drove away.

* * *

The bus stop was only a block away from Frankie's apartment and was often his preferred method of traveling to a job. His aging, bent body blended in with the other senior riders and offered an additional level of cover. Tonight, Artie rode the bus back to Frankie's apartment, the blue cooler resting on his lap in front of his newspaper. It seemed the entire paper was devoted to crime stories. Most of them seemed due to heroin traffic. Twenty five years in prison had educated him on this new world. He studied the pictures of the suspects and marveled at how young they were. Punks.

Two women riding in front of him gossiped about a friend who had highly insured the lives of her children and sent them to live with relatives in the hood. The plan paid off several times as the friend was currently living the good life in Hawaii and pregnant with twins. Artie looked at the cooler in his lap. Had this poor chap's fate been any crueler than bearing children for the purpose of collecting insurance money?

Artie made his way up the two flights of stairs to Frankie's apartment door and let himself in. He sat the cooler on the counter and listened. Loud snoring escaped Frankie's door and Artie sighed with relief. He was exhausted after working at Momma's and carting that 15 pound head around Chicago.

Artie removed the head from the cooler and placed it in Frankie's freezer. He scratched out a Post-It note for the freezer door that simply said, "I can explain this." He removed a yogurt and a bottle of water from the refrigerator, and headed for his room. He wasn't looking forward to Frankie's reaction.

* * *

Nick called Lacey on his way home to his townhouse. He was tired and emotionally drained. Lacey answered on the first ring. "Hey, handsome. Did I see you on TV at a bank robbery?"

Nick chuckled, "You probably did. Good day though, no cops died. I'm heading to my place to crash, is that okay?" Nick still didn't know what was expected of him from Lacey. He had told her he would make their relationship a priority, but it seemed his job got in the way more every day. Nick parked his car in his garage as he waited for Lacey's reply.

"No problem. I have some news. My sister Joyce's daughter, Kamber, has come to stay with me for a bit. We're getting reacquainted right now."

Nick asked, "This was a surprise and you can't really talk, right?"

"Handsome and smart! I'll touch base tomorrow and we can adjust our plans."

Nick unlocked his townhouse door and threw his keys on the kitchen counter. "Adjust plans? Oh, I can't be sleeping over can I?"

Lacey giggled, "Not very easily, no."

Nick undressed to take a hot shower and noticed that his jeans and shirt had taken quite a beating in the robbery. There were blood stains on his shirt sleeves. Nick looked at his arms and found road burn from his wrists to his shoulders. He tossed his clothes in a trash bag, grateful he hadn't been in a suit.

The hot shower stung at first and then gently lulled him to relax. His head rested on the shower wall while the hot water beat on his shoulders and back. A realization struck him: he hadn't been abandoned by his mom after all. She had been right to remove herself from their lives. It had saved them. She didn't leave. She couldn't stay.

* * *

Tommy Albergo and Anthony Jarrett sat in the back corner table of Cindy's Pizza. "Remember when we used to meet here to collect the skim?" Tommy took a big bite from a pizza slice and let the grease run down his chin. "I've dreamt about this pizza for 25 years."

Anthony nodded as he swallowed. "Where did the crew put you up? I'm in a sleep cheap hotel on Washington. I was kind of thinkin' I had earned somethin' a little homier."

"Me too, I'm in Room 227 in the same hotel. At least we don't have to bunk up like Artie. He got stuck roomin' with Frankie Mullen."

Anthony rolled his eyes. "Artie best sleep with one eye open."

Tommy wiped his chin and nodded toward the door, "We've got company."

Anthony turned in time to see a man in a black suit, probably FBI, walk in and stride toward them.

"You boys aren't supposed to mingle. Remember?" Agent Phillips flashed his badge and sat at the small table. "You heard about Emil Carson, right?"

Anthony leaned back in his chair and pointed his index finger at Agent Phillips. "Gettin' popped two blocks from prison? Yeah, we heard. I figured it was FBI cleanin' house." Anthony lacked the edit button most people used when talking to authorities.

Agent Phillips frowned, "We don't work like that. I stopped by to let you boys know our info points to Dom." He took a slice of their pizza and savored the greasy cheese almost as much as he savored the shocked expression on Tommy's face. Agent Phillips grabbed a napkin from a pile on the table and stood to leave. "Watch your back."

They watched as Agent Phillips left the diner and Tommy whispered, "You think he's right about Dom?" Suddenly Tommy felt sick to his stomach. It would be just like Dom to have them hit once they got out of prison. Save the crew the cost of keeping them around in their old age. Tommy glanced out the window as a new fear assaulted his thoughts: what if Dominick knows about the plan?

Anthony took another slice of pizza from the plate. "Think about it. Dom would have to have permission from the Outfit boss to hit us." Anthony chuckled, "With what I've negotiated with Milo, there's no way. More than likely, the government is screwin' with us. Feds are like that. By the end of this week, it won't matter."

Momma placed a hot herbal tea next to her recliner chair. Her apartment above the sandwich shop was small but well appointed. She slid open a small drawer in the end table and removed an envelope taped to the underside. She opened the flap and removed a piece of yellowed paper. A quick sip of tea and she lifted her phone and dialed. She let it ring a few times and hung up. She took another sip of tea, replaced the envelope in its hiding place and waited.

Her phone rang and Momma answered, "Darlin', I might have something useful for you." Momma proceeded to tell the story of the blue cooler and her rekindled friendship with Artie. After listening for a moment, Momma ended the call with, "You stay safe, love. Sophia? Let's pray we're almost done."

CHAPTER 8

Wednesday 7:00 a.m.

*R*enee tried each of her keys to unlock the door to Room 47. None of them fit. She spoke into her shoulder radio, *"Ryan, answer."*

A moment later her radio crackled back, "Ryan here, what cha need?"

"I don't seem to have a key for Room 47. Can you come here and let me in?"

Ryan answered, "He's not there anymore. Got transferred last night."

"Transferred where?"

"I don't know, just somewhere else. Was that it? I've got Jane running down the halls nude again."

Renee sighed, "Yeah, that's all."

Ryan exhaled. He had moved the patient from Room 47 to another room in a different vacated ward. He didn't know how much longer he could keep his secret. Too many eyes were peeking.

* * *

Renee had heard rumors that Building D had patients transferred out in the middle of the night. More than a few of the staff from Building A believed the patients were simply driven to the city and let go. Once the state transferred a prisoner to a private facility, most of the accountability vanished. Employees that transferred to Building D usually quit within the first week. Not just to transfer back to another building, quit the facility all together. Renee had made it nearly a month and was determined to stay until she had earned enough to buy a decent car.

Blood curdling, animal like screams suddenly assaulted the air. Renee ran to the adjacent hall to see Ryan and two patients pull a man off from Jane's nude, bleeding body. The knife wielding man's name was Joshua. He was a schizophrenic and normally docile when taking his meds. He could often be found helping the grounds crew.

The huge knife dripped Jane's blood as Joshua screamed "whore". Ryan and one of the patients frantically tended to Jane. The remaining patient struggled valiantly to hold Joshua back. Joshua glanced at Renee and froze. For just that brief moment she saw extraordinary sadness in his eyes. The next instant he twisted free of his captor, blew her a kiss and defiantly slit his own throat.

* * *

Frankie woke to the sound of dishes clattering and remembered he had a roommate now. His heart sunk when he also remembered his precious head was gone. Decades of protecting it, now lost forever. Frankie grabbed his robe from the closet and headed to the bathroom to shower. Just the fact that he had to put a robe on in his own house annoyed him. His depression made him feel even older. It seemed his legs weighed twice as much as yesterday. At least the place didn't stink today.

After he showered and dressed he went to the kitchen where Artie was cooking up a storm. "Good morning, sir. I made bacon and scrambled eggs. There's plenty to share if you would like some?" Artie's voice was far too cheery. Frankie found it annoying.

Frankie poured himself a cup of coffee and grunted that food sounded okay. He noticed the note on his freezer door. "Explain what?"

Artie winced, "Look in your freezer. We have company."

Frankie opened the freezer door and couldn't believe his eyes. He blinked a couple of times and prayed his mind wasn't playing tricks on him. His head! He pulled it out and held it up to the light. "What...where did you get this?" Frankie was so excited he wanted to kiss it. He imagined that would be hard to explain to Artie.

Artie told him the story about Momma and feeding the tunnel people. Then he retold Sirus' story about finding it in a dumpster. Artie pointed under the sink. "I put the cooler down there. I didn't know where else to bring the head last night. I know it can't stay here."

Frankie frowned, "Why not?"

Artie smiled, "Well, for one, I expect a visit from my parole officer today or tomorrow. I'd rather not explain our partial guest."

Frankie had to hide the fact that he was practically giddy about his head being back. What a twist of fate. This did pose new problems though. Now Artie knew of the head's existence. So did this person named Momma and her son and his buddy. Frankie sat down and realized the entire tunnel population knew, too. He couldn't have Artie blabbing around Chicago that he had put the frozen head in Frankie's freezer. At least, for now, the current location of the head was still secret. Frankie had to give this serious thought. Dom had entrusted Artie's safety to him. He ate his breakfast in silence as Artie gushed about the wonders of the tunnels.

Frankie's dentures were having trouble with the bacon. Only one person knew the head was in his freezer. Frankie could only think of one solution. Artie had to die.

* * *

Travis Cummings checked his reflection in the mirror. His first order of business today was to view the office camera images of who had made changes to his computer. He also had to determine exactly what had been done. Travis looked at his watch: eight o'clock. Perfect. He had a couple of hours before he planned to arrive at Brookfield Place.

Nick and Jen sat in their car outside of Bruno's Bar. Agent Phillips had said Dom held court here every morning with his crew. Jen looked at Nick, "If I understand this right, you're hoping to provoke Dom into making some kind of mistake."

"That's my goal." Nick glanced at Jen and winked, "This might get physical. He probably has a couple of guards around him."

"Good, I haven't had guard for breakfast in a long time." Jen smiled. She was highly trained, mostly by Nick. He had wanted to be sure she could take care of herself. She had often proved herself to be a valuable backup. Her petite size and feminine appearance were a useful distraction.

Nick put his hand on the door handle and stopped. He looked at Jen, "Help me watch his face. I'm going to give him some information I don't think he knows somewhere in the conversation. It should cause him to show his 'tell'. Watch his body language, too."

Jen smiled, "I love these body language studies."

"They could save your life. Closest thing to mind reading we have."

Nick and Jen walked into Bruno's and walked straight to the back table. The group of six men at the table and two bouncers were the only non-employees there. Nick held up his badge, "Chicago Homicide." He guessed which one was Dom by the positions of the chairs. He looked at Dom and said, "I need everyone but you to leave."

Dom leaned forward, "You can't walk in here and tell my guests to leave."

"I was trying to be nice. It's here or downtown."

Dom glared at Nick and then motioned for the men to leave. The guards stood firm.

Nick looked at Jen, "Before we send these two out, check their carry permits. They're both packin'."

Jen walked over to the larger of the two and held out her hand. "Let me see your permit."

The big man had a smile growing across his face as he stared down at her. He looked at Dom. Dom pointed at Nick. "These are my boys. I'm sure they have permits somewhere."

Nick shook his head. "Sorry. Not good enough." Nick looked at Jen, "Take their guns, issue citations and get them out of here."

Jen smiled. "No problem."

The big guy looked at Dom who stood. "What do you mean 'take their guns'? Besides, it's their job to stay with me at all times."

Nick stood, "They're leaving without their guns. I don't know what you think is so special about them. Anyone can see they're useless."

Dom's neck had turned red. He looked at the two guards and then snarled toward Nick, "Give her your guns."

The one big guy took a menacing step toward Jen. That was all she had been waiting for: any sign of aggression. Jen stepped forward and punched his groin. She removed his hand gun and tossed it on the bar as he doubled forward. When he bent over, she applied pressure just behind and below his ear that caused him to drop to his knees in pain. She chopped the inside of his elbow with the side of her hand and snapped cuffs on his wrist before he could recover.

She twisted his other arm behind his back, cuffed that wrist and applied pressure just left of the base of his spine with her index and third finger. He went flat to the floor on his stomach, screaming in pain. Jen rested her boot in the small of his back and looked to the other guard. "Which way are you leaving here?"

The second guard placed his gun on the bar and walked backwards to the door.

Nick had returned to his seat and motioned for Dom to do the same. "Like I said, I don't know what you think is so special about them. I have to admit I'm disappointed. It seems to me you would want skilled bodyguards protecting you."

Dom watched as Jen ushered the cuffed man to wait outdoors with the others. She returned to the table and sat to the side of Dom.

Dom had regained his composure and asked, "Did you say homicide? Who died?"

Nick leaned forward, "Your banker's wife for one. Seems your 'crew' can't protect anyone." Nick shook his head, "Again, very disappointing. What do you know about that murder?"

Dom twisted his mouth to a snarl, "I don't know anything."

Nick spoke to Jen, "He doesn't know anything." Nick looked back to Dom, "How about your attorney? James Baxter? Know anything about his murder last night?"

Dom repeated, "I don't know anything about that murder either."

Nick chuckled, "Seems you don't know much about your own people. How about Carson? Got out of jail yesterday and got murdered. I suppose you don't know anything about that."

Dom smiled, "You're right, I don't know anything."

Nick smiled back, "I'm sure you think you are coming across as clever. I don't buy it. I believe you really don't know. It might be time to admit that you have lost control of this 'crew' of yours."

Dom stopped smiling and leaned forward, "Do you have what you need? Have I answered all of your questions?"

Nick stood, "Just one more. Were you aware that your attorney was a middle man for hits? We've documented ten this year and we've just begun digging."

Dom's eyes narrowed and his nostrils flared almost instantly. "I wouldn't know what our attorney did in his free time."

"Making 50 grand a pop and paying the shooter 25 grand cash each time. What would your piece of that be? Or has that been going on under your nose, too?"

Dom lowered his chin and looked up at Nick with lasers. "If I hear anything, I'll call you. What's your name?"

Nick pulled a card from his pocket, "I've been waiting for you to ask that. The name is Stryker."

Dom's nostrils flared. He lifted the card and read the name again. He looked at Nick. "I might have heard that name before somewhere."

Nick motioned for Jen to leave. He leaned over the table and put his weight on his fists on the table top. He was within inches of Dom's face. Nick lowered his voice. "You *have* heard the name before." Nick glared at Dom. "Now you're going to hear it until you go to hell."

Nick lifted the two guns from the bar. "These are mine. Have your girls get permits."

Nick joined Jen in the car. Jen was talking fast in her excitement. "That was awesome! Thanks for letting me take the lead." She smiled, "That big one will be teased about that for a while." Jen giggled.

Nick chuckled at her excitement and pulled the car from the curb. "What body language did you notice?"

Jen got thoughtful. "I think when you mentioned Baxter ordering hits, he was surprised. His eyes narrowed and his nostrils flared. He also started to bounce his right foot."

Nick nodded in agreement. "I couldn't see the foot from where I was, but I agree the nostril flare is his tell." Nick glanced over, "Have you found out anything about Billow?"

"I've found out that our prison system is a mess. Since the budget cuts in 2012, the state has shifted as many of the mental prisoners as possible to private facilities. That includes troublemakers they want to get rid of. They just have the prison shrink declare them crazy and away they go. The prisoners know this, too. It's their 'get out of jail' card. When it comes to the criminally insane, nobody wants them. Nobody is prepared to deal with them. Did you know those prisoners have the right to refuse medication? So far I've tracked Billow to four different facilities. At least in our system he is still classified as dangerous."

Nick wasn't convinced that Billow was crazy. He was a killer with a vendetta. He had been raised in a good family, but was an underachiever and certainly demonstrated personality disorders, but that's not crazy.

"I know what I saw, Jen. He's out."

* * *

Gus could only think of one guy that would pay what he wanted for the guns. Alex. Alex's drug business was growing by leaps and bounds. He had already toppled four competing gangs. Alex was the 'man' if you wanted pharmaceuticals. He had everything the street wanted, including an endless supply. Gus pulled up in front of the known safe house and waited for someone to come outside. Moments later a young man walked over to his driver's window and asked, "What you need?"

Gus pointed to the back of the Jeep. "I've got some guns to sell to Alex."

"I'll be back, man. You wait here."

Alex walked out the front door clutching a handful of raw broccoli. Gus met him at the Jeep's back door and pulled out the long rifle.

Alex took a huge bite of the broccoli and nodded. "Old school. Best made sniper gun ever. How much you want?"

Gus swallowed, "I'd like five grand for all three guns."

Alex tossed the remaining broccoli in the street and examined the guns closer. "I ain't even interested in these other two. What kind of history I got to worry about?"

Gus smiled, "Belonged to an old man that be dead now. It's been stored in an attic for at least 20 years."

Alex smelled the rifle. "With the numbers filed off? Been kept clean and shot recently. I was gonna offer you two grand 'til you lied to me. Five hundred bucks. Take it or leave it."

Gus sighed, "I'll take it."

Alex lifted the rifle and looked at his friend. "Pay the man."

* * *

Jake Billow watched as Alex talked to some guy in a Jeep. He looked at his watch and moaned. He was running late. Elmhurst would be furious. He had spent hours last night on his computer researching everything he could find on Nick Stryker and had overslept.

Finally Alex went back in the house and the guy in the Jeep drove away. Jake parked in the drive, grabbed the pillowcase and knocked on the door.

A young man opened the door and yelled, "The man be here."

Jake pushed his way in and met Alex in the kitchen of the house. Jake sat the pillow case on the table and said, "I want 300 grand for these drugs, and that rifle." Now that Jake was close enough to see the rifle he wanted it.

Alex wasn't going to argue. Not many people scared him, but this guy had passed crazy three miles back. Alex looked in the pillowcase and smiled. "Pay the man."

CHAPTER 9

Wednesday 10:00 a.m.

*H*e rubbed his temples in the hope that it would stop the ringing sound in his ears. Light blasted through his fluttering eyelashes. This room was much larger than the one before. On the wall across from his cot, a door was partially open. He leaned to the left to see what was in there. It looked like the side of a shower stall. There was a pile of folded clothes on a bench, a pair of shoes sat waiting on the floor. A stack of towels had been crowned with a folded note. He fought to sit up straight. He had to get to that note. It felt as if his head had been shot with a machine gun. Wincing in pain, he lowered himself slowly back to the mattress and pulled the blanket over his head. More sleep, just a little more sleep.

* * *

Renee knocked a second time on Dr. Elmhurst's door and then slowly turned the knob to enter. She was surprised it wasn't locked and that he wasn't at work yet. She had just spent the last hour updating patient charts. Many had not had any entries for over a month. Others had entries that didn't make any sense. Surely Dr. Elmhurst could explain to her if they had changed systems or something.

Renee noticed a file on the corner of the desk that had a tab that said "Budget". She glanced at the door and used her pen to lift the cover just enough to read the top page. The report was covered in childlike cartoon drawings. A red pen had been used to make deep hash marks over many entries. Names were written in the margins with skulls drawn next to them. Obviously someone had vandalized his reports. She let the file cover drop and walked to the door. She opened it and came toe to toe with Dr. Elmhurst.

Startled, Renee stuttered, "Dr. Elmhurst, I was going to leave you a note and decided against it."

Dr. Elmhurst smiled, "Please, take a seat and we can discuss whatever your concern is." Renee cringed when Billow followed them into the room. She had met him when she first transferred to Building D. He seemed to follow Dr. Elmhurst around the facility and do little else. He gave her the creeps more than the patients did.

"You know our Assistant Administrator, Dr. Bates, don't you?" Dr. Elmhurst gestured toward Billow and seated himself at his desk. He nearly chuckled at introducing Billow as a doctor. Billow nodded at

Renee and took a position to lean against the wall. Renee could feel the heat of his stare on her face and travel down her body. She couldn't imagine his bedside manner as a doctor.

Dr. Elmhurst opened his center drawer, pulled out a file and opened it. "You've been with Brookfield Place for two years. RN, transferred to Building D from Building A almost a month ago. This has been quite a culture shock I would imagine."

Building A was for the highest functioning patients, many having been placed there by other mental health agencies and not the courts. They had the largest staff and were located the closest to the campus police.

Renee nodded.

Dr. Elmhurst continued, "We were fortunate that our offer to double your pay rate was attractive enough for you to transfer to us. What can I help you with today?"

Renee didn't appreciate the way Dr. Elmhurst pointed out her financial status. His tone clearly indicated that her pay rate should trump any complaints she might have.

"The medical charts for the patients are incomplete. Some are missing. Half of the patients are not wearing identification bracelets. I've left notes for the other shifts but no one has responded." What she wanted to say was that in three weeks she had concluded the entire place was in chaos.

Dr. Elmhurst smiled. "Well, I believe you have discovered why Nurse Nancy is no longer with us. I found her a nice enough gal, but a procrastinator on the paperwork. Of course, you know that many of our patients don't really require medical monitoring and many refuse medications. Dr. Bates and I have been discussing the need to get records and communications more in order, however, I appreciate your initiative in volunteering to take this project on."

Renee was stunned. She had not volunteered and was not remotely qualified. "Perhaps we can have a meeting of the full medical staff for assistance and input?"

Billow chuckled from across the room.

Dr. Elmhurst smiled, "At the moment you, Dr. Bates and I are officially the entire staff for Building D. I have been waiting for authority from the state to make the needed additions."

Renee was shocked. "I am the only staff nurse for Building D? Who does my duties when I'm not here?"

"We utilize staff from Buildings B and C when needed. We also have some highly functioning patients that fill those needs. Like Ryan."

"Ryan is a patient?" Renee's mind was reeling. "Did you know that Joshua killed Jane and then himself this morning? Ryan and two patients tried to intervene to stop him."

Dr. Elmhurst nodded. "Yes, the campus police sent me a text earlier. A most unfortunate incident. That's what I mean about some of our patients being high functioning. Many of these people were professionals before they became prisoners. Proper medication can make all of the difference. With our budget, we need them."

Dr. Elmhurst interrupted Renee's thoughts. "I believe another 30 days will show some marked improvements. Dr. Bates and I had just been discussing the extra burden that has been placed on you. We have decided to double your pay for this next 30 days. Does that satisfy your immediate concerns?"

Renee glanced at Dr. Bates and back to Dr. Elmhurst. Something was beyond crazy at this place and it wasn't the patients. Dr. Elmhurst had just offered her a bribe to stop asking questions. She decided to say whatever would get her out of the office. "That would go a long way in satisfying my concerns."

Dr. Elmhurst's crooked smile sent a chill up her spine. She closed the office door behind her and took a deep breath. She was going to find out what was really going on at Brookfield Place.

After Renee left the office Billow took her seat and said, "She's a problem. It won't take her long to figure out that I'm not a doctor."

Dr. Elmhurst opened the file on his desk marked 'Budget', grabbed his red pen and wrote Renee's name in the margin and sketched a skull next to it.

Billow smiled, "When?"

* * *

Lacey had made arrangements to take the day off from work to deal with her niece, Kamber. Nick had taken the news of Kamber's surprise visit well. He probably was so tired he hadn't really been listening. Lacey smiled as she made herself another cup of tea. She had practically burst with pride when the news announcer described Nick as a fearless hero for the people of Chicago. Lacey thought he was movie star handsome with his dark hair and cobalt blue eyes, yet he didn't seem to know it. There wasn't a vain bone in Nick's body. He wasn't a hero, it was his job, his duty; he was a part of a team.

Lacey's phone rang and the caller ID displayed her sister Joyce's name. Lacey had called Joyce last night to let her know Kamber was okay. "Kamber is in the shower. Tell me what's going on." Lacey sat down and listened as Joyce explained her frustrations with Kamber this last year.

"Lacey, I don't know how to thank you. Maybe you can help her 'find herself'. She's all over the place emotionally. She doesn't listen to me."

"You know I'll do whatever I can. How long do you think she'll want to stay?"

"Forever is what she told me! She thinks Chicago has the answers to all her problems. All she talks about is living near you in a real city. She has my financial support if she wants an apartment of her own. Just make sure it's in a good area."

Lacey was surprised by her sister's attitude. It sounded as if she had already resolved to accept Kamber never coming back. She sounded defeated and broken.

Kamber stood in the kitchen doorway, wrapped in a towel and dripping water on the hardwood floors.

"Is that mom? Tell her I'm not a baby. She doesn't have to call and check up on me!" Kamber turned around quickly and slammed the bathroom door.

Lacey sighed, "Did you hear that?"

"Yeah. You know she left and didn't even leave me a note? By the time I heard from you, I was ready to call the police."

Lacey remembered her own stage of independent rebellion and smiled. "Look, Joyce, let's give this a couple of weeks and see where things go. I haven't even had a chance to talk to her much yet. Remember how I used to be?"

Joyce gave a short chuckle. "That's my problem. I do remember how you used to be."

Lacey used the time that Kamber was in the shower to place a call to Nick's dad, Martin. She had explained to him that Kamber had moved to Chicago to become a famous photographer and film director, but had no formal training. Martin had suggested that she take his creative film class that had just started. He said he could help her enroll under a special audit status.

Kamber joined Lacey in the kitchen and waited silently while Lacey finished reading a legal brief. Lacey looked up and Kamber blurted, "I'm sorry. I don't know why I spout off like that. And I slammed your door. I'm acting like a child."

Lacey frowned, "You just took all of my fun away. Now I can't scold you." Lacey watched as Kamber prepared a bowl of cereal and took a seat at the small table. Kamber exploded in excitement when Lacey told her about Martin's class.

"Are you serious? Oh, my God! When can I start?"

"Let's give him a call when you finish your breakfast and find out what documents you need to register. One thing at a time, pretty girl." Lacey smiled and Kamber lifted her bowl and drank the rest of her cereal.

Kamber had a milk mustache across her face as she took a deep breath and then declared, "Done."

* * *

Dom hung up from a troubling call with his number two investment banker. The banker had spent last night going over Travis Cummings' computer files. There was only one irregularity, a big one. The skim from Brookfield Place had not been posted for the month, 70 thousand dollars.

Dom hadn't even had five minutes to think about the implications of that call when Tommy walked in. Dom leaned forward resting his elbows on the tabletop. He was furious that Tommy would presume he could talk to him without making prior arrangements.

Dom shouted, "Don't you know the Feds are probably following you? You bring those problems here?"

Tommy held his hands up in despair. "I have to tell you something urgent. I didn't know what else to do."

Dom couldn't imagine any information that Tommy would have that could be so important. Tommy had been in prison for 25 years and they hadn't even missed him.

Tommy asked, "Can we speak alone?"

Dom nodded for his bodyguard to frisk Tommy and then move toward the door.

Dom exhaled, "What's so urgent?"

Tommy clutched the edge of the table for support. He was shaking so badly Dom held his glass to keep it from tipping over. "There is a plan to kill you, Northside boss, Milo. Anthony is supposed to deliver you to an ambush."

Dom reached across the table and clasped both of Tommy's hands to steady them. "Tell me more about this plan. Your loyalty will be rewarded." Dom listened to Tommy for 20 minutes and then told him to leave. Dom motioned for the rest of his crew to stay away.

He had to think. He had to fit this new information into what he knew. If Milo wanted to take over the Westside crew, he would certainly kill Dom's lawyer. He might also kill Cummings' wife to ensure the cooperation of Cummings during the transition. Of course, he would kill Cummings after he understood Dom's operation. Milo might have worried that Carson was too loyal to Dom to be trusted. That's probably why Carson was shot. It all made sense.

Maybe it had already started. Maybe Cummings had given Milo the skim from the hospital. Dom leaned back and lit his cigar. He was a crew boss. The Outfit boss would have to approve Dom's retaliation. Dom dialed the number. He was confident his request for revenge would be granted. He was 'The Golden Boy' of the outfit; had been since 1975. Nobody would ever come close to accomplishing what he had done that summer. Nobody.

* * *

Jen and Wayne were reviewing ballistic reports on the hits that were tied to Baxter. Nick had secured the homicide files for the same victims. Some had been delivered from the cold case file unit. Nick was convinced there was a witness buried somewhere in the case boxes that could identify the shooter. Nobody is perfect and this shooter had to make mistakes. Attorney Baxter's bank records clearly demonstrated he was making money outside of his legal practice. More than likely it was the reason he had been killed. Find the motive, find the killer.

Jen walked over with a list. "Eight of the Baxter hits were done with the rifle that shot Reggie Lomas."

Nick quickly pushed his chair from the desk to lean back. "Lomas? He was the only one not mobbed up. Karen Lomas did not pay Baxter any money. But Baxter's hit man killed Reggie Lomas?"

Wayne walked over to Nick's desk. "As crazy as it sounds, our first idea might have been right."

"Lomas was a mistake."

Jen was staring at her computer monitor. "You guys are starting to convince me. New topic: come look at this camera image from the Starke hit. The surveillance camera across the street took this. Starke is leaning heavily into the wall there, probably just got shot. See that flash up in the corner of this picture?"

Nick smiled, "Sniper flash. We need to locate a camera to show us that other angle."

Jen smiled, "That's not all, look at this." She clicked on another tab at the top of her screen and pulled up a different video. "This is footage from the Miller shooting seven months ago. Miller falling backwards...look up there."

Wayne yelled, "Sniper flash. Why didn't they see these before?"

Jen shrugged, "The 109th just sent this stuff over this morning from cold case. I think it just got missed."

Nick's phone at his desk rang, "Yeah?" Nick glanced at Jen as he stood. "Chief wants me again."

Nick found Agent Phillips in the Chief's office. Nick's Chief had a half smile on his face. "We have an issue we need to deal with."

Nick said, "Okay," as he lowered himself in a chair.

His Chief continued, "I got a call from the Mayor's office. Seems someone there wants you publically punished for the destruction you caused on Michigan Street yesterday."

Nick raised an eyebrow, "Punished? What did I do?"

The Chief cleared his throat and read from a paper, "Ninety grand estimate for repairing hole in the middle of Michigan Street. Thirty grand reimbursement to city's bond company for the cost of four storefront windows, and 50 grand repair to an iron gate at the alley next to Newman's."

Agent Phillips snickered at Nick's expression. "Your conversation with Dom had immediate impact. Obviously someone in the mayor's office has ties to Dom. I'll be following up on that. It was suggested that your Chief need only inflict a three day penalty. That protects you from anything negative entering your personnel file, and it still gives them something for the newspaper."

Nick looked at his Chief. "Is this serious? Dom calls the Mayor's office and gets me punished for helping at a crime scene?"

The Chief answered, "More than likely Dom called a 'friendly' at the Mayor's office and demanded something negative happen to you fast. He wants to send you a message. The Mayor's office has already released a statement to the newspapers that you faced a penalty hearing today. This is the penalty hearing."

Nick couldn't believe what he was hearing. "So, this isn't anything real, we're just appeasing the mob?"

Agent Phillips interrupted, "Oh, this is real. We now know Dom still has someone in the Mayor's office. Your visit with him moved him to make this request. Dom made a mistake. This will come back and bite him."

The Chief smiled, "I'll let you pick your own punishment. What can you do without for three days?"

Nick went back to the squad room where Jen and Wayne looked at him expectantly. Nick said, "The Mayor's office has put out a newspaper report that I'm being punished for the collateral damage at the robbery yesterday." Nick smiled, "This is revenge for ticking off Dom two hours ago. At least I got to pick my own punishment."

Jen rolled her eyes, "Can't wait to hear this."

Nick said, "No grenades for three days."

Wayne roared. Sam and Jen just shook their heads.

CHAPTER 10

Wednesday 11:00 am

*T*he note said 'Be ready to leave at 8 pm. There is a watch in the pants pocket'. He sat on the toilet while he dug into the pockets of the pants and found the watch. 11 a.m. Next to the shower was a tray of three sandwiches and two glasses of juice. He moaned as he devoured the first sandwich. His legs were shaky, but he couldn't resist the lure of a hot shower. He reached for the safety grab bar and pulled himself in. He couldn't stand any longer and sat naked on the cold tiles of the floor. He reached up and turned on the water. Once the temperature was hot, he scooted over to be under the water spray, grabbed the soap and winced at how frail his body looked.

Ryan entered the room, locked the door behind him and peeked into the bathroom. "Good, you're up. Spend the afternoon trying to exercise your legs. You're going to have to walk some tonight."

Whatever drugs they had been giving him must have been very powerful. The simplest of thoughts seemed to vaporize in seconds. He looked at Ryan, "What's my name? Where am I? Who are you?"

Ryan exhaled, "They're holding you prisoner. I'll tell you everything when we get out of here. I have to leave now."

* * *

Travis Cummings stopped at the iron gate, so the guard could check his identification. The guard filled out a visitor ID for him. Travis studied the map of the campus from the brochure the guard had given him. He had assumed there would just be one building for administration. It appeared from the map there were a dozen buildings scattered across the 150 acre complex.

Travis looked at the guard and asked, "Where would I find Dr. Elmhurst?"

The guard flipped a few pages on his clipboard and then answered, "He's the administrator for Building D. Drive clear to the back."

The gate opened and Travis followed the service road back to Building D. He could think of any number of places he would rather be this morning. He grabbed his briefcase that had his reports of the history of payments in case Dr. Elmhurst tried to claim there had been some new agreement. Inside, a large bronze sign showed Dr. Elmhurst's office was on the first floor, Section A.

A pleasant looking woman approached him. "May I help you?"

"Yes, I'm looking for Dr. Elmhurst. Could you direct me to his office?"

Renee answered, "I'll walk you there. When you are ready to leave, have Dr. Elmhurst page either Renee or Ryan. You don't want to be unescorted."

Travis thought she was being overly dramatic. As they made their way to Dr. Elmhurst's office, he quickly changed his mind. People peeked at them from partially opened doors. Some made noises and pointed at him, some began to follow them. Two people ran crisscross from door to door in the hallway; slamming doors behind them, only to peek out a moment later.

Renee said, "It's a game they play when they're in a good mood."

Travis nodded and clutched his briefcase closer to his chest. Odd singing crept through the air and mixed with occasional yelps. A rhythmic clanging could be heard behind the closed door labeled 'Kitchen'. There wasn't enough money in Chicago for him to work here. They turned to the left and at the end of the hall Travis saw a door with Dr. Elmhurst's name on it.

"Thank you for the escort."

Renee walked away and Travis knocked on the door as he opened it. He wasn't in the mood to afford Dr. Elmhurst any social courtesies. Dr. Elmhurst sat at his desk. A man stood across the room looking out the window.

Travis announced, "I am Travis Cummings and we have an issue that must be resolved this morning."

Dr. Elmhurst gestured for Travis to take a seat. Billow turned from the window. Travis stared at them both. "Well? Why haven't you returned my calls? This is not an optional fee we have discussed. I have brought reports to remind you that this has been paid every month long before you obtained employment here three years ago." Travis started to reach in his briefcase and Dr. Elmhurst stopped him.

"It won't be necessary to produce any documents. I have to confess that we have had a lot of problems here, not the least of which are some delays in receiving our state funding. Now that we are speaking in person, remind me what this fee is for."

Travis couldn't believe his ears. Was this man crazy? "It's your percentage that's paid for 'protection'. The mob, get it? You wouldn't have been awarded this contract from the state without them. What did you think it was? You've been signing the monthly checks and mailing them to me for three years." Travis didn't need the aggravation of Dr. Elmhurst playing innocent. He wanted the money.

Dr. Elmhurst glanced at Billow. Billow had raised his eyebrows at the mention of the mob. That was trouble they didn't need.

Dr. Elmhurst unlocked the bottom drawer exposing a large amount of cash. "What is the amount we owe, Mr. Cummings?"

Travis answered, "It hasn't changed since last month." Now he was beyond annoyed. "Seventy grand that you should have paid three weeks ago and another 70 due next week."

Dr. Elmhurst grabbed four large piles of cash from the bottom drawer. He had just placed his half of the money from Alex there less than an hour ago.

"Let's count this out and take care of next month too." Dr. Elmhurst counted ten thousand to return to the drawer, and counted out the remaining 140 grand for Travis. "I'm most embarrassed that you needed to make a personal appearance. I assure you this will not happen again. May I make a photocopy of your visitor pass in order to verify to security that you arrived safely?"

Travis stuffed the money in his briefcase, handed over his visitor pass and asked, "Could you have Renee escort me out?"

Billow stepped away from the wall, "I'll escort you to your car."

Billow returned to Dr. Elmhurst's office ten minutes later. He sat opposite of the desk and leaned back. "I'm guessing you wanted his visitor pass so you could get his address."

Dr. Elmhurst chuckled, "45 Dalton Street. Expensive address. He's probably king of his little townhouse neighborhood. Wonder if any of his neighbors suspect he's all mobbed up?"

Dr. Elmhurst knew he would have to convince Billow he had done the right thing by giving up the cash. "The last thing we need is the mob in our business. Giving him this cash just bought us another 30 days. If I double up on pills for Alex we can make 600 grand a week. I say we made a good deal." Dr. Elmhurst sighed, "You probably need to plan on being completely independent of this place within 30 days. That's when I plan to leave and all hell will break loose."

Billow thought letting Cummings keep the cash was stupid. There was only so much the mob could do. The only contact the mob had was with Elmhurst. The mob wasn't his problem. Billow decided he'd get that money before Cummings could give it to the mob.

Billows asked, "Is that ID for me ready yet? I'm getting tired of crawling in and out of your trunk."

Dr. Elmhurst opened the center drawer. "Got it yesterday."

He slid it over and Billow pinned it to his jacket. Elmhurst had simply ordered a replacement state ID through the state's printing contractor and had it mailed.

Billow smiled, "I'm going to test this with the guard and borrow your car."

Dr. Elmhurst had reservations, but tossed his keys across the desk. "When you get to the guard, just look impatient. Have my car back by six."

"I can do that."

After easily making it past the guard Billow pushed the car to the speed limit. If he was lucky, he could catch up with Cummings' car and not get stopped by authorities. He drove for almost five miles and hadn't seen Cummings' car yet. The 'Ride Share' lot was just ahead. He pulled in next to the blue van and parked. After switching vehicles he proceeded to head toward town. The rifle peeked out from under the passenger seat. A new box of ammo beckoned him to play.

Finally Billow saw the silver BMW weaving between lanes trying to outmaneuver the increasing traffic congestion as they neared the city. Billow smiled as the BMW slowed to merge around a highway construction project. He quickly caught up to Cummings and followed a few cars behind.

Billow had all afternoon to get that money. The information he found on Stryker from his computer had been copied to a small notebook in his breast pocket. After he took care of Cummings he could start crafting his plan for Stryker. By the time authorities pieced things together, he would be out of the country and living the good life as Dr. John Bates.

Lacey and Kamber stood in the large hallway of the Liberal Arts building and waited for Martin's lecture to finish. It had been years since Lacey had been on the campus. She couldn't believe how much things had changed. Thankfully, the south campus where Martin's office was located still looked the same. Lacey worried about Kamber navigating the city's transit and bus system to get there.

"You know, we need to get Nick's advice as to the safest way for you to get around. I'm not comfortable turning you loose in this city until you know it better."

Kamber watched a young man walk toward them. She had barely listened to Lacey. "Whatever you say is fine." Kamber smiled at Lacey and Lacey knew she had just been politely dismissed.

The young man stopped at Martin's door and asked Kamber, "Are you Kamber Fry?"

Startled, Kamber answered, "Yes."

The young man nodded, "Professor Stryker asked me to be here and see if we might work on a documentary project together. I'm Chad Wilson."

Kamber was so excited she couldn't quit smiling. Her first assignment and it was a documentary. Chad and Kamber quickly began to assess each other's equipment knowledge and expertise. Lacey enjoyed watching their animated exchange. Chad was pleasant and seemed very bright, but Lacey suspected he was going to find Kamber a challenge to keep up with. It was decided that Chad had more technical experience, but admittedly lacked the creative elements possessed by Kamber.

Martin's students poured out from the classroom and Lacey, Kamber and Chad went in. Martin gave Lacey a hug and shook Kamber's hand. He reviewed the documents Kamber had prepared and finally looked at the two young students and smiled.

"Before you leave here, I want to know you have a plan. This assignment is already a week old, so you are behind the bus on this. Pick an issue for a short documentary. The assignment is only going to require a 15 minute film, but it must show off your technical skills and deliver a powerful social message." Martin watched as Chad shrugged and glanced at Kamber.

Kamber quickly took the lead. "I would like to focus on runaways in Chicago, or the homeless."

Chad's face brightened. "Either one works for me!"

Martin directed his next comment to Lacey, "These topics will lure these two into the underbelly of the city."

Lacey felt her stomach sink. If this is what motherhood feels like, she wanted no part of it. Lacey looked at Kamber, "You don't know the first thing about the real Chicago. Maybe a story about Navy Pier or the museums would be a better start."

Chad touched Kamber's arm before she could respond. Chad offered, "I've lived here all of my life and I know how to read the neighborhoods and the people. We can be very careful and I have my own car. Please?"

Frankie listened to Artie talk about how he was going to help some lady he kept calling 'Momma' take blankets and pillows to the tunnel people tonight. Evidently some non-profit had collected the items for the community. Because the location of the community had to be kept secret, they could not deliver them. Frankie couldn't understand Artie's motives. Who cares? Artie had been rambling for about ten minutes thinking that Frankie was listening. Frankie was trying to decide the best place to take Artie to kill him.

Artie suddenly asked, "You didn't answer me. Have you decided what we should do with that head?"

Pounding at the front door shattered the silence. Frankie moaned as he slowly rose from his chair and walked over to open the door. A cop, in a suit.

The man held up a badge, "Agent Miller, FBI. I'm here to do a parole compliance check on Artie Corsone."

CHAPTER 11

Wednesday 3:00 p.m.

*H*e had fallen asleep directly after his shower. Ryan had told him to exercise but the influence of the drugs had made it impossible. Now he was staring at the tattoo on his forearm with pride. It was the only information he had as to his identity. The drugs he had been given made him feel as if he were in a dream. Fragmented memories of his life were quickly pushed aside as a hallucinated army of beetles charged toward him to attack. They oozed from the walls and raced toward his cot only to vanish one second before reaching him.

He tried to drink some of the juice that his captor had brought. His tongue felt numb and made it difficult to swallow. Juice poured from the corners of his mouth and stained his shirt. Extreme exhaustion beckoned him back to the cot even though greater demons waited for him there. He fought falling asleep. He remembered he was supposed *to exercise his legs. He was getting out tonight; he had to be ready.*

His head pounded, his eyelids dropped and then refused to open. He would exercise later. He had time.

* * *

Travis Cummings glanced over to his passenger seat at the bulging briefcase. He was stuck in construction traffic, but proud of himself for collecting Dom's money. It needed to get into Dom's account as soon as possible. He suddenly realized he couldn't deposit 140 thousand dollars in cash without a lot of questions. Questions he didn't want to answer. Travis fumbled his fingers around in the console until he found his hidden pack of cigarettes. He cracked his window open and took a long drag. He would have to take the cash directly to Dom.

Travis couldn't chance calling Dom from his cell phone. Not with that Detective Stryker accusing him of murder. His phone records were already going to be a problem. He would have to stop somewhere for a burner phone or deliver the cash unannounced. The prospect of just walking in to speak to Dom after Dom had told him to stay away didn't seem smart. He would call and arrange a meeting.

At the first available exit Travis turned off from the highway. He never noticed the blue panel van behind him. Another two miles toward the city and Travis spotted a strip mall that had a liquor store sign boasting cheap prepaid phones. He pulled in, tucked a spare jacket carefully over his briefcase and locked the car. Travis impatiently waited while the clerk rang up a bottle of wine and some jerky for an old man.

Travis paid for his phone and walked toward the door just as a car horn started honking in the parking lot. He looked to the space where he had parked his car and saw that his BMW lights were flashing. His alarm had been triggered. Travis bolted to his car and found the passenger window had been shattered. His briefcase was gone. He unlocked the driver's door and simply sat down. It wasn't possible. He had only been gone a few minutes and he had covered his briefcase carefully. Now what? A full five minutes passed as he tried to plan his next move. He didn't have a choice; he would have to use his own money to pay Dom. He couldn't get the hospital to pay twice.

Travis turned the key to start the engine at the exact moment both his windshields exploded. First the rear, then the front. He couldn't imagine what was happening. Seconds later he felt the buzz of something pass his head. He watched as the rear windshield of the car parked in front of him exploded. My God! Someone was shooting at him!

* * *

Jake Billow cursed under his breath. He had missed Cummings' head twice. He knew he couldn't blame the rifle, it was perfection. Billow casually drove the van back into traffic from the other side of the parking lot. No one watching would have guessed that he had anything to do with the chaos in front of the liquor store.

He should have been able to make that shot. No matter. He really didn't need to kill Cummings anyway, he had the money. It had just seemed like a fun idea even though he preferred to shoot cops.

Before he confronted Nick he would need to spend some time at the firing range and get used to this rifle. He smiled at the dark leather briefcase sprinkled with tiny remnants of shattered glass. Next stop was to his apartment to put the cash in a safe place.

He glanced at his watch. He still had a few hours before Dr. Elmhurst would need his car. That gave him plenty of time to verify some of the internet information he had discovered about Nick.

✳ ✳ ✳

Nick and Jen drove to 121 North LaSalle Street where the communication center for Chicago's Office of Emergency Management was located. Operation Virtual Shield was the city's nickname for the estimated fifteen thousand cameras connected in a fiber-optic video network loop. Operation Virtual Shield was not monitored in real time but used to recall valuable evidence when needed. A tech located the street for the dates and times of the sniper flashes from their other videos. Nick and Jen watched silently as the monitor displayed the sidewalk scenes of both shooting locations for fifteen minutes prior and then fifteen minutes after the actual shots were fired.

Nick looked at Jen. "Did you see?"

Jen shook her head, "See what?"

Nick asked the tech to play the video backwards. Nick suddenly said, "Stop right there."

Jen leaned closer, "All I see is an old man walking to the bus stop on the corner."

Nick looked at the tech. "Take the other video back to ten minutes after that shot."

Jen leaned in close again. "I see an old man waiting for the bus, a couple of kids on bikes and a lady that obviously just spent her whole paycheck shopping. What am I missing?"

Nick asked, "Do you notice how rigid the old man's right leg moves? See his arm tucked tight to his waist?"

Jen turned to face Nick. "He has a rifle in his right pant leg. He's holding the stock with his right hand. We're looking for an old man?"

Nick remembered what Agent Phillips had said about his mom. That she was a master of disguise. Was it possible? Nick shook the thought from his mind. Any hit man would be a master of disguise, too.

Nick sighed, "I'm not sure what we're looking for yet." He asked the tech to make them a copy of the videos. Nick asked, "What do you have by 45 and 54 Dalton Street Monday night around seven?"

The tech keyed in the addresses. "Cameras are concentrated in the heavy crime areas. All I have over there is a bus stop cam."

"Let's see it."

The tech pulled up the available footage and stopped when Nick asked him to.

Jen smiled, "Got an old man getting on the bus. But his right knee is bent."

Nick said, "Alexia and Baxter were shot with a pistol. Where does this bus go from here?"

The tech switched to the bus terminal schedule. "Stops over by Madison West."

Nick smiled, "One block from Baxter's townhouse."

Nick's phone rang, he looked at Jen. "Travis Cummings." Nick answered.

Travis sounded frantic as sirens screamed in the background. "You're going to have another homicide. Someone is trying to kill me!"

* * *

Lacey invited Chad to lunch with them at the student cafeteria. Kamber and Chad had hit it off well. Lacey could barely get a word in the conversation.

Kamber had come prepared with a notebook and insisted they schedule their plan for proceeding. After deciding that addressing the homeless issue would be easier than locating runaways, Kamber and Chad abruptly stopped talking. Obviously they were both deep in thought for a next step.

Lacey seized the moment with a suggestion. "Nick has a friend that is involved in helping the homeless that live in tunnels under the city."

Kamber jumped in excitement spilling Chad's drink on the table.

"Sorry. Oh my gosh! We have to talk to him!" Kamber looked at Chad, "Can you imagine the film we could get from people actually living in tunnels?"

Lacey put her finger in the air to stop Kamber. "These are people. They deserve respect and privacy. I'm not so sure that your cameras would be welcome."

Chad said, "We could talk to this guy that Nick knows and find out what they would let us do."

Kamber clapped her hands together, "Maybe they would let us stay over a couple of nights to get the real feel of it?"

Lacey moaned. What was she going to do with this girl? "Kamber, this isn't a pajama party. These people are living day to day trying to survive. You have no concept of the dangers they face every minute."

Kamber looked serious. "You're right, I don't. Most people don't understand because it's all a dirty little secret. Our documentary might make them care."

Chad looked at Kamber and said, "Wow. You really know how to get your point across. This documentary is going to be awesome."

Lacey took out her phone and dialed Nick for Mitch's number. She could tell from Nick's voice he was in the middle of something and it made her feel guilty.

Nick gave her the number and said, "Don't tell me you're dumping me for Mitch."

Lacey laughed, "No. Kamber thinks she wants to spend the night with the tunnel people."

Nick took a moment before responding. "I think I need to make time to meet Kamber fairly soon."

"I'm so glad you said that."

* * *

Frankie stepped back to let Agent Miller into the apartment. Artie busied himself feverishly wiping the tiny countertop around the sink. Agent Miller walked in, pointed to the sofa and asked, "May I?"

Frankie nodded and said, "I'm in the middle of breakfast. You two do what you have to."

Agent Miller glanced around looking for a blue cooler. He couldn't believe the Bureau actually believed their tip that Artie had brought a frozen head in a blue cooler to Frankie's apartment last night.

Artie walked in and took a seat across from the couch. "I was told that you would be visiting soon."

Agent Miller produced a small notebook from his pocket. "Mr. Corsone, how is it that you ended up here, sharing an apartment with Mr. Frankie Mullen? It is Mullen right?"

Miller was looking toward the kitchen at Frankie. Frankie grunted and continued to eat. His mind was racing on how to keep the cop from finding the frozen head in his freezer.

Artie smiled. "Frankie and I had been friends back in school, decades ago. I took the chance he would be willing to do me a favor and let me stay here a bit."

Miller nodded as he wrote. "Frankie, what school was that exactly?"

Artie swallowed. Damn. This cop was smarter than he thought.

Frankie looked over his fork and answered, "I don't know what he's talking about. I quit school in eighth grade. He used to hang out in the hood from time to time. Artie has memory problems these days. And he stinks."

Artie smiled. "It's true. Sometimes I stink."

Miller asked, "How long will you be staying at this address?"

Artie answered, "I'm thinking a year or so, right Frankie?"

"Hell no. You better give him instructions on what to do when he moves. It'll be soon."

Miller smiled to himself. It was refreshing not to get rehearsed answers. Miller handed Artie a printed form. "Here are the rules and conditions of your parole. Instructions on notifications are on the back in case you do move." Miller stood, "I'm required to do a search of the premises for drugs and weapons."

Artie frowned, "Oh, dear. I just refilled a pain prescription. I never even thought about that being a problem."

Miller walked to the kitchen, straight to the freezer and opened the door. Frankie nearly had a stroke. He had a mouthful of scrambled eggs and spit them into a paper towel. Artie started to breathe deeply and clutch at his chest. Miller slammed the freezer door shut and started to open cabinets. "You probably should just throw that roast away. Freezer burn."

CHAPTER 12

Wednesday 4:00 p.m.

There was no mirror above the sink. He could feel facial hair and wondered if he had always worn a beard? He ran his fingers past his forehead grateful to feel he had a full head of hair. How old was he? There was a toothbrush and toothpaste on the sink, which he used. He bit gently on his tongue again. Parts of it were still numb. His legs were still weak, but he wanted to take another shower. It seemed no amount of soap made him feel clean. If he could stand through the whole shower, he might be ready to exercise.

In the middle of his shower a name came to mind. Ryan. That's what his captor's name was. Was he really a captor? Tonight, Ryan was going to save him. He dressed again and began walking slowly from one side of the room to the other. It wasn't long before he needed to rest. He sat on the toilet instead of the cot. The cot made him sleepy and he was running out of time.

* * *

Nick and Jen arrived in front of the liquor store to find Travis Cummings sitting in the back of a patrol unit. The entire strip mall had been evacuated and crime scene tape outlined the parking lot nearly to the street. A uniformed cop greeted Nick. "He won't tell us anything but his name. He says he'll only talk to you."

Jen walked over to the BMW. Crime Scene Unit techs said they were finishing up. One of them held up an evidence bag. "We've got your two bullets. Good thing the shooter missed, these babies would have done some serious damage. Long range rifle probably shot from over there." He pointed across the parking lot to where Billow had been parked.

Jen looked around for cameras. The tech shook his head. "If you're looking for cameras, we've got three, all pointed in the wrong direction. The liquor store camera is just for show."

Nick walked over to the patrol car to speak to Travis. "What happened?"

Travis focused on Nick's eyes. "After I talked to you about Alexia, I checked up on you some. You're not half bad for a cop. I trust you, is what I'm trying to say. I can tell you a lot, but I need a deal and protection. Federal, as in FBI. You won't regret it."

Nick nodded, shut the patrol unit door and dialed Agent Phillips. Nick relayed the message from Travis. Agent Phillips responded, "Get him back to your building before he changes his mind. If any-one sees him in your building, they will assume it's because of his wife's murder. I'll meet you there with a deal. Nick, his info is for the FBI."

"I want this, too. You can trust me."

Agent Phillips didn't respond right away. "If he's willing to say what I think he is, you're not going to be able to act on any of the information. The mob is an FBI case."

"At least I would know what the problems are. Who knows? You might find me useful."

Phillips was well aware of Nick's skills. His train-ing in the SEALs taught him to follow orders and respect authority. Phillips sighed, "Just bring him in; I'll see what I can do."

Nick opened the patrol unit door again and spoke to Travis, "You can ride with me. Your deal is being put together now. The FBI is going to meet us back at the station." Nick noticed Travis shaking. "Are you alright? Do you need something?"

Travis smoothed his suit pants with his palms, probably to remove perspiration. "I'll never be alright after today."

* * *

Mitch hefted a large black garbage bag stuffed with blankets through the tunnel door in the basement to drop on the other side. Joseph knew to check every couple of days to see if donations had been made for the community.

Momma came up behind Mitch and startled him. "I got one more bag here."

Mitch bumped his head in the opening. "Dang. You would make a good spy, you know? Didn't even hear you sneak up behind me."

Momma chuckled and handed him the bag. "I got a favor to ask. Well, actually I have two favors."

Mitch leaned against the basement wall and said, "I know, don't mention to anyone that Artie has a frozen head in a cooler." Mitch rolled his eyes for comic effect.

Momma smiled, "You're a smart boy. I just don't want Artie gettin' into trouble when he was just helpin' us out."

Mitch nodded. "Yeah, Eli and I talked about that. We figured we really didn't see anything anyway."

"Thanks. Nick's girlfriend, Lacey, called. She has a niece that is going to the University to study film makin'. She and her friend want to do a documentary on the community. Could you go ask Joseph what he would allow?"

Mitch scratched his head. "What do you mean? What kind of stuff does she want to do?"

Momma handed Mitch a list. "I wrote down the things she mentioned. He can cross off any he wants."

Mitch read the list out loud, "Interviews, filming, spending the night. Spending the night? Is she nuts?"

Momma laughed and patted Mitch's shoulder. "You go and talk to Joseph and get back here in time for the dinner rush. From what you told me 'bout visitin' that place where Renee works, it sounds like the 'community' is practically a church!"

* * *

Renee glanced at her watch and knocked on Dr. Elmhurst's door. At four in the afternoon he should be deep into the daily reports from yesterday. His voice beckoned her to come in and she found him standing at his window with the same few files at the corner of his desk.

"You have to admire the beauty of these grounds. Did you know that with 120 acres we have the largest facility of this type in the Midwest? Amazing." He turned and sat at his desk. "Prime real estate this close to Chicago. A little construction to move the security wall and a lot of money could be made with an upscale housing project on the North side quite easily." He smiled.

The guy was loony tunes. Who would want to live next to a prison for the criminally insane? Renee nodded in agreement and said, "I need about an hour to go over to Building A and fill out some reports I missed. If you don't mind, I want to go now so I can be back by the time our patients go to the dining room."

"You know, I think there is a little creek over on that side, too. That always bumps the price up. Sorry, you asked about Building A? Go ahead, we're fine here."

Renee made a quick half smile and left the office. She clutched her purse close to her side as she made her way to her car. Inside her purse was a list of all of the passwords to get into Building D's administrative records and communications with the state. She had found them stuck in the break room cubby marked 'Nancy'. It seems the previous nurse had some questions about Building D, too. Renee pulled in front of Building A and parked. Even the landscaping showed more life on this side of the campus.

Renee made her way to the Administration office and knocked on Tyler's door. Tyler yelled, "Come in."

When he saw Renee he jumped up and ran over to give her a hug. "I knew you'd be back. God, we missed you!"

Renee started to cry. Tyler backed up and then shut his office door. "What's wrong?"

Renee composed herself with sheer will. "You're going to help me find out what's going on in Building D." She told Tyler what she had witnessed and pushed copies of the papers she had confiscated across his desk. "I'll check out half and you take half. I can work on mine tonight at home. Will you help me?"

Tyler recognized a list of security codes for Building D's Administrative and state reports. "I.... we could get fired over this. What are we looking for?"

"I don't know. For one, we don't have any narcotics. If I need something for a patient, Dr. Elmhurst says he'll see to it." Renee was having trouble defining exactly what troubled her so much. "I know he has staff from Buildings B and C helping, but wouldn't I see someone eventually? I've been there three weeks! Please trust me. Something is very wrong."

Tyler shook his head, "You're mistaken about staff from Buildings B and C taking shifts there. You must have misunderstood Dr. Elmhurst. The state won't allow that." Tyler leaned back in his chair. "You know the rumors. Building D changes people. Maybe you're just upset?" Renee frowned at him. Tyler added, "What does Nancy say about this? Have you talked to her?"

Renee said, "Nancy? She quit three weeks ago. That's how I got the transfer. I'm the only nurse for the whole building."

Tyler entered a few keystrokes to his computer. "She's still getting a paycheck. And she's still sending email reports to the state. I've got one she sent this morning. Here, a narcotics order." Tyler's brow furrowed. "That's odd. She's placed two narcotics orders this week. One was delivered yesterday." Tyler made a couple of more entries and exhaled. "She's made six narcotic orders in the last three weeks." Tyler stared at Renee. "These entries were made during the day shift. You really haven't seen her?"

* * *

Dom did not appreciate Joey arriving late. "Your boss calls so you decide to take a nap? What's your problem? You think because your name is Joey Lacastra you can make me wait? You're worthless to me if I can't have you when I want you!" Dom purchased Joey's contract from the Gambino family in New York. He had been a sniper in the Army and decided to follow his family's footsteps with the crew after his discharge.

"You need to learn to relax." Joey stuck a toothpick in the corner of his mouth and grinned.

Dom lunged forward and yelled, "You need to learn respect!"

Joey pulled back from Dom's fury. Dom's eyes said it all. He was a full blown maniac. It was a look Joey had seen before on his dad and it never ended well.

Joey composed himself and muttered, "Sorry, Dom. It won't happen again."

Dom glanced around to make sure no one would hear. He slipped a piece of paper to Joey. "This guy disappointed me. Take him out. He's a hot shot banker downtown; I put home and work addresses for you there at the bottom." Dom smiled, "No sniper shot. I want you up close and personal. Make him hurt. You make sure he knows where it's coming from."

✳ ✳ ✳

Before Agent Phillips acknowledged the presence of Travis, he took Nick aside. "That bug you managed to plant at Dom's bar this morning just picked up an interesting conversation about our guy here."

Nick asked, "What?"

"Dom just put a contract on Cummings. Joey Lacastra, he's a New York boy, Gambino family. Dom didn't get him cheap."

Nick shrugged, "New name to me. If this conversation just happened, it means Cummings has two people trying to kill him."

Phillips nodded, "Well, should we see what Mr. Cummings has to say?"

Frankie stood at the kitchen window waving the fresh air inside. He was certain he had experienced heart palpitations when Agent Miller had been there earlier. A flash of light outside at the street caught Frankie's attention. In an SUV down the block the parking mirror was angled wrong. It was bent too far outward. The sun blasted from the top rim of the mirror. The driver was watching the sidewalk across the street. Probably the entrance to Frankie's building. Frankie looked down the street in the opposite direction. A pickup truck was parked and the driver reading a newspaper. A passenger in the truck was talking on a cell phone and looking toward Frankie's building. Suits. Black suits.

Artie was in the living room still yacking about tunnel people.

Frankie broke the silence. "Say, I'm not saying you have to, but could you take that cooler under the sink and go down to Sutherland's Butcher Shop for some fresh fish? The bus will drop you right at the door. Bus should be out front in about seven minutes."

Artie was surprised at the request, but felt he owed Frankie something for letting him stay there. "I suppose I could, but why take the cooler?"

Frankie smiled, "I don't like my fish to get warm. That's about a thirty minute bus ride. I can fry them for our dinner."

Artie didn't have the heart to tell Frankie that he loathed fish. He went to the closet and pulled his jacket on.

Frankie quickly grabbed the cooler from below the sink and handed it to him. "Thanks."

Artie smiled to himself as he walked down the steps to the street. Perhaps he was making progress with Frankie after all.

Frankie watched as Artie left the building with the cooler. The man in the SUV grabbed the car mirror, straightened it, and put a phone to his ear. The man reading the newspaper folded it and straightened up behind the steering wheel. His passenger leaned forward intently watching Artie. Artie climbed the steps into the bus as both the SUV and pickup pulled from the curb.

They had been watching, waiting for Artie to leave. That cop knew exactly what he saw in Frankie's freezer. They believed it belonged to Artie and they knew about the cooler. Frankie didn't know how, but someone had tipped off the Feds. Frankie closed his kitchen window. When they stop Artie and find out there's no head in the cooler, they'll be back. He opened the freezer door and pulled the head out. On his closet floor was another small, blue cooler.

Frankie packed the head in the cooler and made his way to the parking garage below. As he pulled his car out, he looked for suspicious vehicles and drivers. There were none, they were all chasing Artie's bus. He headed for his storage unit. As much as he worried about Artie and the cops, he worried more about the head being out of his sight. This was his life's trophy, his insurance policy. He wanted to look at it every day and know it was safe. He couldn't do that now. Because of Artie, the Feds knew a frozen head had been in his apartment.

He stopped at a convenience store to buy a bag of ice. While he stood waiting to pay, he noticed a small freezer unit with ice cream sitting on a counter. It was small enough to fit in his trunk.

"How much do you want for that freezer there?"

The owner of the store raised an eyebrow, "You mean the ice cream? Or the freezer?"

"The freezer."

"What'll you give me? Three hundred bucks?"

"Make it three fifty and you load it in my trunk."

As Frankie plugged in the freezer and listened to it hum in his storage unit, he felt better. Now that he had the freezer he wouldn't have to come back with ice. You never knew when someone was watching.

CHAPTER 13

Wednesday 5:00 p.m.

*H*e was dressed and ready to go. The drugs were wearing off and every hour he was thinking clearer. He remembered how he knew Ryan. Ryan had been his friend for years. Ryan and he had both been at this place for years. He was a doctor and this place had become his whole life. He rubbed his temples in the hopes that it would improve his memory. How could he know he worked at this place and not know what this place was? Nothing made sense. Surely he had more to his life than his job. Did he have a family? Where did he really live? Why couldn't he remember his name?

A siren sounded in the distance. Not a siren like the police would use; a warning siren that reminded him of old German movies or tornados. There was a danger nearby. For some reason he desperately wanted to hide. He went to the bathroom and closed the door. Crouched in the corner of the shower floor, he wondered what horrors were happening outside of the walls.

* * *

Lacey, Kamber and Chad sat on mats in the gym. Nick had given Lacey a membership for her birthday. It wasn't just any gym; it was owned by a group of retired cops and specialized in teaching self-defense. Lacey was a familiar face to many of the people there because she worked out at least every other week. Many of the trainers knew that she was Nick Stryker's girlfriend.

Today she had begged one of the trainers to give a crash course to Chad and Kamber. Lacey had a feeling that in spite of Chad and Kamber's promises to stay clear of trouble, trouble was going to find them. Kamber leaned back on her elbows on the mat and looked at Chad who had not moved for five minutes.

"Are you dead?" Kamber smiled when she saw his head slowly rise from the mat and turn to look at her.

"Yes." Chad dropped his head back on the mat.

The trainer walked back in the room. "Okay, everybody up! Now that we've warmed up we can start your training."

Chad pulled himself to stand slower than Kamber had. He looked at Lacey and said, "My mom's not going to appreciate you killing me."

* * *

Artie stepped off the bus and walked across the street to Sutherland's Butcher Shop. It was right where Frankie said it was. He walked straight to the counter and asked the butcher to recommend a fresh fish that would not taste fishy. Artie didn't notice the man standing behind him until the man moved in a little too close. Artie was fresh from prison and knew to maintain his personal space. Artie took a step sideways and glanced back, definitely a cop. Now he realized why Frankie wanted him to take the cooler. Artie smiled to himself, he actually liked the excitement of being used as bait. He liked the idea of messing with the cops even more.

Artie clutched the cooler close to his chest like a treasure. The butcher placed the wrapped fish on top of the counter. Artie just looked at the wrapped fish. He wanted it to look like he was afraid to set the cooler down. The cop grabbed the wrapped fish and said, "Here, let me help you with your cooler."

The second cop moved in closer.

Artie smiled, "Well, thank you, young man. I don't want anything to smell fishy."

Artie lifted the lid to the empty cooler and nearly laughed out loud at the cop's expression. The two cops exchanged glances and quickly left the store. Artie put the lid back on the cooler after paying and walked back to the bus stop bench to wait. He couldn't help but chuckle every time he pictured the cop's expression. Frankie was every bit as good as his reputation, maybe better. Artie was quite sure the head was long gone by now.

✳ ✳ ✳

Joey Lacastra placed a call to Travis Cummings' office. The secretary informed him that Mr. Cummings would probably not return to the office until Monday. His murdered wife was being buried tomorrow.

Joey said, "I'm sorry to hear that. Where are the services being held? I would like to pay my respects." Joey wrote down the information and entered the address into the GPS in his car. He drove past the funeral home slowly, twice. Other than a back parking lot and a back door for family use, the building was far too exposed. He decided to head over to 45 Dalton Street.

Joey watched the street activity in front of Cummings' townhouse to get a feel for the neighborhood. He guessed that most of the residents were professionals, because there was little to no activity on the entire block. It almost seemed too easy. That worried him.

✳ ✳ ✳

Agent Phillips had Travis Cummings sit in a secure, private room for his interview. Nick sat well off to the side of the table and Agent Phillips sat directly across from Travis. Phillips placed a recorder on the table and pulled a file from a briefcase.

Phillips looked at Travis, "I have more than one deal here. The one you get depends on what you can deliver. Any deal we make is void if we catch you in a lie. Even a small one."

Travis glanced at Nick and then answered, "I understand. What would I get if I gave you all of Dom's real books for the last ten years, complete with names and bank account numbers, for both the skims and the gambling business?"

Phillips raised an eyebrow. "We already have quite a bit of that. You're asking for immunity, a new identity and protection from the mob. That's a big package considering you've been knee deep in this over ten years. I need something special."

Travis leaned forward, "How special is proof that every major private prison and mental health facility in Illinois is paying skim to the mob and some are supplying narcotics to dealers?"

Phillips was surprised. "You have proof?"

"Do I have a deal?"

Nick asked, "Wouldn't you only know Dom's operation? How could you know about the entire state?"

Travis smiled, "I supervise the books for the entire Chicago Outfit. Dom is just a crew boss, a side ledger. He gets what the Outfit feels like giving him."

Phillips was stunned. Travis Cummings was in deeper than any of them had imagined. Securing whatever documents Cummings had was now the priority. Phillips pulled out a document that displayed the seal of the United States Justice Department at the bottom. "This is the best deal, everything you've asked for. Read it and sign, then we'll start recording."

Nick offered, "I think we need to get his records fast. You can interview him while I pick up his records."

Phillips frowned at Nick, "The FBI is capable of retrieving documents and protecting Mr. Cummings."

Travis pushed his chair back and stopped reading the deal from the Justice Department. "I've got stuff scattered all over my house. I'll have to be there. I want him watching out for me." Travis pointed at Nick. "No offense, but I trust Stryker more than the FBI. That's got to be part of the deal or I'm out. I'll take my chances getting out of the country."

Nick knew Phillips had just been put in an impossible position.

Nick addressed Travis, "Look, I have a job already. I can't become your personal bodyguard. You said that you trust me; the FBI can keep you safe. I can assist, if everyone agrees, for special situations. Could you live with that?"

Travis smirked, "I suppose no pun is intended when you ask if I can live with that? I sure hope so. Yeah, I just want you involved in this and watching my back."

Nick glanced at Phillips who was not happy with the turn of events.

Agent Phillips looked at Nick, "I'm not the only one that won't like this."

Nick knew he meant his mom.

Frankie arrived home from the storage unit, hung up his coat and went to stand at the kitchen window. Like clockwork, the pickup truck and SUV that had followed Artie's bus pulled up in front of Frankie's apartment building. He watched Agent Miller and another man take the front steps two at a time. Neither man looked very happy.

Frankie waited. The apartment door shook with pounding. Frankie opened the door and Agent Miller pushed his way in and walked straight to the kitchen. He stood with his hand on the freezer door and said, "You think you're pretty clever, don't you?"

The other agent stayed in the living room and watched as Agent Miller opened the freezer door and then slammed it shut. "Where is it?"

Frankie sat on the arm of his couch, "Where's what?"

Agent Miller wanted to shoot Frankie. "The head. We know Artie brought a head here in a blue cooler last night. I saw it in your freezer an hour ago!"

Frankie whistled, "They are working you boys too hard these days. I sure hope you didn't tell your boss that you saw a head in my freezer and left it there. Boy, I sure wouldn't want to explain that, especially since you already had a felony probation warrant. If a head was in our freezer, why didn't you say so? I'd have given it to you. What the hell would I want with a frozen head?"

Frankie walked into the kitchen and opened the freezer door. Only he and Agent Miller could see what was inside, which was nothing. "I bet you thought that big beef roast in there was a head after hearing that rumor about Artie having a head in a blue cooler. Sounds like an honest mistake to me."

Agent Miller was furious at himself for not taking the head earlier. He thought the rumor had been hogwash. When the rumor proved real, he decided to see what Artie would do with it. The potential had been there to get more evidence. Now there was nothing. Miller's mind raced for a way out. He wasn't going to leave there with a frozen head no matter what. Frankie was right; he certainly didn't want to admit he had lost the head to his superiors. The smart career move would be to expose the rumor of a frozen head as being false. There never was a head, it was a beef roast.

Agent Miller stared in the freezer and then shut the door. He looked at the other agent and then to Frankie. "I guess I owe you an apology, Mr. Mullen."

Both agents left. Frankie laughed so hard he wet himself. Another little issue old age had blessed him with.

* * *

Joseph had agreed to meet with Kamber and discuss her documentary assignment. Mitch had told Joseph he would bring Kamber and her friend, Chad, to the tunnel after seven when the sandwich shop closed. Joseph cautioned Mitch that Kamber should be made to promise not to mention the entrance from Momma's basement. Keeping the location of the community secret was vital to its survival. Ultimately, he had to protect the community and preserve their trust in him.

Mitch called Lacey with the good news that Joseph would meet with Kamber and Chad. Lacey trusted Mitch to keep Kamber safe, but warned him anyway. "If something happens to them, you're going to have to answer to Nick."

Mitch imagined what a confrontation with Nick would be like and shuddered. "Don't worry. You just have them here at seven. No cameras allowed."

"Thank you, Mitch." Lacey hung up and glanced at Chad and Kamber's anxious faces.

Kamber spurted, "Well?"

Lacey smiled, "Nick wants to see you both first, but you can meet with the 'mayor' of the tunnel community at seven."

Kamber was literally jumping in place while Chad just watched her.

He turned to Lacey, "Is she always like this?"

"I have no idea."

* * *

Agent Phillips looked at his watch; it was almost six. "We have to go to your house and get whatever documents and computer information you have. You can pack your personal items and we'll take you to a safe house."

It was apparent that Travis had not thought about having to leave his home. "Can't you just guard me at my house? Do I really have to move?"

Phillips nodded, "At least for now, you really have to move. Dom took out a contract on you a couple of hours ago. That was after someone else had already tried to kill you. It looks like two people want you dead."

"Three, if you count my mother-in-law. Am I going to miss the funeral tomorrow?"

Phillips stood to signal it was time to leave. "How important is it to you that you go?"

Travis stood and put his suit jacket back on. "The only reason I would go is to make sure she was really dead."

Agent Phillips turned to Nick, "I'm going to send an advance team to his townhouse and have another agent come here to help with transport. If you want to follow us, I'll let my guys know to look out for you."

Nick had promised Lacey he would meet Kamber before seven. That wasn't going to happen. "I'll tag along in case you need me." Nick smiled, "Travis, you're in good hands. Try to relax."

"I'll relax when I'm in the Bahamas."

Agent Phillips chuckled, "You're going to have to go farther away than that when this is done."

Nick called Lacey and explained he would have to come over later tonight to meet Kamber. Lacey understood as usual. "Nick, I know you worry that you are disappointing me when you have to change our plans. I really understand. I love you."

Nick's heart swelled, "I love you, too."

Nick walked into the homicide room to find Wayne, Sam and Jen all staring at the large white murder board. A long column on the left was titled 'Ballistic ties to Baxter'. In the center under the title 'Mob Ties' was the name Lomas, circled, and under that Attorney James Baxter and Alexia Cummings. The right hand column was titled 'Suspects'. Under the title 'Suspects' was written old man in film and Dom's hit man.

Jen heard Nick come up behind her. She said, "As you can see, we haven't made much progress."

Nick pointed to 'Dom's hit man' on the board and said, "Joey Lacastra out of New York is Dom's new guy. He flew in today to hit Travis Cummings. We need to find out who he's replacing." Nick sat on the corner of Jen's desk, "We should also put Travis Cummings up there as a 'homicide potential'. Lacastra has been hired by Dom to hit Cummings and someone different tried this afternoon. This is all tied together somehow."

Sam added Nick's suggestion to the murder board and said, "We should have ballistics from this afternoon's shooting fairly soon. Glad I'm not this

Cummings guy. I've heard of Joey Lacastra. Gambino Golden Boy and nobody you want to be close to."

Wayne waved a file in the air, "I'm chasing down Attorney Baxter's phone calls around the dates of each hit. He makes a lot of calls to burner phones. We're probably not going to get much from them. I'm also going to see if we can get video from the other hit scenes. Maybe I can find this old man."

Nick looked at Jen. "Why don't you call it a night and have dinner with John for a change? I'm going to back up Phillips at Cummings' place and then head over to Lacey's."

Jen nodded and held up a stack of papers. "Give me one minute before you leave. This is what I have found out about the prison mental health situation in Illinois. You're not going to like it."

Nick looked at the stack of papers in Jen's hand and smiled. "You can summarize all of that in one minute?"

Jen said, "Yes, I want you to know that I can't locate Billow. The last information I found was that he had requested a release hearing. The doctor that filed the petition for release is a Dr. Elmhurst at Brookfield Place. I left a message for Dr. Elmhurst, he hasn't called back. I didn't realize that the burden of proof is on the prosecutor, not the medical expert, in a release hearing. The prosecutor has to prove Billow is not ready for release. If the prosecutor doesn't act within 30 days of the request being filed, it's automatically granted."

Nick felt an instant flash of anger. "Thirty days? What prosecutor has time to review that kind of request that fast? Who makes these laws? Shouldn't the shrink have to prove he's not crazy? How long ago was the request? How much time is left?"

Jen leaned back in her chair. When Nick was upset, his questions came out like gunfire. "I'm guessing that the real purpose behind this new law is to move people out of the prison system and save money. That's the law, 30 days. I called the prosecutor's office to see who had been assigned the file. Nobody has responded yet. We have two days left."

Wayne had been listening and shook his head. "Billow kills nine cops and walks away free in four years? He was sentenced to nine life terms. Some prison shrink appeals his conviction with an insanity defense."

Sam offered, "How about Jared Loughner? He shot Arizona congresswoman Gabby Giffords in 2011 and has filed for a release. Some people say he will get it. The whole system is broken! Some nut is convicted of murder and sentenced to life and then the prison shrink declares them mentally ill. The mental health facility declares them cured to get rid of them and lets them go. The people that really need mental health care can't get it because there are no beds."

Nick sighed and grabbed his bike keys from his desk drawer. "I'm taking my bike, its better in traffic. You can have the unit car. If Lacastra shows up at Cummings' place, maybe we can cross one name off the board."

Sam added, "Too bad you can't take a grenade."

CHAPTER 14

Wednesday 7:00 p.m.

*I*t was almost time for his big escape. The drugs were wearing off, his mind was clearing. Memories bombed his brain. Some were pleasant, many were horrific. Which ones were real?

* * *

Mitch held the door of the sandwich shop open for Kamber and Chad and then locked the door behind them making sure the shop sign was turned to 'Closed'. Mitch was only 30 but their eager young faces made him feel old. He motioned them to follow him. He stopped abruptly at the door to the basement and turned around.

"If word got out about this entrance to the tunnel, the cops would come and make everyone leave. These people have nowhere to go. I trust you both because of Nick and Lacey. You have to promise to keep this secret."

Kamber nodded. "We promise. Where is the entrance that the community people use?"

Mitch frowned, "I never asked, you shouldn't either. You'll understand more after you speak to Joseph."

Kamber and Chad followed Mitch through the sandwich shop basement to a far corner where Mitch stopped in front of a large cabinet on wheels. He motioned to Chad, "Help me roll this over." Chad and Mitch rolled the cabinet to the side exposing what looked like a large ship wheel made of brass.

Kamber's heart began to pound. "Oh, my gosh! This is just like in the movies!"

Mitch smiled, "My buddy Eli is an engineer for the City and he said these tunnels housed the fresh water lines from Lake Michigan to service the city. Once the city vacated these for a new system, the tunnel maintenance doors were sealed off. Eli found an old map of this first tunnel system and last year we broke through the wall. This door leads into the main junction hall, it's enormous!"

Chad said, "This has to be the coolest thing I have ever seen!"

Mitch laughed, "Wait 'til you get on the other side. You won't believe it! Remember, no cameras."

Kamber and Chad promised. Chad went through the opening first and helped Kamber crawl through.

Mitch stayed in the basement, but pointed to the left. "Walk over that way. When you see the steam vents, stop. Joseph will come out to talk to you. There's a table and some chairs there. Be back here in exactly one hour! I've got a dart game I don't want to miss!"

The room was cavernous and each sound they made echoed. Kamber turned her lantern on and held it high in front of her. Chad turned on a high powered spot light that he slowly passed over the ceiling, floors and far walls.

"Holy Moly! Can you believe this?" Chad stopped his light at what looked like a wall of fog.

Kamber pointed and said, "Those are the steam vents we're supposed to walk to."

Kamber instinctively grabbed Chad's hand when a large figure of a man walked toward them from the steam cloud. Kamber's throat made an involuntary moan and Chad's grip on her hand became crushing.

Joseph walked up to them and smiled. He gestured for them to take seats at the small table. "I understand you two young people have a documentary assignment and have chosen to focus on the plight of Chicago's homeless population, specifically, this community." Joseph's voice was deep and soft. He articulated each word as if it had been laced with honey. Chad wished they could talk him into narrating their video.

Joseph didn't wait for a comment. "I am a law professor at the University. I became acquainted with the community when I was seeking to help my brother. I guess you could say that these people have changed my life. I have been trying to do the same for them."

Joseph continued, "This community has survived because of the carefully constructed rules we have put in place. I must insist that we come to an agreement before we proceed. At best, there will only be a few of the people who live here that may be willing to provide a filmed interview. The location of the community, even the mention of the tunnels, cannot be disclosed."

Chad and Kamber both promised to abide by the rules.

Joseph leaned forward, "I feel guilty every night that I leave here to go to my home. It has been five years now since I first found the tunnel. In that time we have accomplished a great deal. Seventy five percent of the residents here have jobs. That would surprise most people. Each one of them now has a bank account using my home address. In the past, whatever money they had saved was stolen from them."

"You'll find that many have developed partnerships with each other. While one works, the other guards their belongings. It is hard to get a job if you are pushing a cart everywhere you go. Last year, 50 of our residents were able to save enough for a security deposit and a few months' rent. Having a home address made it easier for them to find better jobs. They're no longer homeless."

Kamber asked, "I think it's important that we really understand how they feel. I was hoping we could spend the night here one night."

Joseph looked thoughtful and then answered, "This will be a human interest story. Let's make sure that your listeners can relate to the suffering of the homeless at a personal level. Perhaps you can challenge your viewers to have just one 'authentic' homeless night. You should probably have this experience yourselves and report how it affected you."

Kamber and Chad both reached for their notebooks and started taking notes.

Kamber asked, "Can you give us some suggestions on keeping our experience authentic?"

Joseph stood and began to pace. "There is no real way you will really understand the depth of despair of the homeless. You will know that your life will return to a secure place in just one day. They live with the fear that tomorrow will be even worse. For your documentary to make people understand, you must find a way to make people remember that."

Joseph smiled and returned to his seat. "I am very hopeful that your efforts will be noticed and make a difference. Let's list out some of the basic things you will need to do for your experiment. You two sleep with at least three layers of clothes and a heavy coat. No sleeping on a mattress, now. Open your window wide; it's going to be cold tonight. Remember to wear mittens. You will still be warmer than the people in the community."

"Let's see, today is Wednesday, so from nine until midnight there is a portable shower van on the corner of Wilson and Tucker. There are only four of these vans for the entire city of Chicago. You'll have to wait about an hour for your turn. If you get there early, the water might be warm. Go there for your ten minute shower. Walk home and find a place to dry your towels. They must get perfectly dry or they will mold. Some people wave them in the air and dance for about 30 minutes. That usually is enough time. The shower van won't be back until Sunday."

"You might share an orange or an apple for a snack. Fill your knapsacks with shampoo, soaps and extra clothes. That's your pillow. Before you go to sleep, tape newspaper over your mirror. There are no mirrors here and most homeless only see them-selves in window reflections. In the documentary, you might mention a distorted image for a distorted life.

"Get yourself a bucket to use as a toilet. In the morning, carry your bucket to a sewer drain and empty it. If you're lucky, you'll find a kind shop owner with an outside faucet. Clean you bucket well with soap, fill it up and bring it back to your space at home. You'll need that bucket for brushing your teeth and washing up."

Kamber and Chad listened carefully and took notes. Joseph smiled. "In the community we watch out for each other. Alcohol and drugs are prohib-ited. The homeless people that live 'up top' live in another world. They must carry weapons to protect themselves. Most people have seen the homeless sleeping in doorways and alleys. They assume that they are drunk or on drugs. Sometimes they are. What people don't realize is that the homeless that live on the streets have to sleep in the daytime. At night, they must keep moving in the shadows to avoid becoming the prey."

Joseph looked at his watch. "I can't believe it has been an hour. Let me know how your experiment goes. You have the comfort of knowing that this is just an experiment. Try to imagine that you have lived like this for months, maybe years. Imagine that tomorrow will be more of the same, maybe worse. In the meantime, I will discuss your request with our residents. If you get a moment, Google 'Homelessness in Utah'. I think you'll be surprised."

Joseph walked back to the wall of steam vapors, and Chad and Kamber slowly walked toward the entrance to the sandwich shop. Joseph had already touched them deeply.

Kamber looked at her watch. "Maybe Mitch will give us some towels, so we can go to the showers."

Chad thought about the prospect of showering in a van at the corner of Wilson and Tucker Street. He guessed the temperature outdoors was about 40 degrees and falling. Chad could tell from the tone of Kamber's voice that they were going.

Chad winced. He knew Kamber's answer before he asked the question. "So, you want to start the experiment tonight?"

Kamber stopped and looked him in the eyes, "Please say you will. I want you to stay at Lacey's place with me tonight. We can stop at your house first to get your three layers of clothes and your essentials."

Chad rolled his eyes, "You mean my bucket?"

* * *

Joey Lacastra parked his rental car on the street adjacent to Cummings' back yard. If he had to leave quickly, there was only one fence to jump. Joey shot out the corner street light and the camera for the bus stop. His silencer had made the popping of the shots barely audible. The corner was now enveloped in complete darkness. The bus runs were done for the day and traffic was practically nonexistent.

Joey walked through Cummings' townhouse assessing the risks of shooting Cummings when he arrived home. A sliding glass door led to a small patio encased by a six foot privacy fence. Joey moved a wooden patio table to rest against the fence, just in case he needed to jump the fence in a hurry. A large window in the den was only four feet from the fence and sheltered by a tall shrub. Joey unlocked the den window.

In minutes he had removed the screen and placed it behind the desk. It was a cool night but not yet cold, so he decided to leave the window open. In his job a few seconds of time could save your life. He counted the steps from the den doorway to the corner of the kitchen island. From that corner he could clearly see the front door, the glass slider in the dining room and his escape was only fifteen steps behind him. This would be his spot. He glanced at his watch. It almost seemed too easy. If Cummings didn't get home shortly, he would get him tomorrow.

Nick arrived in front of the townhouse before the FBI agents. He decided to circle the block. Nick slowed his Harley to a crawl as he approached the Cummings' townhouse from the side street. If he were doing the hit he'd park here and shoot out the lights. Nick noticed the shattered remnants of the street light and camera. It looked fresh. Across the street was a sedan with rental plates. Nick walked toward the fence he knew was Cummings'. The grass was damp from the evening dew and slightly bent from someone recently walking to the fence.

Nick raised himself over the fence. A screen was removed from what Nick knew was the den. He had carefully studied Cummings's home while at the crime scene the night before.

Nick dialed Phillips, "Stop your guys from going in! He's here." Just then two bright flashes could be seen through the windows. Gunfire. More flashes. The crack of automatic weapons mixed with the ping of silenced bullets. Nick ran for the den window and jumped in.

Agent Phillips and Travis had just pulled in front of the townhouse and had seen the flashes just as Nick called. It was too late. His two agents had already entered the building. Agent Phillips yelled to Travis, "Get down! Don't move. I'm getting you out of here."

Travis had been in the back seat and rolled to the floor. He couldn't see where they were going, he just heard the roar of the car's engine as they sped away. Agent Phillips was on his phone ordering more back up and EMTs. Travis heard him curse.

Travis asked from the back, "Did Stryker get there yet?"

Phillips answered, "He's in the middle of it."

Nick could see one FBI agent on the floor bleeding from his neck. Nick quickly moved to the kitchen, where he caught a glimpse of a shadow moving to his right. Nick yelled, "Chicago PD, freeze!"

The shadow seemed to vaporize into the curtain of the sliding door. Nick glanced back to the agents. One of them waved him on. Nick ran through the door opening in time to see the shadow man leap over the fence toward the side street. Nick raced to close the gap. Bullets flashed past him as Joey desperately sought to gain advantage. Cummings' elderly neighbor had stepped outside her back door in time to be grabbed by Joey. She screamed as Joey held her to his chest with his forearm and continued to fire at Nick.

Nick couldn't fire without endangering the woman. He rolled quickly to the right to force Joey to turn. Nick saw a clear shot to Joey's knee and fired. Joey screamed, pushed the woman to the ground and stumbled to regain his balance. Nick leaped and disarmed Joey as he wrestled him to the ground. Joey twisted to attack, but he was not skilled in close combat and was no match for Nick. Nick paralyzed him with a chop to his neck, rolled him over and cuffed him.

Sirens screamed from all directions. An FBI agent scaled the fence to assist Nick. An EMT crew began working on Joey.

The agent had been called to the scene from the Special Cases task force. He had barely been briefed as to what was happening. He asked Nick, "You must be Stryker. Is he dead?"

"No. He's just stunned. Keep a close eye on him. I don't know what you've been told, but he's a professional hit man for the mob. How are your men inside?"

"Alive."

Nick walked over to the older woman and wrapped his hands around hers. "Are you hurt, ma'am?"

She looked tearfully at Nick's face. She was shaking badly, but answered, "Oh my, you're a handsome young man." Then she fainted. The EMTs started working on her.

Nick called Phillips, "We've got him. Ask Travis where this paperwork is and I can start finding it."

Phillips said, "My guys should be doing this."

Nick sighed, "Your guys are kind of busy right now. Let's fight about territory when this is done."

Phillips was still driving, so he handed Travis his phone. "Here, tell Stryker what to look for."

Nick kept Travis on the phone with him as he located a stack of binders, a bank bag full of flash drives, and ten years of recorded telephone calls. Travis was into covering his butt. Travis directed him to a desk computer and was listing the file folders for Nick to copy when a flurry of gunshots and shouting rang out from the street.

Nick hung up on Travis, jumped over the EMTs working on the fallen agents, and ran outside. FBI agents were shooting down the street at a fleeing car. An FBI agent and two EMTs were motionless in the ambulance. The agent in charge was screaming orders to his men. Nick glanced at the massacre in the ambulance. Lacastra was better than he thought.

One of the EMTs had been outside of the ambulance and suffered only minor wounds. "He needed an IV. I talked the FBI agent into cuffing him in the front. This is all my fault. I thought the guy was unconscious."

Nick holstered his pistol and went back inside. Once seated at the desk computer again he dialed Phillips. "Lacastra escaped. I was told he took your guy's gun, shot him and two EMTs. All three are dead. Lacastra played possum to put them off guard. It isn't pretty here."

Nick paused, he felt guilty for stating the obvious. Agent Phillips had just lost at least one man and had several others wounded.

Nick sighed, "I'm sorry, the last thing you need is hot air from me. I'll finish this with Travis. Who do you want to take this stuff? There is a lot."

Agent Phillips couldn't believe what he was hearing. His men were having a bad night. Because of the secret nature of the assignment, the other agents didn't even know what was going on. Nick was right, people were making mistakes. He had to have those documents. "I'm not that far from you. Can you bring the stuff here? I'll give you the address."

"No problem."

* * *

Dominick Guioni settled back in his leather chair, sipped on his scotch and listened to Etta James singing 'At Last' on his sound system. A loud buzzer from the front gate blasted from the intercom on the end table. Dom scowled as he turned down his music and answered. "What?"

The voice of one of his guards replied, "There's a Mr. Lacastra here. He's bleeding and says you'll want to see him."

Dom wondered why he was bleeding already. He had only arrived in the city this afternoon. "Let him in and call the Doc."

The guard at the gate took Joey's small .22 and motioned him through. Joey drove down the long, dark drive toward the mansion and readjusted his pistol in his waistband. The escort guard walked alongside the car obviously talking to a girlfriend. The gate guard hadn't even patted him down. Sloppy, they were all sloppy. Joey wondered how men like Dom had survived in positions of power.

Dom watched as Joey was ushered into the doorway of his study leaning heavily on one of the guards. His pant leg was soaked in blood. Dom motioned for him to sit in the leather chair. He knew from experience that blood cleaned easily off leather.

Dom frowned, "What happened?"

Joey tried to put the best light on the situation he could. "Obviously, I've been shot. I went to do

Cummings at his house and the damn FBI showed up."

Dom raised an eyebrow. "How do you know it was FBI?"

Joey raised his voice. "They told me! I think I killed a couple of them."

Dom stood and shouted, "So you decide to drive here? To my home? Were you followed?"

"I was careful." Joey could see that Dom was not reassured. "There was some ninja Chicago cop that shot me and roughed me up. You never mentioned the FBI was crawling all over this Cummings when I took the job."

Dom shrugged. "I didn't know. Did you get Cummings?" Dom realized that Travis Cummings more than likely went to the FBI to make some kind of deal. Now he had both the Northside crew and the FBI gunning for him.

Joey answered, "Cummings never even came home. I'm the one that was set up. I'm telling you there must have been ten FBI agents and that crazy cop there."

Dom wondered if the crazy cop wasn't Nick Stryker. One thing was for sure, he wasn't going to get to Cummings in time to stop him from talking.

CHAPTER 15

Wednesday 8:00 p.m.

*H*e heard Ryan's key in the lock. The excitement of escaping was almost too much to bear. He smoothed his clothes with his palms to remove the dampness of his sweat.

Ryan closed the door behind him. "We've hit a snag. I need to take care of something before we can go."

He felt the disappointment wash over him in waves. Ryan must have noticed. "Trust me; I'm getting you out of here."

* * *

Renee sat in her car in the employee lot of Building D. She dreaded going back inside and running into

171

Dr. Elmhurst. She was just about ready to open her car door when Dr. Bates walked out of the employee entrance in the back. Renee slid down in her seat. She didn't want him to see her.

She watched in shock as Dr. Bates released the trunk lid of Dr. Elmhurst's car and crawled into the trunk. A moment later Dr. Elmhurst walked out the door, glanced around, slammed his trunk lid and drove away. Renee didn't know why, but she started crying. Nothing here seemed real or logical. Why would Dr. Bates get in the trunk of Dr. Elmhurst's car? Could it be her? No, she knew what she saw. She just didn't know what it meant.

Ryan knocked on her driver's window and nearly gave her a heart attack. Renee lowered the window and Ryan asked, "Where have you been for the last hour? I've been looking for you!"

Renee got out of her car and answered, "I had some business to attend to." They started walking back toward the building. "Can I ask you a personal question, Ryan?"

Ryan looked nervous, but answered, "Sure, anything."

"Are you a patient here? What is your diagnosis?"

Ryan's cheek twitched, but he calmly answered, "I'm a paranoid schizophrenic, but I take my meds. I've been in the Independent Living Program for two years now."

The Independent Living Program allowed patients to live outside of the facility. Most patients in that program secured employment from the facility they had been assigned to. It was a convenient way to continue the monitoring requirements and the patients realized fewer socialization adjustments.

Renee thought Ryan's answer was reassuring. She asked, "Why were you looking for me?"

Ryan's cheek ticked again, "I have to show you something important."

Ryan led Renee into Dr. Elmhurst's office and closed the door behind them.

Renee said, "We're not supposed to be in here, Ryan."

"First, who doesn't lock their office in this kind of place?" Ryan had his hands on his hips. "Second, the only file Dr. Elmhurst looks at is this one." Ryan moved the file marked 'Budget' from the corner of the desk.

Renee recognized the file, but didn't want to admit she had peeked at it earlier.

Ryan opened the cover to expose the top page. The red ink drawings and scratch marks were as Renee remembered them. Renee said, "He probably keeps this on top of his desk as evidence that someone tampered with his file."

Ryan said, "He has a red ink pen in his center drawer and when I walked in this afternoon he was doodling in that right hand margin. Look close at what is there." Ryan pointed to the far right column.

Renee leaned closer and saw a skull with her name next to it. She looked at Ryan. Ryan could have done this. Renee started to edge toward the door.

Ryan shook his head. "I'm not doing this. Look at the other names next to skulls…they're all gone."

Renee walked back to look at the list. "What do you mean? Gone?"

Ryan pointed to the top name on the list: Nancy Logan. "I haven't seen her in a month. Dr. Bates had a tow truck come get her car. He said he was giving her a ride home." Ryan thumped his finger next to her name. "Nancy hated him! She said he stalked her from the first day she transferred here. She would never have gotten in his car."

Ryan pointed to the next name with a skull. "Joshua Jones."

Renee interrupted, "You know that Joshua killed himself after he killed Jane. You were right there when it happened." Renee was thinking that Ryan's paranoid issues were not as controlled as he thought.

Ryan said, "Dr. Elmhurst told me to stop giving Joshua his meds about a week ago. Joshua was fine on his meds." Ryan lowered his voice to a whisper. "I heard Dr. Bates in Joshua's room yesterday morning telling him that Jane was a whore and someone should kill her. I heard Dr. Bates tell Dr. Elmhurst they would increase their profits by two thousand a week with those two gone."

Renee didn't know whether to believe Ryan or not.

Ryan pointed to the next skull. The name was John Bates. "This is Doctor John Bates, the real one. The guy calling himself Dr. Bates now came here in an armored ambulance over a month ago."

Renee felt her knees weaken. What if all of this was true?

Renee swallowed, "Where is the real Dr. Bates?"

Ryan shrugged, "Disappeared overnight. He's been gone for a month. He told me once that Brookfield Place was his only family. His car was towed, too."

Renee leaned against the wall for support, "Dr. Elmhurst wouldn't allow a patient to pretend to be a doctor."

Ryan nodded, "I agree, I think the real Dr. Elmhurst has been locked away and drugged. You saved him yesterday, remember? I think they are keeping him alive so he can sign some court paper. At least that's what Jane told me before she was killed."

Renee knew immediately which patient Ryan was talking about. She had noticed the tattoo and thought it strange. Much of what Ryan was saying fit with what she already knew. Now her name had a skull next to it.

"Wait. How would Jane know anything? She was in her own world."

Ryan shook his head. "She wasn't like that until they started drugging her. Bates caught her listening at Dr. Elmhurst's office door. I think that's why they changed her meds and got Joshua to kill her."

Renee asked, "Then who is pretending to be Dr. Elmhurst?"

Ryan looked thoughtful. "I'm not sure. I guess I don't know."

"Ryan, what should we do? Call the police?"

"I thought about that, but what do we tell them? I have no real proof. Except the real Dr. Elmhurst has been drug free for 24 hours now and is waiting for me to help him escape. I figured I'd get him out of here and let him tell me what to do."

Renee rubbed her temples; she was getting a headache. Ryan was right, they had no proof. The real Dr. Elmhurst would know what officials to call at the state. He could also identify who they were dealing with to the police.

Renee looked at Ryan, "I still don't know what we should do."

Ryan begged, "Please help me get Dr. Elmhurst out of here. I thought I could smuggle him out in my trunk, but it's too small. I saw your new car and…please?"

Renee's mind was spinning. The thought of smuggling a person out of a facility for the criminally insane made her sick to her stomach. What if Ryan is wrong?

The list of names with skulls drawn next to them made her shiver. Where were Nancy and the real Dr. Bates? What had happened to them? Was Joshua tricked into killing Jane to increase profits or because Jane knew something she shouldn't? Now her name was on that list. It was true that Dr. Elmhurst didn't act like any doctor she had ever been around. What if Ryan is right?

* * *

Tommy Albergo sat in his car waiting for Anthony to show up. Anthony had said he had something important to tell him. Tommy wiped beads of sweat from his forehead with his wrist. He knew that Anthony was knee deep in a plot with Milo's Northside crew to take over Dom's crew. He had warned Dom this afternoon and Dom had promised him protection. Yet here he was waiting for Anthony. It was possible that Anthony was who he needed protection from. Tommy turned the key to start his car. What had he been thinking to agree to meet Anthony in the dark?

His passenger door opened and Anthony slid in. "You weren't going to leave without meeting me, were you?"

Tommy swallowed, "I got cold. I just wanted the heater on. What's up?"

"I know you were worried that Dom had Emil Carson shot right when he got released from the joint. I know Dom didn't have it done. I told you that Fed was messin' with us."

Tommy was relieved to hear it wasn't Dom. He was never sure how safe he was with the crew. "Who did it then?"

Anthony leveled a pistol at Tommy's head. "Me."

* * *

Jake Billow had spent the last hour at the firing range. He was finally starting to get the feel of his new rifle and loved it. There was a slight pull to the right that he now adjusted for.

The firing range manager tapped him on the shoulder. "We're closing now, you'll have to leave. I noticed it didn't take you long to start killin' those targets. You're pretty good!"

Billow raised himself to stand. "New rifle, I had to get used to it."

The manager held out his hand, "May I?"

Billow handed the rifle over. The manager lovingly ran his hands over the stock and barrel. "This is a sweetheart. It's the best sniper rifle that was ever made in my opinion."

He handed the rifle back to Billow and said, "Got a cop that comes here that would love to shoot that sometime. He's military sniper trained. Nick Stryker, maybe you've heard of him?"

Billow smiled, "I have. Stryker and I go way back. When you see him, tell him Billow would like to show him his rifle."

"Will do. I'll write that down so I don't forget. You have a nice night now."

Billow chuckled to himself as he pulled the van into traffic. He wanted to scope out the neighborhood of Nick's girlfriend's place. He took a piece of paper down from behind the visor. He had done a 'people search' on the internet and discovered Lacey had moved about six months ago. The Google map search had provided him a street view of her new townhouse. Lacey Star was in a picture with Nick at some award dinner. The article said she was Nick's significant other. Billow smirked as he entered the address into the van's computer. Lacey was now significant to him, too.

* * *

Nick delivered the items he had collected at Cummings' house to Agent Phillips at the safe house. Nick wasn't impressed with what the FBI had arranged, but the last thing Cummings needed to hear was that the safe house wasn't safe. Nick thought of his mom. No wonder she didn't think the FBI could protect the family from the mob.

Agent Phillips met him at the door and stepped out to a guarded terrace to talk to Nick.

"It went worse than I had thought back there. The first two agents that entered Cummings' house: one was seriously injured and the other will recover soon. He had an armored plate under his vest and took three shots to the heart. He said if you hadn't arrived when you did, he would've been killed. Lacastra had his brains targeted for the next shot. Outside, we lost one agent in the ambulance and had two more wounded. I'd call this a bad night."

Agent Phillips tried to read Nick's expression, he couldn't. "Spit it out, what's on your mind?"

"This place sucks. You need to be rural, long driveway, a place to hide cars, some kind of perimeter security. A pizza delivery guy could tell this place was being used by Feds for something. Could you park another black SUV on the street?" Nick figured if Phillips asked, he deserved an answer.

Agent Phillips sighed, "I agree. This came about too fast for an ideal solution."

Nick said, "My dad has a rural place about 30 minutes south of here. He built it for his and mom's retirement. It's vacant, rural, and I installed security there myself last year."

"What kind of security?"

Nick smiled, "Cameras, mass and thermal detectors, detonators, every whistle I could think of. There's also a barn with a hidden trap door to a safe room that has a tunnel escape to the woods. The tunnel can be tripped to explode and collapse if needed."

Phillips stared at him in disbelief. "All that for a retirement house in the woods? What the heck did you do all of that for?"

"Dad told me he worried about retaliation from the criminals I deal with. He wanted me to have a safe place if I needed it. I never gave his reasoning much thought. It was fun setting the place up like that, reminded me of my military days." Nick's expression turned thoughtful. "Knowing what I know now, I think he hopes that mom will come back and they will live there. He wants her to feel safe."

Agent Phillips stared at Nick. "This offer is too good to refuse, but I do have one concern."

Nick nodded, "Me, too. Mom's really not going to like this."

Nick called his dad, drew a map for Agent Phillips and gave him instructions on the security system.

While taking notes, Agent Phillips interrupted him, "Wait a minute. Did I hear that right? The fourth large oak tree in from the street has a security panel hidden in the bark exactly five feet up from the front exposed root? Are you serious?" Nick laughed. It did sound ridiculous hearing it out loud and Phillip's expression was priceless.

"It's kind of James Bond, isn't it? I got it from some CIA tech nerds. A full camera system runs through the trees, but squirrels are an issue. Seems they like to make videos. That first panel only controls the driveway and a perimeter warning system. Once you get in the house to activate the primary system, it will trigger the perimeter system to reset. Call me when you get there if you have questions."

Phillips shook his head, "Expect a call. That's all I need is to blow us up. Are the utilities working? Should I have men pick up supplies?"

Nick answered, "Someone should get food and general supplies. The entire 80 acre camp is self-sustained. Generator, a deep well, a couple of ATVs in the garage, and an old pickup truck. The house is all modern. I think it's the only thing that my dad has spent money on all of these years. There's a satellite dish that is programmed to government and civilian bands." Nick smiled, "It brings in the entertainment channels. You can watch soaps."

Phillips grinned, "I won't be there. We have special people for that type of duty. They've had all the Rambo training, like you. I'll be leaving as soon as our interviews are done. I'm more interested in digging into those files."

* * *

Artie had just arrived at Frankie's apartment. He was surprised Frankie wasn't there. It was already dark outside. Artie's cell phone began ringing and he struggled to find the right button to receive his call. The call was from an old buddy still active in Dom's crew.

"Hey, just wanted to let you know somebody just popped Tommy Albergo, not 30 minutes ago. That makes two, countin' Carson, been shot right out of the joint. You'd better watch your back. What's going down?"

Artie assured his friend he had no idea and hung up. It was a most troubling call. Now it was just Anthony and he left. Who would be doing this? Once again, Artie wondered about Frankie being gone after dark. Artie had heard the rumors that Frankie had been Dom's favorite hit man. Was that why Dom wanted him living here?

Frankie opened the apartment door and grunted a greeting. He had purchased a top notch lock and installed it at the storage unit. His arthritis in his knees was screaming in pain. Seeing Artie just reminded him that his head would still be in his freezer if it wasn't for his guest. Artie watched as Frankie removed a pistol from his coat pocket and laid it on the coffee table. Frankie walked to the kitchen and poured himself a short scotch. He grabbed a shoe box from on top of the refrigerator and declared his gun needed cleaning.

Artie decided it was a good night to find a different place to live.

* * *

Joey Lacastra winced as Dom's doctor dug in his leg for Nick's bullet. Dom watched from his leather chair as he sipped his scotch and twirled a pen in his hand. The longer Joey watched Dom, the more repulsive Dom looked. Joey was furious that he had been hired to hit someone under the watchful eye of the FBI. Now the Feds would be after him.

His status with the Gambino family was compromised now, too. They wouldn't want FBI heat either. His only salvation would be to do the impossible: hit this Cummings guy before he could testify. Joey had to find out what this guy was going to testify about, before he could figure out who would benefit the most from his death.

Joey asked Dom. "What's this guy got that the FBI wants?"

Dom considered not answering, it wasn't any of Lacastra's business, but the scotch was taking over his judgment. "Cummings does books for the entire Chicago Outfit. Our skim, gambling, everything we do. He has the 'real' books on collections. It's my job to keep him in line." Dom finished his drink and poured more.

Joey's mind swarmed. There are four crews in the Chicago Outfit. The Outfit had barely recovered from the Family Secrets trial of Frank Calabrese Sr. in the summer of 2007. If he could deliver the hit of

Cummings to the Outfit before any trials, he could name his price.

Joey was sure the Outfit boss would be as displeased with Dom as he was. Dom should have known there was a problem with Cummings sooner. Key people are supposed to be on a short leash. Joey glanced around the room. None of the security he would have expected was there. Dom was old school. He thought his goons and his reputation were enough to keep him safe. Joey considered his choices. This might be his best opportunity to level some justice for the Outfit boss on Dom. If all goes well, he'll be talking to his new boss in the morning.

The doctor finished the last stitch on Joey's leg, gave him some pills for the pain and walked over to bid farewell to Dom. Joey pulled his pistol from his waistband, attached the silencer and shot the doctor in the back of the head. The doctor fell across the desk, his blank eyes staring at Dom. Dom's shocked expression made Joey chuckle.

"You made a mistake setting me up with the Feds."

Joey shot Dom twice in the heart.

Dom's two house guards proved to be worthless. They assumed Joey was no threat since he had passed through the guard at the gate and Dom had granted him entry. Joey popped them as he exited Dom's sitting room. They simply slid down the walls of the foyer. Neither of them even had time to draw their weapons.

It was even easier outside. He just shot each guard as they approached his car. The silencer kept the noise to a minimum. Joey's headlights steadily advanced toward the estate's main gate. The massacre behind him was hidden in the black of the night. The guard at the gate leaned toward Joey's window to clear him. Joey noticed him glancing back for the escort guard.

Joey put his hand out the window, his pistol aimed at the guard's head. "They're all dead. If you want to die, try to stop me." The guard put his palms up and stepped backwards.

Joey pulled away from the estate and headed for his hotel in the city. In the morning he was either going to be a hero or a dead man.

Lacey was curled on the couch as she listened to Kamber beg for permission to do the homeless experiment in her townhouse. Kamber explained they had already had their showers in the street van, picked up Chad's clothes, and now needed to dry their towels by dancing. Lacey almost burst out laughing at Kamber's appearance. She wore a knit cap with leather flaps that covered her ears, mittens, three layers of clothes, and boots. Her hair was stringy and wet and her makeup was streaked. Chad also wore three layers of clothing and was holding a bucket.

Lacey pulled an afghan up around her shoulders. "Do you have a window open in your room? It's freezing in here."

Kamber's eyes opened wide, "Sorry! I'll go shut my door. We have to sleep in the cold. Please say we can, Lacey. This is going to be the best documentary ever!" Kamber raced from the room to shut her door.

Lacey asked Chad, "I'm not sure I want to know, but what's the bucket for?"

Chad made a sour face. "It's our toilet."

Kamber returned to the living room. "I also put newspapers over the mirror in my room."

Lacey shook her head and smiled. "Of course you did. Does your experiment allow you to eat spaghetti?"

Chad and Kamber smiled at each other, the aroma of the spaghetti was inviting, and then they both frowned. Chad answered, "I don't think so. We have two oranges."

Kamber asked, "So, we can do it? It's okay?"

Lacey nodded her head. "Your mother is going to kill me for letting you have a boy here all night."

Chad blushed.

Kamber said, "You don't have to worry about Chad. We're just going to sleep together."

Lacey's eyebrows went up and Kamber started laughing. Chad spread his hand over both his eyes.

Kamber said, "We have to dry our towels before they get moldy. Can we turn on your sound system?"

Five minutes into watching Chad and Kamber dancing with their towels, Lacey thought she heard her door buzzer. She opened the door to Nick, gave him a kiss and pointed to the living room.

"Well, there she is: my niece, Kamber."

Nick tried to figure out if Chad and Kamber were having a towel fight or dancing. Both of them were dressed strangely. He tried not to chuckle.

Nick asked Lacey, "Do these tendencies run in your family?"

Kamber suddenly stopped dancing and stared at Nick. He was so good looking her mind went blank. Nick smiled at her and she realized what she must look like. She wanted to run to her room and hide. Instead, she reached over and shut off the music.

Lacey held Nick's hand and walked him to the kitchen counter. "You're just in time for spaghetti. Our homeless guests can't have any, they have oranges." Lacey smiled at Kamber's expression.

Chad and Kamber each sat on the counter stools across from Nick. Chad knew that Nick was some sort of cop and Kamber knew that he worked in homicide. Nick draped his jacket over the back of the stool and said to Lacey, "Spaghetti sounds great, I'm starving. I can't stay long, tomorrow is going to start early." Nick smiled at Chad and Kamber, "I'm glad you two are still up. I'm sorry I didn't get here sooner. So, you're both in my dad's class?"

Chad nodded, "He is the best professor at the University! He suggested that we partner up on this documentary. Lacey hooked us up with Mitch at the sandwich shop and he got us an interview with Joseph in the tunnel."

Kamber couldn't stop staring at Nick and wishing she could run to the bathroom, blow-dry her hair and fix her makeup. Lacey noticed Kamber's glazed over look. She often felt that way around Nick when they first started dating. Now she found his other qualities overshadowed his good looks. Nick seemed totally oblivious to Kamber's loving stare.

Nick said, "I brought you each a canister of pepper spray. The department hands them out to the homeless. If something does happen, this will give you time to run. You have to stay alert and aware of your surroundings. The homeless are often victims of violence."

Kamber spoke. "Oh, we know. Joseph told us that most of them had to stay awake at night and keep moving or they would be attacked."

Nick looked at Lacey, "I hope I'm not out of line, but I brought something else I think they need." Nick pulled a leather case from his breast pocket and unzipped it. There was a strange type of tool and three tiny metal squares.

Lacey nodded. "I thought about asking you to bring those but I didn't want to cause you any hassle with the department."

Chad leaned in to get a closer look. "What the heck are they?"

Nick answered, "GPS locators. I want to install these in your watches."

Chad looked puzzled. "But we're going to be in tunnels. They probably won't work."

Nick smiled, "These are CIA. They can locate you within a 50 foot radius through concrete, iron, or water. You can watch a man move in a submerged submarine from a helicopter. They track from a government band and are practically indestructible. When you want to remove them, it's a simple procedure." Nick installed the GPS devices in each of their watches. He then installed an app on their phones to show them that they were activated.

Nick left the third chip on the counter. "This is an extra chip in case one of you has your watch stolen. If you get separated from each other, this will help." Nick looked at Lacey, "You should keep this extra chip somewhere safe, maybe your jewelry box? Never hurts to be prepared." Nick leaned over and kissed her.

Nick ate two plates of spaghetti and visited with Lacey while Chad and Kamber finished their towel dance and discussed their plans to interview street people later.

Nick and Chad made a list of neighborhoods they should stay away from, and Nick walked over and kissed Kamber's cheek. "I have to leave. Lacey will give you my number if you need me."

Nick shook Chad's hand and said, "You've got your hands full, buddy."

Chad lowered his voice, "Don't I know it."

CHAPTER 16

Wednesday 9:00 p.m.

Jake Billow parked his van down the street from Lacey's townhouse. Not long after arriving he saw Nick walk from Lacey's front door to a Harley parked at the curb. He watched as Nick rode away. The powerful roar of the engine echoed in the near empty street. Billow hated cops. He thought all cops were arrogant. Especially cops like Nick. Billow waited a moment and then pulled from the curb to follow Nick. Just as his van was directly in front of Lacey's townhouse, two young people came out of her door. Billow eased back to the curb to watch. The young couple walked down the street and disappeared into the darkness.

Lacey was home alone. He turned his van around to park on Lacey's side of the street. It was exciting to be this close to Nick's 'significant other'. Something caught his eye in his peripheral vision. There it was again. The corner of a curtain waved out an open window. Billow looked up and down the street. It was quiet. There was no sign of the young couple coming back.

He walked to the back of the van, reached in and grabbed a roll of duct tape and a steel rod. He crossed the street quickly and stood outside the window listening. There was a bed under the window and the door was closed. At the bottom of the door a band of light suddenly got brighter. Lacey had turned on a light closer to this room.

Billow lifted himself through the window and listened at the door. He heard noises in the distance, kitchen noises. Lacey put the leftover spaghetti in the refrigerator and rinsed the plates for the dishwasher. She wiped the island countertop and dropped the extra GPS chip into her jean pocket. A sudden rush of cold air sent a chill up her spine. Kamber's door must have blown open. Lacey turned from the sink to see a man standing behind her, his arms raised above his head, his eyes crazed. A metal rod came crashing toward her.

Billow watched as blood ran from Lacey's forehead onto her nose, trailed across her pretty lips to drip steadily on the white marble floor. Billow injected her with Rohypnol, wrapped her wrists in duct tape and carried her to the back of his van. Once Lacey was secured with rope, Billow pulled from the curb and drove toward his apartment.

At a stop light Billow looked through a small window to the back of the van. Lacey was in a fetal position, duct tape on her wrists and mouth, unconscious from the drug. An involuntary giggle escaped his lips. He felt electrified.

The light changed to green and he could hardly keep from speeding home. He couldn't stop giggling. This was just like the good old days when every cop in Chicago worried they would be his next target. The rush of excitement was intoxicating. He wondered if he had time to kill a couple of cops tonight, too.

* * *

Kamber and Chad returned to Lacey's after about an hour of interviewing people they met on the street. Many of the homeless were glad to tell their story on camera. Some admitted to having problems with drugs and alcohol. Many were victims of circumstance. What they all had in common was little hope for the future. Kamber traded boots with a young woman and Chad traded boots with an old man. By the time they were back in Lacey's neighborhood, they were both exhausted.

Chad said, "The hardest part of this documentary is going to be the editing. These are powerful stories. I wish it wasn't limited to 15 minutes." Chad stared at Lacey's front door and sighed, "I also wish I was going to take a hot shower and crash on a soft mattress."

Kamber twisted her mouth, "Oh, yeah. I guess it's the floor tonight. Can you believe how cold it is outside? This is hard work being homeless and we're just pretending!"

Kamber opened the townhouse door and looked around. She put her finger over her lips to signal quiet. Lacey must have gone to bed, because her bedroom door was closed and the townhouse was quiet. Chad and Kamber tiptoed to Kamber's room, closed the door, and went to sleep.

* * *

Momma had just finished her shower and put her nightgown on when her cell phone rang. The caller ID said Artie Corsone. Momma was surprised that Artie was calling at that hour.

She answered, "Hello, dear. What has you callin' so late?"

Artie took a moment to gather his courage, "I was wondering if I might sleep on your couch this evening? I will be looking for an apartment tomorrow; but this evening I seem too tired to bother."

Momma was surprised by the request. "Artie, my love, there's no reason to explain a thing. My couch makes into a comfortable bed. I'll get it ready for you. When will you be here?"

"I'm at the door to the sandwich shop right now."

Momma chuckled and told him she'd be there in a minute. She dashed to her room to get a nice robe and slippers. She fluffed her hair on the way down the stairs and held the door open for Artie.

"I am so sorry to trouble you so late in the evening." Artie was pulling his bags behind him. Momma took the smaller of the two bags and pointed to the back.

"Don't you worry 'bout the time. It's only ten o'clock for heaven's sake!"

Artie looked out the picture window of the store. "It gets dark so early it throws me off."

Momma giggled, "Me, too! When you called, I must have dozed off in my chair. I thought it was midnight!"

Once settled upstairs, Artie told Momma about his troubling call about Tommy Albergo getting shot. Momma had just brought Artie a cup of tea. Artie slowly stirred the tea bag in the hot water and said, "Four of us were released this week from prison and already two of us are dead." Artie felt comfortable talking to Momma. She knew the score on the Westside crew and she certainly knew Artie wasn't an angel. "You know Dominick arranged for me to stay with Frankie Mullen until a suitable apartment could be located."

Momma's eyes opened wide. "I wouldn't close my eyes with that man around. Frankie Mullen is a smart, old fart. Never got caught for nothin'. Some people think he was Dom's secret hit man." Momma was rocking up a storm in her chair.

Artie smiled, "Today I heard rumors that there was bad blood growing between the Northside crew and the Westside crew. I suppose it's possible that Milo is picking off the weak links before he goes after Dom. Maybe it was Milo that had Tommy and Carson hit."

Momma set her tea cup down and smoothed her robe. "This is just my opinion, but there is so much mistrust, ego and greed in these crews that by the time the finger pointin's done, everybody's gonna be dead. Most times they're all wrong in their thinkin', too."

Artie's phone rang. He excused himself to stand in Momma's small kitchen at the other end of the apartment. Momma could tell from the tone of his voice that something was very wrong. Artie returned to the couch.

Momma asked, "Is everything alright, dear?"

Artie put his phone back in his pocket. "No. Someone hit Dom at his estate tonight. Killed Dom, his doctor and all but one guard. This is real bad. Guess it just happened about an hour ago." Artie thought about what he had just said about Milo and the Northside crew looking to take over Dom.

Momma pretended to take the news in stride. "Well, you live by the sword, you die by the sword. You knew someday this would happen to Dominick. I can guarantee you that he didn't see no bright light when he passed! They got plenty of guys waiting in the wings to take his place. Life and crime goes on. Why don't you go freshen up for bed and forget all this killin' nonsense? I've got a couple of things to do downstairs before I call it a night."

Artie kissed Momma's cheek. "I should have fought harder to steal your heart; beautiful and wise." Artie grabbed his small bag and walked toward the bathroom. "I shall try to leave some hot water."

"You don't worry 'bout that. I've already had my shower. You sleep tight now."

Momma waited until she could hear the water running in the shower and got the envelope with Sophia's number out from under her drawer. She slipped her cell phone and the envelope in her robe pocket and walked clear down to the basement where she locked the door behind her and walked to the far corner. It was important her call not be heard. She dialed Sophia's number, let it ring three times, and hung up.

A full ten minutes passed. Momma was just about to dial again when her cell rang. "Darlin', I've got some breakin' news."

* * *

Renee glanced at Ryan as they drove past the guard at the gate and headed away from Brookfield Place. Dr. Elmhurst was in the trunk. Renee was near panic. "I don't know if I can do this, Ryan. I'm tempted to turn around and go back."

"I'd rather make a mistake than have someone else come up missing or dead." Ryan's face was twitching.

"Ryan, have you taken your meds today?" Renee didn't know if Ryan's twitch was because of stress or his disorder.

Ryan rubbed his hands over his face. "I couldn't find the drug order. I should have taken my meds at noon. I've got two doses in my pocket. I was trying to hold off until later before taking one."

Renee's heart sank. Her partner in this little adventure was a paranoid schizophrenic, off his meds, and she had a drugged up doctor in her trunk. Renee thought of Tyler from Building A. Tyler would give her meds for Ryan.

"The Administrator for Building A will give me meds for you, don't worry." Ryan's face twitched again. "For God's sake, take a dose now! Both of us can't be paranoid!"

Ryan smiled, dug in his pocket and popped one of his pills. The 'Ride Share' parking lot was just ahead.

Ryan said, "Let's pull over in there and get him out of the trunk."

Renee pulled into the lot and drove to the far back corner, away from the parking lot light. The other cars in the lot were empty. Renee popped the lock on the trunk and watched through her side mirror as Ryan helped Dr. Elmhurst steady himself. Moments later, Dr. Elmhurst was seated in the back seat. Renee and Ryan sat silently waiting for him to speak.

Finally Renee spoke. "Dr. Elmhurst, Ryan and I have committed a crime by removing you from the facility without authorization. We'll need your help explaining what has happened to the police."

He wondered why Renee had called him Dr. Elmhurst. That must be his name.

"Ryan called you Renee. Thank you, Renee, for saving me. You too Ryan. I don't want to be difficult, but I don't want to see the police yet. I need to get my memory back first. If I could just rest somewhere for the night, I'm sure my mind would be better. Couldn't we go in the morning?"

Ryan looked at Renee. This was a turn of events he hadn't expected.

Renee turned to look at Dr. Elmhurst. "I don't know what kind of drugs you have been on or for how long. You're either going to a hospital or the police station right now, no debate." Renee hoped she sounded more in charge than she felt.

Dr. Elmhurst leaned toward the front seat. "Wouldn't a hospital or the police need me to fill out forms? I don't even know my first name? Do you?"

Renee answered, "We can easily find that out. What's important is not to make a bad situation even worse."

Ryan asked Renee, "Wasn't that your brother that brought you this car? Would he let Dr. Elmhurst spend the night?"

Renee spoke to no one in particular. "Yeah, all I need is to involve my family in this little prison escape." Renee was close to breaking down from the stress of what she had done and now the pressure from Dr. Elmhurst's begging was pushing her to the edge. The mention of Eli gave her an idea.

Eli had just finished his shower, put on his boxers and grabbed a beer from his refrigerator when his phone rang. "Hey, Sis. What's up?"

Renee sputtered, "We need your help! I just helped a doctor escape Brookfield Place in the trunk of Momma's car. He's been held prisoner and drugged. People are missing, maybe dead, and my name is on a skull list! Another patient, well ex-patient that pretends to be a nurse, is with me. What's that cop's name you know?"

Eli sat his beer down. What the heck was she talking about? "Are you okay? You sound high or somethin'."

Renee started to cry. "Eli, I need you! Call that cop friend of yours and tell him to meet us at your house."

Eli freaked, "My house? Hell no! Take these people to the 107th Precinct. I'll get Oink there and I'll meet you."

Renee started to calm down. "What's this cop's real name? I've got enough to explain without walking into a police station and asking for Oink."

* * *

Nick had gone back to the station after dinner at Lacey's. He felt restless and knew he couldn't sleep anyway. For the last hour he had reviewed the stack of papers that Jen had left on his desk regarding Billow. She had also made a chart showing all of the places Billow had been assigned to in the last five years.

The quiet of the homicide room was interrupted by Jen walking in and plopping her purse on her desk. "I see you couldn't enjoy your evening either."

"John's going to think you don't like him anymore." Nick rolled back his chair and stretched his back. "Thanks for getting all of this together."

Jen turned her computer on and twisted her chair to face Nick. "I just can't get Billow out of my head. Assuming you really saw Billow at the bank robbery, which I believe you did, then he is probably in what they call an Independent Living Program. I can't confirm it, because this hospital, Brookfield Place, hasn't updated their reports to the state in two months. The latest news about Billow was Dr. Elmhurst requesting a release hearing 28 days ago."

Nick took out a small notebook from his pocket. "Travis Cummings said he had just left a meeting with Dr. Elmhurst at Brookfield Place before someone shot at him in that mall parking lot. I still don't understand why he went there. He's holding something back. I need to talk to Cummings again."

Nick punched in the number for Agent Phillips. After a couple of rings he finally answered. "Phillips."

Nick asked, "How can I talk to Cummings?"

Phillips asked, "Why?"

"Because I think he knows more than he's told us. I'm trying to pin down who shot at him in the parking lot."

Phillips gave Nick a number. "By the way, I'm heading to Dominick Guioni's estate right now."

Nick looked at his watch, it was after ten. "What's up?"

Phillips answered, "We have a tip that there's been a massacre there. Gotta go." The line went dead.

Nick looked at Jen, "This is going to be a long night. The FBI is on their way to Dom's estate. They have a tip that there's been a massacre there."

Jen had walked up to the murder board and now stood facing Nick. "How would that fit with what we know the Westside crew has been up to?"

Nick looked at the murder board. "Humor me for a minute. I still think the original hit on Reggie Lomas was a mistake, and Attorney Baxter and Alexia Cummings were killed to cover it up." Nick pointed at the board. "Let's put Lomas, Attorney Baxter and Alexia Cummings in with all of the hits that Baxter got paid for and ballistics matched to that rifle. Keep them to the side. Then let's start a column titled Brookfield."

Jen nodded her head as she changed the murder board to reflect its new structure.

Nick said, "Let me make a quick call to Cummings before it gets much later." As Nick waited for someone to pick up the line, he pointed at the murder board. "We might as well start a victim column for Dom. Evidently somebody wanted him dead, too."

Jen squeezed in Dom's name for another column. She realized that they had filled the entire nine foot murder board, except for a small space in the middle. Jen picked up a red marker and put a big question mark in that space. She plopped down in a chair, stared at the board and listened to Nick talk to Cummings on the phone.

"Travis? This is Nick Stryker. Tell me again why you went to Brookfield Place?" Nick listened a while and then said, "You're not playing straight here. You could have told them they were late paying the skim by phone. Remember, your deal blows up if you lie or fail to cooperate. Why did you drive there in person?"

Nick clicked his pen as he listened. "Who was there?" Nick wrote on his desk pad. "How much did they give you?" Nick wrote again. "That was two months' worth? Didn't you think it was strange they gave you cash? What were you going to do with it?" Nick listened quite a while and then asked, "You're sure the only people that knew you had that money were Dr. Elmhurst and this other guy? You say your briefcase with the cash in it was stolen while you were purchasing a phone?" Nick looked at Jen and rolled his eyes. "Why didn't you mention this missing cash before?" Nick stopped clicking his pen and frowned. "You were afraid to admit that you lost Dom's money? That's bull. You offered to turn over all of that to the FBI, remember? What else was in that briefcase?"

Travis Cummings was many things, but a fool wasn't one of them. Stryker was going to kick this nest until something came out. He couldn't afford to have the FBI back out on his deal. "What else was in the briefcase that was more important than the cash? My personal ledger tracking my kickbacks from Milo Spulane. Milo wants to incorporate the Westside crew into his own and needed to know specifics. I gave them to him. The real reason I don't want the FBI getting my notebook is my offshore account numbers are in there. That notebook never left my sight. I planned to use that money to hide after I testified."

Nick said, "So, you didn't mention the notebook because it could lead the FBI to your assets."

Nick hung up from his call with Travis and walked over to the murder board. He wrote Dr. Elmhurst and mystery man under the heading Brookfield. He drew a red line from Cummings' name to Brookfield and from Cummings' name to Joey Lacastra's name under the mob heading.

Wayne walked in the room, followed by Eli, and smiled at Jen and Nick. "Well, at least I don't have to chase you two down. Sam is on his way in." Wayne sat at his desk and rolled his chair toward the murder board. "We need a bigger board. We have got a whole group of people on the way here to report murders, missing people, and a kidnapping at your Brookfield Place."

Jen looked at Wayne, "We also have a massacre at Dominick Guioni's estate."

Wayne stood and headed for the door, "I'll go steal the white board from the Chief's office."

CHAPTER 17

Wednesday 10:30 pm

Jake Billow secured Lacey in a closet. Her mouth, hands and feet were duct taped. He injected Lacey with what was left in the syringe. He had no idea if he was overdosing her or not. He didn't care. The gash on the side of her forehead had stopped bleeding and now had swollen into a good sized goose egg. Too bad, she was quite the beauty otherwise. Billow felt a chill rush up his spine. He imagined Nick's rage finding out his precious Lacey now belonged to him. Satisfied that Lacey was properly secured, he locked the closet door and pushed the tall chest back in front of it.

He was too wired to sleep. It was time to mess with Nick. He wanted Nick furious. What better way than to shoot a few cops? He always killed in threes. He was sure that Nick would remember. He grabbed a handful of ammunition and dropped it in his coat pocket. Billow headed outside to his van. Nick would know he was back when he heard that third call.

* * *

Agent Phillips stood outside Dom's house and watched as the Crime Scene Techs and Coroner's team investigated the scene and the bodies. A fellow agent walked up and shook his head. "He's not here."

Phillips said, "Then he's not dead."

Agent Phillips walked over to where the one surviving guard was being interrogated. He grabbed the guard's shoulder and turned him. "Where did you take him?"

The guard looked puzzled. "Take who?"

"You know who: Dom. You've had plenty of time to take him somewhere." Agent Phillips looked around. "Or maybe he drove himself out of here. Or maybe he's been kidnapped. Did you check the shooter's trunk?"

Phillips looked at the other agent, "Do we have a handle on what cars might be missing from here?" The agent turned and walked away quickly as he talked into his cell phone.

Agent Phillips studied the guard's face. Phillips didn't know if he was scared to death, in shock, or in on some plot. "What's the mob's punishment for a guard that lets something like this happen?"

The guard had dead eyes and answered, "I'd rather be one of them right now." He pointed to the bodies waiting to be loaded into the coroner's wagon.

Phillips responded, "You'll be safe for a while. Turn around; you're under arrest for accessory to murder." Phillips cuffed him and then pushed him toward another agent. "Read him his rights."

* * *

Frankie woke to the ear blasting shrills of his new phone. He turned on the bedside light and saw that the caller had blocked the ID. It better not be Artie wanting to move back in.

"Yeah?"

It was Dom. Frankie listened for a very long time, all the while trying to dress. Finally Frankie spoke, "Your trust is not misplaced. Give me the address." Frankie had Dom repeat the address a second time. This would not be the time to make another mistake.

Dom said, "I'll be in touch. Only a trusted few know I survived tonight. I expect you to keep it that way. Punk didn't think I'd wear a vest and plate inside my home." Dom coughed, "I don't want him to see daylight." The line went dead.

* * *

Renee, Ryan and Dr. Elmhurst arrived at the 107th Precinct and were escorted upstairs to the homicide room. Wayne was already talking to Eli at a long table they had set up in the center of the room. Nick, Jen and Sam were at their desks working.

Sam suddenly shouted to Nick. "Hey, ballistics just confirmed the rifle used to shoot out Cummings' car was the same rifle used on Lomas and the rest of those mob hits you have in the big red circle."

Wayne turned his head, "What? If there was already a mob hit man out for Cummings, why was Joey Lacastra hired?"

Nick and Jen exchanged questioning glances.

Nick said, "Same gun doesn't mean the same shooter."

Jen raised her arms in a stretch. "Could this case get any stranger?"

Renee, Ryan and Dr. Elmhurst entered the room. Eli looked at Jen. "Yep."

Sam, Wayne, Nick, Jen and Eli listened as Renee and Ryan ticked off every strange thing that had been happening at Brookfield Place. When they finished talking, Eli rested his head in his hands and moaned.

Wayne asked Renee, "Your decision to remove Dr. Elmhurst from the facility was based on your belief, and some evidence, that he was in grave danger, correct?"

Renee nodded and answered, "Yes."

Wayne glanced at Nick and then said, "I don't think you two have to worry about being in trouble, especially since you came straight to the police."

Nick asked Renee, "Who is taking care of the patients in Building D now?"

Renee and Ryan answered together, "No one."

Nick directed his next question to Ryan, "Are you a nurse there, too?"

Ryan's cheek twitched when he answered, "I'm a paranoid schizophrenic. With my medications I function well and live off campus. I have a job at Brookfield to assist with patient care. I'm not really a nurse."

Eli whispered to Wayne, "He's a patient?"

Wayne ignored Eli and directed his next question to Dr. Elmhurst. "You were the Administrator to Building D before being abducted?"

Dr. Elmhurst answered, "I believe so, yes. At least that's what Ryan and Renee have told me. I don't remember much. I'm so sorry, but I just don't have my memory back yet; there are too many drugs in my system. Could I lie down somewhere?"

Nick had wanted to ask Dr. Elmhurst about the release hearing request for Billow, but realized that Dr. Elmhurst was in no condition to give an answer.

Jen offered, "We have a holding room that's mostly used by us for naps. Would you like to go there?"

Dr. Elmhurst shrugged, "I've been in a cell for weeks. The prospect of going in another one doesn't sound very appealing."

Jen smiled, "What if I leave the door open?"

"That would be fine."

Jen escorted Dr. Elmhurst to the end of the hall where the holding room was. Dr. Elmhurst collapsed on the bed and covered himself with the thin blanket. Jen shuddered at the thought of what he had been through over the last month.

Renee looked at Wayne and said, "I have a friend who is the Administrator of Building A; his name is Tyler Goodman. I went to him earlier today with my concerns. He promised to look into things and help me. I think he needs to know what is happening, so he can get some staff and security in Building D until we straighten this out."

Wayne looked at Renee and said, "We'll call him in a minute."

Wayne excused himself and walked over to Jen, Nick and Sam. "I think we need to have this Tyler guy meet us at the crazy farm. We should take Renee and Ryan, too, since they know these people. How much force should we bring with us?"

Nick shrugged, "I think we need enough manpower to make a statement. They have 120 acres we have to search, missing people, and maybe some bodies. We don't know what we'll find and this is a state sanctioned facility. Call the Chief, but I think this warrants at least a level two status. We want SWAT and State Troopers, too. Our initial goal is to secure the environment we have to investigate."

Wayne nodded and said, "I'll make the calls to the Chief and Central." He suddenly stopped and asked, "What the heck do I call this?"

Nick answered, "A mutiny at the insane prison."

Eli watched a tear roll down Renee's cheek and walked over to give her a hug.

She hugged him back and said, "I'll never tease you again about the trouble you used to get into."

Eli smiled, "Yeah, you crashed right through that benchmark."

Wayne told Renee to call Tyler and tell him they were coming to Brookfield Place with police.

Renee reached Tyler and told him the police were on their way.

Tyler answered, "Good. I'm still here at my office going through reports and calendars. You were right, Renee. Building D is worse than a mess. I'll start putting together photo bios on who is supposed to be there: both staff and patients."

Wayne asked to speak with Tyler. "This is Detective Dunfee. What can you tell me?"

Tyler said, "Renee told me a nurse named Nancy Logan was missing. I didn't believe her, because I had seen numerous emails and reports being generated by Nancy's employee code. I called Nancy's mom to get a good phone number. She told me a male friend of Nancy's called her three weeks ago and told her that Nancy won a vacation. Nancy's mom hasn't been able to reach her since. Detective Dunfee, I think Renee is right; something sinister is going on."

Renee broke down when Wayne told her what Tyler had said about Nancy. She remembered the red skull list and told Wayne that Nancy's name had been on it.

Ryan interrupted, "Renee's name got added today with a red skull. The file is on Dr. Elmhurst's desk."

* * *

Frankie double checked the hotel name and room number before he entered the lobby. The service staff at the desk ignored him as he walked to the bank of elevators, entered, and pushed the button for the third floor. In the elevator, he turned his jacket inside out and mussed up his hair. He had a small flask of whiskey that he splashed on his face, took a swig and then checked that his silencer and pistol were ready in his pocket. Room 337. Room 337. He glanced again to make sure that was what was on the paper. Yes, Room 337.

A hotel maid had a housekeeping cart at the far end of the hall. The room door was open, the interior light bright and casting shadows in the dimly lit space. Dom never was one to spend much money on accommodations for his 'guests'. It didn't surprise Frankie at all that he had put Joey Lacastra in this flea bag hotel.

Room 337 was dead center in the hall. Frankie took a couple of deep breaths, rolled his shoulders forward and started making the sounds of a drunken old man. He watched the doors along the hall to see if anyone reacted to his performance. Nothing. He leaned heavily against the door for Room 337 and began pounding. "I'm home, Mable. Let me in."

Frankie glanced both ways down the hall as he continued pounding. It was still clear. He pounded louder and shouted louder. "Let me in, Mable. I'm back."

Suddenly the door to Room 337 opened a crack and a man's voice said, "You've got the wrong room, old man." The door shut.

Frankie pounded again. "Who are you? What are you doing in my room?"

Joey was almost finished packing and in no mood for this drunk. He certainly didn't want attention drawn to his room. Joey opened the door wider and Frankie fell forward halfway into the threshold. Joey pushed back on the door to send Frankie stumbling backwards into the hall. Joey's nostrils were assaulted by a strong whiskey odor.

Frankie stumbled back toward the door and shouted, "What cha doin' in my room?"

Joey opened his jacket with his right hand to show his gun. "You've got the wrong room, old man."

Frankie pretended to stumbled to his left as he aimed his pistol at Joey's forehead from inside his coat pocket. "You've got the wrong old man."

An almost inaudible 'pop' left Joey bleeding on the floor. Frankie took two steps into the room and shot him again in the head. He kicked Joey's lifeless foot out of the way and closed the door. Frankie looked both ways once back in the hall. The housemaid exited the far room with a stack of towels on her arm. As Frankie passed she smiled and said, "Good evening, sir," and went back to her work. Frankie entered the elevator, reversed his coat back and left the building.

The housekeeper pushed opened the door to Room 337, took Joey's pulse, and left the room. She removed her housekeeping apron, placed it in the laundry sack on the cart and left the building. As she drove toward the city she placed a call. "Joey Lacastra was just hit. Grand Manor Hotel, Room 337. Frankie Mullen."

The night lights of the city danced across her dashboard. She glanced at her reflection in the rearview mirror. The strain of the last 25 years was showing tonight. She was so close. Sophia wiped a tear from her cheek with the back of her hand. She exhaled and her jaw set firm in determination as she drove through the night traffic. This was no time for weakness.

* * *

Jake Billow sat in his van across from the corner convenience store. He readied his rifle and checked through the scope one last time. Where he was parked, it was dark and an easy escape back to the main road traffic. He had just called in an anonymous tip that the store was being robbed.

Like clockwork, two patrol cars screamed into the lot. The officers had their guns drawn and cautiously made their way toward the store's entrance. Billow whispered, "One more step." He squeezed off a shot and saw the officer go down. He shifted the van into drive and eased into traffic.

"One."

Billow drove twelve blocks to the 109th Precinct building and waited. The 'Officer Down' call would be answered by anyone available. Billow watched an officer dash from the parking lot door and jump in a unit. As the officer looked to his left to merge traffic, Billow squeezed the trigger again.

"Two."

He laughed as he pulled from the curb and headed toward the 107th Precinct, Nick's precinct. He parked some distance down the road and carefully rolled the van forward and back until he had the perfect angle for the front entrance. This precinct had some parking behind the building, but shift officers often used the angled parking at the front. Billow watched as two, three, four squad cars pulled in and parked. Only one space was still open; that would be the winner.

A squad car came from around the corner and landed in the spot. Billow raised his rifle to aim. The officer got out of the car and turned toward the building. Billow squeezed the trigger. The officer dropped to the sidewalk.

"Three."

Billow pulled from the curb and headed home.

✳ ✳ ✳

Nick and Jen road together to Brookfield Place. Nick had put extra ammunition and two high powered rifles in the trunk in case he and Jen needed them. The closer they came to Brookfield, the more police cars had joined the caravan. Blue and red flashing lights were ahead of them and behind them as far as they could see.

The unit radio broke through with "10-24! Officer Down, Officer Down!" dispatch gave a south side address.

Jen shook her head, "This job sucks sometimes."

The last code any cop wants to hear is a 10-24. Nick knew that plenty of officers were available to answer the 10-24. He tried to focus on picturing the murder board in his head. "If the motive for shooting Cummings in the mall parking lot was to steal the skim cash, how did a mob hit man know that Cummings would be there, at that time, with 140 grand in cash?"

Jen answered, "You said Cummings was surprised Dr. Elmhurst gave him cash. He was usually paid by check."

"There were only two people that knew Cummings had cash. We have Dr. Elmhurst and whoever that second man was in his office. That rifle's history isn't fitting anymore, Jen. Attorney Baxter certainly didn't order this hit; he's dead. Dom's shooter, Joey Lacastra, hadn't even been assigned the job yet when Cummings was shot at."

Jen said, "This is driving me crazy. Let's assume that you and Wayne are right that Lomas was a mistake. We've got an old man in those pictures from the other hit scenes. What if this old man is really the mob hit man Attorney Baxter used? If he made a mistake shooting Lomas, let's say he covered it up by killing Alexia, because she had ordered a hit that didn't happen. Maybe he was worried she'd start trouble."

"Let's say Alexia's name was on the check because she had ordered a hit on her husband, Travis, through Attorney Baxter. She orders a hit on him because she hates him. This has nothing to do with the mob. This old man then kills his partner, Attorney Baxter, to keep him from disclosing the mistake to any mob guys. If we think he did all of that because of a stupid mistake on an address, maybe the old man also lost his rifle? He might be getting dementia or something. His rifle could have been stolen or sold to anyone."

Nick nodded, "If we use that theory, then whoever shot at Cummings just happens to be the new owner of the rifle. He doesn't really have anything to do with our other mob hits. We're back to Dr. Elmhurst and his buddy. They just ended up with the old man's rifle."

The radio broke through again. "10-24! Officer Down, Officer Down!" Dispatch gave the address.

Nick glanced at Jen. "That's the address for the 109th."

Jen tapped her index finger on her pistol handle. "Not many people are crazy enough to shoot an officer in front of a police station."

Nick said, "That second call was exactly fifteen minutes after the first. That's about how long it would take to drive from the first call. This is the same shooter."

The tension in the car was palatable. Both Jen and Nick expected another call. They rode in silence another ten miles. Nick glanced out his side window at the total blackness of the night and his memory took him back five years and his hunt for Billow. He had killed nine officers before Nick and Jen caught him. Always in groups of three. That was his unique M.O.

"10-24! Officer Down. Officer Down!" The address was the 107th.

Jen looked at Nick, "Billow."

Nick pulled his phone from his pocket and dialed a number. "Chief? Stryker. I thought I saw Jake Billow at the bank robbery scene, couldn't catch him. He saw me. Jen and I have been tracking his current status. At best it's cloudy. I believe he's out. We just had three 10-24's in less than an hour. That's his M.O. My gut says Billow is sending a message." Nick listened a few moments and then said, "Thank you."

Jen was impressed that Nick had the personal phone number for the Chief memorized.

Jen knew that every fiber of his being wanted to be on the hunt for Billow.

Nick said, "The Chief isn't sold that it's Billow on these 10-24's, but he wants Billow arrested if in fact he's out. The Chief's putting out an All-Points Bulletin. He's calling in the Feds, too. He wants to use the Marshals for the take down."

Jen could read Nick's thoughts and said, "You and I will find him first."

Nick looked at Jen, "Billow has a lot of ties to Brookfield Place and we're here. Maybe we'll get lucky."

They rode in silence for the next few miles. She knew that every cop in the caravan was cursing and slapping their steering wheels. It was a helpless feeling to be committed to a case when a 10-24 goes out from Central. It's in every cop's blood to want to join the chase.

They finally arrived at Brookfield Place and watched as the line of police cars crawled through the iron gate and into the campus. Nick drove their car to the back and parked in front of Building D, where Wayne had instructed them to go. Wayne had just arrived with Renee and Ryan.

Nick glanced around at the chaos and exhaled. "This is a dangerous situation. These cops are already hyper because of the 10-24's and no one is able to identify the good guys from the bad guys. Somebody has to take control."

Jen asked, "Got any ideas?"

"Yeah, in absence of control, manipulate chaos."

Jen could always see Nick's SEAL training kick in. His focus and thinking became laser sharp. She had no doubt he would have this situation manageable in short order.

Wayne walked over. "That last 10-24 was Jeff Turner. Rookie, tomorrow would have ended his first week at our house. Got two kids, and another on the way. Sniper was a bad shot on the other two; they're going to make it." Wayne looked at Nick. "Are you thinking what I'm thinking?"

"Billow. It's going to be a very long night. Find me that guy named Tyler."

Nick started barking orders establishing perimeter search teams, building guards and information reporting procedures. He ordered the campus police to contact all employees to return to Brookfield Place and report to the campus police building. SWAT arrived and Nick asked them to secure all unoccupied buildings and perimeter gates.

Jen helped Wayne and Sam set up a command post inside Building D. Renee and Ryan worked to keep the patients calm. Wayne and Sam moved tables from the cafeteria out to the reception hall and in a nearby conference room. The large number of officers arriving required a central location to receive orders that minimized any impact on the patient areas. As officers reported themselves available, Jen recorded their names and phone numbers and wrote down whatever assignment Nick gave them.

Within 30 minutes Nick had sequestered staff from the other buildings to help with the patients. Temporary staff, that had been brought in to help with patients, reported their needs and Jen, Wayne and Sam worked to locate what was needed for them. Wayne had requested that Control Central contact the local hospitals for volunteers and supplies.

Jen looked at Wayne, "It seems we have manipulated the chaos successfully."

Sam laughed, "You're hanging around Stryker so much you're starting to sound like him."

CHAPTER 18

The campus police dialed the number they had for Dr. Elmhurst. After a few rings he answered. The campus cop thought he sounded as if he had been sleeping.

"I'm sorry to disturb you, sir, but you have to come back to Brookfield right now. I'm not sure what's going on but there must be a hundred cops from the city here. I'm not exaggerating and they brought SWAT. The police are demanding that all employees come back in."

He thanked the officer for the call and sat up in bed. Well, that's that. He got out of bed, grabbed his suitcase from the closet and called the airline. He had one hour to catch a flight out of O'Hare to Orlando. A three hour layover and he would be on his way to Belize. He pulled up his bank information and wired the remaining funds he had to his offshore account.

He checked that he had Dr. Elmhurst's driver's license, passport, and medical records. It had been pure luck that he and Dr. Elmhurst actually resembled each other. His weeks of planning were paying off. He would have loved another month's worth of income, but it felt good to know it was over.

* * *

Sam was in charge of assigning cops copies of photos to verify the identities of staff and patients. Tyler had given Sam the code to get into the computer and print out bios and photos. Sam also borrowed two doctors from Building C to review patient medication records and determine what was needed.

Nick had asked Wayne to secure medication and food from the other buildings at the facility to Building D. Some patients were terrified of the police presence in the building. Others were merely curious. All of them complained that they were hungry and needed their medication.

Nick could see why Ryan had been hired as an employee of Building D. He was excellent at calming the patients and multi-tasking. Renee had reported to Wayne that the kitchen had no food. What little had been there had been raided by the patients for snacks. She was grateful to hear that arrangements were already underway to get the kitchen working again. It was rumored that the FBI had ordered over three hundred pizzas from around the city to be delivered at the gates.

The FBI agents would be arriving soon and assuming much of the responsibility for restoring order. Nick wanted to hand them as much information as he could. He was glad he had arrived first. The FBI was far more generous with pizza than information. This was Nick's best chance to find out what Billow's status really was.

A conference room to the right of the hall was being used for interviews. Nick had asked Tyler to join Jen and him at a corner table. Tyler had an armload of files that Nick and Jen took from him.

Tyler pointed to a stack of banker boxes on the table near Wayne. "Those are all bio files, too. I haven't had time to check them all off against the state report."

Nick asked Tyler, "Who is responsible for this facility?"

Tyler answered, "I can get that for you from a computer, but I didn't bring that with me. It is a conglomerate company based in Louisiana. This is a private facility that caters to the State."

Tyler noticed Nick's expression and continued, "It gets worse. The State pays per patient and supplies medications. The Department of Corrections also pays per patient and provides some funds for security and facility maintenance. That's it. Once someone is sent here, everyone washes their hands of them. Our company takes anyone the state wants to send. The worse the patient is, the more they are paid."

Nick was stunned. "Do you mean there's no one accountable for day to day operations other than staff?"

Tyler shrugged, "Pretty much."

"Doesn't the state come in and inspect living conditions or patient progress?"

Tyler shook his head. "I'm telling you they don't care or they don't know what to do. Just review the recent legislation and budget cuts if you need proof. I think the general population would be appalled if they knew the real condition of the mental health system." Tyler shrugged, "Of course, maybe they don't care either."

Nick said, "I want to hear what you think is going on, Tyler."

Tyler sighed and glanced over to where Renee and Ryan were dispensing medications to borrowed staff from Buildings A, B and C.

Tyler lowered his voice so Renee wouldn't hear him. "I thought Renee was having a breakdown when she came to my office. Building D has done that to employees before. I told her I would do some snooping. Once I started looking into things, I couldn't stop. That's why I'm still here tonight. I think things started going wrong about a month ago from the looks of the reports."

Nick said, "Get more specific."

Tyler shrugged, "The reports stopped. The only requisitions I can find are for food and drugs. Lots of drugs, six times more than what should have been needed. To tell you the truth, the drug orders have been heavier than they should have been for years now."

Jen asked, "Wouldn't the state have noticed a sudden increase in orders?"

Tyler shrugged again. "Maybe eventually. I'm talking years, not weeks. Like I said, nobody wants to get involved with this type of facility. If duplicate drug orders were found, they might not even be reported. If it was reported, it would be reported to us."

Jen was shocked. "The company that owns this place is who the report would go to?"

"Yes. If a violation is deemed systemic by the state, meaning the activity continues, the state could ask for an investigation by the Justice Department. Trust me, that is a very large pile, and we would be on the bottom."

Nick said, "Let's go through your files. Let's look first at who is missing. How many patients are supposed to be here?"

Tyler answered, "There are 1247 patients in Buildings A, B and C, and 64 staff. Building D is supposed to have 15 staff and 237 patients."

Nick wondered where the other fourteen staff persons of Building D were. The only one he had met so far was Renee.

Tyler opened a file. His index finger pointed to a picture of a woman in her mid-thirties, nice smile. "I've tried to sort out the Building D staff and patients first for you. Nancy Logan, R.N. No one has seen her for three weeks at least. However, I have multiple drug orders done on her ID code to the state over this period. One was done this morning."

Tyler opened another file. "Dr. John Bates. Renee and Ryan seem to think they have been talking to an imposter. I checked with the state and Dr. Bates requested a new ID badge last week that was delivered today. What I could find on him hinted that this place was his whole life. No wife, kids, siblings. He has been the number two administrator for this building for two years." Tyler raised his eyebrows. "Seems kind of fishy he would just stop coming in to work and then order a new ID badge."

Tyler opened a third file, "Dr. Edmund Elmhurst. I understand Renee took him to the police department tonight, so I guess he isn't really missing."

Jen grabbed the file from in front of Tyler and turned it around to face Nick.

Nick glanced back up at Jen, "This isn't the man Renee brought to the police station."

Renee was standing at Wayne's table talking to one of the patrol policemen. Jen yelled for Renee to come to their table.

Nick pointed to the picture of the real Dr. Elmhurst in the file. "Do you know who this is?"

Renee shook her head. "I've never seen that man before."

Tyler said, "That is Dr. Edmund Elmhurst."

Renee's knees went weak and she sat down. "Then who did Ryan and I take out of here?"

* * *

Kamber was starving. She looked at her watch and saw it was only midnight. She felt as if she had been freezing for eight days. Joseph was right. It was one thing to think you understood the plight of the homeless and quite another to experience it. Chad was fast asleep and snoring. Experiment or not, she was going to use a real toilet and find something to eat. Kamber silently raised herself up and tiptoed to the door. She slowly twisted the handle, stepped into the hall and quietly closed the door behind her. She didn't want Chad to catch her cheating.

Kamber scurried into the bathroom and sighed with relief at how warm it felt. She did feel a little guilty for cheating, but decided she'd get over it. She checked her reflection in the mirror and nearly screamed. She looked as if she had aged 20 years in one day. Mascara was smudged all over her face and her hair looked like it had gone through a blender. She did a little repair work with a wash cloth and her fingers. She didn't want to look too good.

On the kitchen counter next to the toaster was a paper plate with garlic toast wrapped in plastic wrap. Kamber unwrapped the plastic wrap slowly as to not make a sound. She picked up a piece of the garlic toast and ran it past her nose. The aroma was irresistible. She stuffed half the slice in her mouth just as Chad turned on the kitchen light and yelled, "Aha! Caught ya!"

Kamber held out the paper plate to Chad as a peace offering. He grabbed two pieces. They leaned against the kitchen island moaning as they ate.

Kamber motioned toward the refrigerator and whispered, "Get us something to drink."

Chad turned and then stopped. "What the heck is this?"

Kamber walked around the corner and froze. A large pool of what looked like blood was on the white marble floor with impact splatters on the cabinet door. Kamber ran to Lacey's door and softly knocked, "Lacey? Lacey, are you okay? There's blood in the kitchen."

There was no answer. Chad walked up behind her and whispered, "Go in."

Kamber turned the knob and opened the door. Lacey wasn't there. The bed hadn't been slept in. Chad turned on the light and said, "Maybe she went to Nick's house. Call her."

Kamber ran to her room and got her phone. She didn't care that it was midnight, Lacey would understand. She dialed as she ran back to Chad. Kamber heard Lacey's phone ringing in stereo. Chad held up his hand; he had Lacey's phone. "Her purse is here, too. Now what?"

Kamber dug in her pocket and found the phone number Nick had given her and dialed. After several rings a woman answered, "Control Center answering Nick Stryker's line."

Kamber wasn't sure what to say. "I need to speak to Nick Stryker please."

The woman answered, "Detective Stryker is at a level two crime scene. He can only receive calls from the Control Center. You'll have to leave a message."

Kamber stomped her foot in frustration. "Ask him to call Kamber, tell him it's urgent."

"What is the number ma'am?" Kamber gave her number and dropped her phone onto the counter.

Chad was staring at the pool of blood and then pointed. "There are drops leading toward the door. Do you think she went to a hospital?"

Kamber ran to the front window and saw that Lacey's car was in the driveway. She yelled to Chad, "Wherever she went, she didn't drive. Her car is still here."

Kamber looked like she had an idea.

Chad asked, "What?"

Kamber said, "That third GPS chip is gone. Nick left it on the counter, remember? I don't see it now." Kamber started searching every place she thought Lacey might have put it. She remembered Nick telling Lacey to put it in her jewelry box. It wasn't there. "I don't see it anywhere. What if she has it on her?"

Chad shook his head, "That would be quite a coincidence, don't you think? Why would she have it on her?"

Kamber raised her voice, "I don't know! I'm just desperate." She grabbed her phone and went to the GPS device app that Nick had downloaded. Nick had engaged all three chips and all three chips were displayed on the top tool bar. Kamber touched device A and device B and device C and then 'map', like Nick had shown her. A map appeared and displayed chips A and B on top of each other and chip C way off to the south.

Kamber turned her phone to Chad and said, "Ha! Let's go find her!"

Chad said, "We don't know that's her. I think we should call the police."

Kamber answered, "I'm going to chase down this chip with or without you. We've already got a message into Nick. We can call the police when we get there."

Chad rubbed his hands over his face. He already knew better than to argue with Kamber. "Let me go to the bathroom first. Why don't you shut that window in your room since we've flunked the experiment anyway?"

Kamber went to her room to close the window. As she was locking it, she saw a dirty shoe print on the comforter. A very large shoeprint. Someone had crawled in the window and that someone had Lacey. Kamber screamed for Chad.

* * *

Renee called for Ryan to come over to Nick and Jen's table. Renee held up the picture of Dr. Elmhurst. "Ryan, this is the real Dr. Elmhurst."

Ryan studied the picture and said, "Yeah, I've seen him around for years. Not lately though. His name is Dr. Elmhurst? Then who…"

Nick slid a stack of files Tyler had prepared across the table and said, "Let's start going through these until we find a picture that matches our guest at the station."

Jen returned to the table from making a call. "Correction, we no longer have a guest at the station. He left. They said he just walked out. I was reminded that we left the door open for him."

Tyler kept pushing files from the banker boxes toward Renee, Ryan, Jen and Nick.

Nick opened a file; a picture of Jake Billow stared back at him. "Well, here's one guy I'm interested in."

Renee glanced over, "That's Dr. Bates."

Ryan glanced over and nodded, "Yeah, a real creep."

Jen exhaled, "He's no doctor. He's a killer; read the bio."

Ryan read the bio and then elbowed Renee, "I told you he wasn't right."

Nick looked at Jen, "Billow is pretending to be Dr. John Bates? Would you call Control with that alias for the APB?"

Jen nodded and placed the call. It was going to be very helpful having Billow's alias. She was beginning to have hope.

Renee frowned at Ryan. "You told me I was smuggling a doctor out of here. Keep looking in the files for our guy's picture. He must be a patient."

Jen yelped. "Oh, God! Here he is! Read the bio."

Nick read a minute. He looked at Tyler. "Am I reading this right? This guy is a delusional psychopath that thinks he's a doctor. He was convicted of mutilating dozens of people while performing his 'surgeries'. It says he actually passed himself off as a surgeon in a hospital which is how he got caught. He's labeled here as highly dangerous, cunning and not likely to improve."

Tyler was speed reading the computer printout next to the picture. "Yes, that's what it says, Marcus Newberry. Let's hope he doesn't reopen his practice before you find him. What's scary is that they know they have nothing to lose. He'll end up right back here."

Nick said, "There's nothing to protect the staff or other patients from people like him. I suppose you just keep them drugged out of their minds. I can't imagine living in this environment." Nick wondered how they ever found medical professionals willing to work there.

Tyler shook his head, "These patients have the right to refuse medications and we can't force them. Only about half of the patients in Building D are taking the recommended meds from what I can tell."

Nick looked at Ryan, "Whatever made you think Marcus Newberry was really a doctor?"

Ryan answered, "He gave medications and stuff, just like me. Everyone called him 'Doc' for years. He was real smart. He took out a patient's tonsils once." Ryan got a serious look on his face. "She died from complications though. I think they were mad at him for that." He started twitching and looked at Renee. "I need some drugs."

Nick's phone rang with a SWAT ID. "Stryker." Nick listened for a while and said, "We're putting together ID files now. Let me know when the coroner arrives. I'll be there shortly."

"SWAT has found a dozen or so remains in the vacated crematorium building. Some of the bodies are fresh. Only a few in the oven." Nick looked at

Tyler, "Did anyone have a partial artificial leg that you know?"

Tyler winced, "Dr. Elmhurst had an artificial left leg from the knee down."

Nick sighed, "We found the real Dr. Elmhurst."

Nick stared at the file for Billow and got an idea. "Wayne, where is the day guard for the entry gate? Is he here?"

Wayne flipped through some notes, "Yeah, he's bitching about it but he's here. I think he's just outside in the hall." Wayne got up and came back a few minutes later with the day guard.

Nick showed him the picture of Billow and asked, "Do you know who this is? What he drives?"

The guard nodded his head, "He's that new doctor for Building D. He just registered a van to the facility for patient transfers."

Nick felt his adrenaline pump, "Do you have that registration form?"

The guard flipped through his clipboard and pulled off a sheet of paper that he handed Nick. "Right there. Got his address, vehicle ID, copy of driver's license; everything I'm required to get."

The guard was getting defensive. He was probably intimidated by the massive police presence at the facility. Nick smiled at him, "Good job. You might have saved the day."

The guard smiled back and offered his services for as long as they needed him. Wayne smiled and ushered him from the room.

Nick called Control with the address for Billow and VIN number of the blue panel van. He was sure the address was phony, but the VIN had to have been checked by DMV for the registration tag. They were making progress. Billow was running out of time.

* * *

Lacey felt like she was in a bad dream. She opened her eyes and realized she was in a small closet with men's clothing. Her head was killing her. Suddenly she remembered the man striking her. Her adrenaline rushed at the thought that maybe the man had harmed Kamber and Chad. She forced herself not to panic, and pretended Nick was giving her step by step instructions. Lacey shifted her body to determine what her situation really was. She had been drugged. Her limbs were weak and her mind was sluggish. She focused on what Nick had taught her. He had told her that there was always an opportunity, you just had to find it.

Study your opponent. Her eyes had adjusted to the darkness and she could see that her abductor had made a big mistake. He had taped her hands in front of her. Nick had taught her how to escape being taped but she had to be able to stand.

She bent her elbows so her fingers were near her mouth and pulled down on the tape that wrapped around her head. Once the tape was below her chin she could open her mouth. She did a few deep breathing exercises and began to feel her head clearing. She used her fingernails to begin sawing through the tape that was binding her ankles. She thought about her kidnapper. He hadn't wrapped her ankles nearly tight enough. Kidnapping wasn't his thing. A narrow light ran the length of the closet door. Lacey bent down and pressed her cheek to the floor. She could tell that some piece of furniture was in front of the door, she could see its thick feet. Beyond that, she could see the bottom of a shabby looking couch or chair. It was quiet in the room.

Lacey willed all of her strength to stand. She examined the clothing in the closet looking for sizes and any hints of her kidnapper's identity. Her attention returned to her wrists. She had to get free. Nick had taught her to raise her taped wrists high above her head and then with one quick motion, use all of her strength to snap them free from the tape when she lowered her arms to her sides. Her first attempt didn't work. Her elbow had hit the wall causing pain to shoot up her arm. She listened to make sure her abductor had not heard the thunk.

She centered herself in the closet and tried again. It worked! Her wrists were free. A loud slam confirmed her abductor had arrived home. He was just outside of the closet door. Lacey braced herself for the inevitable fight.

Billow stared at the closet door frame behind the chest of drawers. He wondered how Lacey was doing. Was she still drugged? Was she awake? He walked toward the chest and then stopped himself. There were other things to worry about tonight and he was tired. He turned and walked into his bedroom.

Minutes turned into an hour. Lacey finally heard the sound of him snoring. She leaned her head back against the wall and wiped a tear from the corner of her eye. She had to stay strong. Nick had taught her well. There was nothing she could do but wait.

CHAPTER 19

Thursday 1:00 a.m.

Milo Spulane wasn't accustomed to someone waking him at one in the morning. As boss for the Northside crew, he expected his men to take care of issues for him. He glared at the waiting guard when he opened his bedroom door. The guard sheepishly handed Milo a phone.

"This better be an emergency." Milo growled into the phone, "What?"

The Chicago Outfit boss was calling him. Milo blinked his eyes awake and listened. The boss was calling a meeting for three a.m. Milo was expected to be there. There had been a massacre at Dominick's estate.

Milo sat on the edge of the bed and collected his thoughts. It would be easier now to get the Westside crew merged with his. It made perfect sense. Milo couldn't believe his good luck. A massacre at Dominick's estate.

The words echoed in his head like music. Milo looked in his closet and selected his best suit.

He got dressed and told his guard to be sure the car was ready at two. He wanted it cleaned and waxed, and he wanted an extra car to follow him to the meeting. He needed to look worthy of his new appointment.

* * *

Chad drove while Kamber tried to learn how to use the toolbox feature at the top of the GPS app. The last instruction Kamber had given him was to go southeast about one inch. Chad was ready to stop the car and scream. Finally after much trial and error she figured out how to feed in a road map so they had street names and mileage marks.

"You don't have to get so emotional." Kamber smiled as she scolded Chad.

Chad glanced at the map on Kamber's phone. "Wait! That's a rough area. Maybe we should call the cops now, so they can get there first." Chad imagined any number of terrifying things that could happen to them in that neighborhood. Nick had specifically told him to never go near there. He could tell by Kamber's expression he wasn't going to change her mind.

Kamber thought about it a minute and said, "Maybe when we get closer it can give us an actual address. Then we can call the cops, okay?"

They rode in silence occasionally pointing to unpleasant surroundings. Chad swore he heard a gunshot. Kamber said it was a car backfiring. Chad kept driving. His head swiveled as he tried to take in everything around them. Finally he asked, "How close are we?"

Kamber pushed her phone over to his face. "Real close." The map suddenly changed to a zoom view with a pulsating dot. Under the dot it said 225 feet.

Kamber pointed, "Pull over to the curb across the street and we can walk. It says 225 feet; I bet it's that little blue house there."

Chad looked at the house she was pointing at. It was little more than a chicken coop with house numbers. "You said we'd call the cops. We don't even know if this chip is Lacey. It could be somebody Nick has been watching. A bad guy. Maybe the chip is showing on our app by mistake."

Kamber started to tear up. "Then where is Lacey? This has to be her chip. Remember the footprint on my blanket? It's my fault she's gone! I'm the one that left the window open. We might not have time for the cops to get here."

Chad parked and Kamber reached for the door handle. Chad whispered, "Wait. We can't just knock on the door."

"I wasn't planning on knocking. Whoever took Lacey is probably in there. What if he's hurting her? We have to get closer, Chad."

✳ ✳ ✳

Billow jerked awake. His doctor had told him that his snoring or dreams kept waking him. They had tried to get him to use some crazy machine for breathing at night, but he refused. Tonight he figured he was just too excited to sleep.

He was still in bed when his phone rang. "Yeah."

"I thought I'd let you know the cops are all over Brookfield. I'm on my way to O'Hare. You've got less than an hour; I have your ticket. I suggest you get here before they find your alias." The line went dead.

There was no way Billow was going to leave town before he took care of Nick. Everything was ready, he had Lacey, and all he had to do was contact Nick to get the game started. He quickly threw a few items in his suitcase and walked it out to his van. When he came back in he stopped in front of the closet door. He wondered if he should check on Lacey.

Lacey had heard him moving around. She had heard him leave and then return. She knew he was standing just outside of the door. She sat silent, praying that he would walk away.

Billow decided she was probably fine and still drugged out. He needed to make contact with Nick. He would either be at home or on a case at this time of night. He might even be at Brookfield. Billow grabbed his van keys and decided to drive to Nick's condo.

Kamber and Chad had slid down in their seats when Billow had brought the suitcase out to the van. Now they watched as he pulled away and drove down the street. His red taillights disappeared at the corner.

Chad looked at Kamber, "It's now or never."

They quickly ran over to the small house and peeked in the windows. They couldn't see anything through the filthy glass. Kamber twisted the knob on the front door. "It's locked."

Chad sighed, "Well, yeah." He pulled a charge card from his wallet and slid it past the lock. The door popped open.

Kamber whispered, "You're pretty good at that."

Chad shrugged, "I used to lock myself out a lot."

Once in the small dark living room, Kamber whispered, "Lacey? Lacey are you here?" The GPS screen indicated that they were standing right on her.

Chad frowned and raised his voice. "Lacey, are you here?"

"I'm here! In the closet!"

Chad and Kamber ran to the chest of drawers and pushed it to the side. Chad picked the lock and Lacey stumbled into Kamber's arms. All three of them were crying.

Lacey grabbed Kamber's shoulders. "Are you okay? I was so afraid he had taken you both, too."

Kamber wiped her tears. "We're fine! Let's get out of here before he comes back."

Lacey stopped, "Wait. Let's push that chest back so he thinks I'm still here."

Chad pushed the large chest of drawers back in front of the closet door and looked at Lacey closer. "We're taking you to a hospital."

* * *

Frankie hesitated before he tossed his pistol into the Chicago River. It was like killing an old friend. He was forced to do that too, in his lifetime. A massacre at Dominick's estate and the killing of Joey Lacastra was going to bring a lot of heat to anyone associated with the Westside crew. That included him. In the morning he would go to the storage unit and get the pistol that was there. There was no history on that gun and he had properly registered it.

The black water of the river swallowed the pistol without making a sound. Frankie walked over to a bench and rested his knees. The bright colored lights of the city danced on the water's surface and brought a flood of memories to Frankie's mind. It seemed he remembered the old days better than this morning. He heard a noise behind him and twisted to see.

A young woman bundled in a winter coat and scarf walked behind him and sat at the far end of the bench. Frankie's breathing returned to normal and he wiped his nose with his hankie. He glanced down at the woman who seemed to be lost in thought.

She must have sensed him looking and said, "Life is certainly a puzzle, isn't it?"

Normally Frankie would have just grunted and left. There was something mysterious about this pretty lady sitting on a park bench in the middle of the night. It reminded him of an old movie.

Frankie answered, "I worked on a puzzle for two months before I figured out two pieces were missing."

The lady chuckled. "You're wiser than you know. I'm sure I'm missing pieces right now."

Comforting strangers and spewing words of wisdom were not phrases anyone would use to describe Frankie. He chuckled to himself that some stranger had called him wise.

The woman asked him, "Do you think things happen for a reason?"

Frankie looked at the bright lights on the water and envisioned his pistol on the river bed.

"Reason has nothing to do with it."

Frankie became curious.

"What are you doing out alone at this time of night? There are killers all over this city."

The woman sat up straighter. "Oh, I know that! My husband was shot dead two days ago. Right in our home, on his birthday! My kids are with their grandparents and I'm trying to understand why I'm not grieving. Maybe something's wrong with me."

Frankie said, "Maybe something was wrong with him."

Frankie stood to leave. "You really should go home."

The woman stood to leave also. "You're right. Thank you for listening to me." She walked over and gave Frankie a hug.

Frankie remembered the last time he was hugged. He was six years old.

"My name is Karen."

"Frankie."

Frankie watched her get in her car and drive off. He never gave his name to strangers, why had he done it now? He never listened to people blab about their problems. Old age was changing him, he didn't like it.

He liked the hug.

* * *

Agent Phillips grabbed a cup of coffee from the refreshment table the facility had set up for the officers. He walked to where Nick, Jen, Wayne and Sam were digging through a table full of files with Tyler, Renee and Ryan. Phillips noticed a short stack near Nick.

Nick nodded as Phillips joined them and handed his files over. "We're still trying to identify 'one' of the Dr. Elmhurst's."

Phillips smiled, "How many Dr. Elmhurst's are there?"

Nick answered, "The real one is dead in the crematorium, there's one that is really a psychopathic killer that we helped escape, and one we haven't identified that paid Cummings the cash."

Phillips opened the top file of the pile Nick had given him. Jake Billow.

Nick said, "He's been using the alias of Dr. John Bates for the last month. The real Dr. Bates is probably in the crematorium. I haven't had time to get over there yet." Nick lowered his voice to a whisper, "You done at the estate?"

Phillips nodded. "Dom's not there." Phillips signaled for another agent to come over and then said, "We got a tip. You can cross Joey Lacastra off your list. He was hit by Frankie Mullen tonight."

Nick shrugged, "Who's Frankie Mullen?"

Phillips answered, "An old retired hit man of Dom's."

Jen and Nick exchanged glances.

Renee and Ryan yelled from the end of the table. "Here he is! This is him, Dr. Elmhurst."

Nick grabbed the file and read the bio. "This is the same bio for the real Dr. Elmhurst, but the picture is different. This doesn't help at all."

Phillips handed the file to his agent and said, "Run this picture through the system." He looked at Nick. "We'll figure out who he is. I see Billow is causing grief tonight, too." Nick knew that Phillips was referring to the 10-24's.

Nick's phone rang. He knew it was Control because they were on a level two case. The Control operator said, "I have a Miss Lacey Star that provided the emergency code. May I patch her through?"

Nick glanced at Jen, "Yes."

Lacey didn't want to alarm Nick, but she didn't want him to hear she had been kidnapped without knowing she was okay. She knew when she heard his voice she would want to cry. She forced her voice to sound steady. "Nick, I'm fine. Perfectly fine. I don't want you to freak out, but I'm at a hospital with Kamber and Chad."

Nick stood, "What happened to Kamber?"

Lacey answered, "Nothing. I was kidnapped this evening but I'm fine now. I wouldn't lie to you. Kamber and Chad found me because I had that extra chip in my pocket."

Nick asked "What hospital?"

Nick's heart was pounding. He looked at Phillips, "My girlfriend was kidnapped tonight. She escaped and is at the hospital."

Jen couldn't believe what she was hearing.

Phillips stood, "Go. Take Jen, we've got this."

CHAPTER 20

Milo's driver pulled into the grand estate of the Outfit boss. Everyone, including Milo, was frisked and relieved of their weapons. Two Outfit guards accompanied each guest into a large conference room. Milo realized the meeting had been going on for some time. Obviously he was meant to be the last to arrive. He surmised the Outfit boss wanted to pave the way for his announcement of the merger of the Northside and Westside crews.

The Outfit boss rose and clasped Milo's hands in greeting. The others around the table nodded. Each crew boss was accompanied by their consigliere (attorney/advisor) and at least two guards. Milo noticed that Dom's underboss was there. Milo guessed that everyone wanted to make sure he understood the merger decision. A seat had been left open at the far end of the table and one near the Outfit boss.

The Outfit boss motioned for Milo to sit next to him. Milo tried to hide his excitement as he took the seat and waited for the meeting to resume.

The Outfit boss stated, "We've been discussing the unprecedented growth in our businesses in the last few years due to the Fed's concentration on terrorism. We'll be honoring our newest associates at next month's regular meeting. I am pleased to report that we have doubled the number of associates that work for us in the last six months."

A brief round of applause instantly stopped when the boss indicated he was ready to speak again. "It's not like the old days, is it boys? Now we have energy companies, cyber teams, international arms partners, and of course, the old standbys of sex and gambling. The longer we remain low key, the longer the government will assume we're dying off."

The boss turned to look at Milo. "I understand you have some ideas for increasing profits you wish to talk about?"

Milo was confused. He hadn't asked to address the meeting.

The Outfit boss continued, "Two months ago you said that you had a profit increasing proposal for my review."

Milo remembered. When he first decided he wanted to take over the Westside crew he had formed an argument demonstrating the benefits of a merger. It must be that the boss wanted the proposal made to the entire outfit. Milo spoke for 15 minutes straight about the benefits of a merger between the Northside crew and the Westside crew. He speckled his proposal frequently with sincere regrets regarding the attack on Dom's estate, but pointed out it demonstrated that Dom had lost control.

When Milo finished the mob boss said, "I have a few questions regarding your vision of this merger. What would be Dom's role?"

Milo was confused. "I don't understand."

Dominick entered the room from a side door and took a seat at the other end of the table. He nodded at Milo. While listening to Milo, Dom had decided there was enough evidence of Milo's greed to accuse Milo of the attack at his estate. Dom had already insinuated Milo was responsible to the Outfit boss earlier.

Dom spoke, "You looked surprised, Milo. Your man missed one; me. You need not worry about punishing him. I've taken care of that."

Milo leaned forward and banged the table with his fist. "I had nothing to do with the attack at your estate. I don't know what you're talking about."

The Outfit boss said, "Dom called me earlier this week with serious concerns about you, Milo. He had verified a plan you had with Anthony Jarrett to set Dom up for a hit."

Milo was scared. He couldn't figure out how Dom could have found out about the plan so soon. "That's a lie."

The Outfit boss motioned his guard at the door. The guard left and returned with Anthony Jarrett being carried by two goons. He was barely alive, his face barely recognizable. Anthony looked around the room through the one eye that could see anything and landed on the Outfit boss.

The boss asked him, "Anthony, were you promised a reward for delivering Dom for a hit?"

Anthony looked like he was going to puke. Finally he tried to straighten his posture and answered, "Yes."

"Who promised you this reward?"

Anthony pointed at Milo.

"Thank you, Anthony."

The Outfit boss motioned for them to take Anthony away. Milo's number two man walked through the door Dom had used and stood. The Outfit boss motioned for him to come take Milo's seat.

Milo looked at the faces around the table for what he knew was the last time. Like he always said, there's only one way to leave the mob.

* * *

Jen would have preferred to be the one driving but she trusted Nick. She had already reminded him that Lacey had said she was fine. "If you don't calm down, you're going to scare Lacey. We'll get him. He's making all kinds of mistakes, he can't shoot anymore, and he never was a good fighter."

Nick glanced over to Jen. "You think it was Billow, too."

Jen said, "It was Billow. Every cop in Chicago is looking for him already. Who knows what that screwed up head of his is thinking?"

Jen said, "I'm going to call John. He left 12 messages with Control."

Nick listened to Jen comfort John about what she had been doing for the last 30 plus hours. He realized that neither of them had been home to sleep since early Tuesday morning and that was only for a few hours.

Northwestern Memorial Hospital's emergency room staff directed Nick and Jen to Lacey.

Nick walked in the room, sat on Lacey's bed and hugged her. Jen, Kamber and Chad turned to give them privacy. Nick finally let her loose and looked at her head bandage. He kissed her tenderly and then hugged her again.

Lacey patted his back, "I'm fine. Really. They're going to let me out of here shortly."

Nick kissed Lacey again and squeezed her hand. "I'm so sorry. He's after me."

Lacey winked, "Then he has a big problem."

Nick took a deep breath and stood. He hugged both Kamber and Chad. "I don't know what to say. You risked your lives and saved Lacey. I'm so grateful you weren't hurt."

Seeing Lacey, Kamber and Chad okay relieved Nick enough to focus on Billow again.

Nick began pacing. "Tell me everything."

Marcus Newberry marveled at the bright lights of the city and the congestion of the traffic. After spending ten years in various institutions even the styles of the cars amazed him. He wondered where all of those people were going in the middle of the night. He had only walked a couple of blocks from the police station when he decided to sit on a step and rest. He still didn't have his strength back. It was cold. He wasn't dressed properly and he was hungry. He suddenly realized he had no money either. He would need to form a plan if he were to survive.

A man walked down the sidewalk toward him. Marcus stiffened. He was in no condition to fight someone and he knew it. Suddenly he was vulnerable again, a victim.

The man stopped when he reached Marcus and said, "You don't look like you belong on the street."

Marcus decided to lie; it had always worked in the past. "I was robbed of my money and my car. I don't even have a place to go. I'm just sitting here trying to come up with a plan."

The man weaved a little as he listened. Marcus figured he was drunk. "How long have you lived in Chicago?"

Marcus answered with a smile, "Just got here this evening. I've been gone ten years. Welcome home!"

The drunk laughed. "So, what're you gonna do? Just sit here?"

Marcus laughed, "Guess so 'til I get an idea."

The drunk sat next to Marcus on the step. "I've got a problem, too. If I drive in my condition and get stopped by cops, it'll be my third drunk driving offense. I'll go to jail for a long time. Why don't you drive me home? You can stay for the night and I'll pay you 50 bucks?"

Marcus stood, "Best and only offer I've had. Where's your car?"

"It's not a car. Got me a brand new Jeep CJ5 and put a lift kit on it, too!"

The drunk pointed to a parking garage across the street. They began the dangerous journey across traffic. Marcus wondered if he'd ever driven before. It seemed likely he had. He wished he could remember.

Agent Phillips reviewed the final report from their initial assessment of Brookfield Place Building D. It appeared that 137 patients were missing according to the state reports. Phillips rubbed his face and wished he could take a 15 hour nap.

He looked at Tyler and asked, "Do you have any idea where these people might be? 137 people don't just disappear."

Tyler shook his head. "I'm sorry. There's very little communication between the buildings in the facility. We all operate independently. I can tell you we're still being paid for those missing people."

Ryan answered, "They might be transfers. That one lady, Maggie, I know for a fact went out on a transfer just last week."

Tyler asked, "Transfer to where?"

Ryan shrugged, "Ask Rudy. He's the one that drives them there."

After several phone calls, the employee named Rudy Jones was located at the campus police station playing cards. Agent Phillips requested he be driven to Building D immediately. Rudy was terrified. He slowly walked over to Agent Phillips and extended his hand. "I'm Rudy Jones. You want me for somethin'?"

Phillips pointed for Rudy to sit and slid Maggie's picture in front of him. "Do you remember transferring this lady last week?"

Rudy held up the picture. "Yeah. That's Maggie." He laid the picture down.

Phillips asked, "Where was she transferred to?"

Rudy chuckled, "The same place they all go. Out. She was transferred out. They give 'em each a week's worth of meds, a hundred bucks and have me drop 'em off at the bus station. I don't know where they go from there."

Phillips asked Rudy to flip through the 137 files of missing patients to determine how many had been 'transferred'.

Agent Phillips walked over to get another coffee. Wayne joined him.

Wayne pointed to the table where Rudy was flipping through files, "I heard that. Now what?"

Phillips stirred his coffee and asked, "Have you ever heard of the Dozier School for Boys or their sister campus in Okeechobee, Florida?" Wayne shook his head and Phillips continued, "Boys and girls were sent to these reform schools for minor infractions: truancies, runaways, petty thefts, things a lot of kids do. Sometimes schools had them sent there, sometimes the families that just didn't know how to deal with them."

"The schools had complaints filed on them continuously from when they opened in the 50s until they were finally closed in 2011. Serious complaints were made to all levels of the government." Phillips shook his head, "Finally, a few investigators took it upon themselves to look into the accusations. They brought cadaver dogs and found 55 bodies in unmarked graves. Behind the dairy barn. Prosecutors claim there isn't enough evidence to prosecute any individuals. It's being fought, but that's how it works with these places."

Wayne was shocked, "This is true? It went on for decades? Where's the oversight?"

"Oversight?" Phillips chuckled. "The discovery of the bodies barely made the news. I only saw one very small newspaper article about it. Nobody wants to think it can happen here, under our noses. Nobody wants to admit that our system considers some people to be disposable."

Phillips took a swig of coffee and said, "Be glad you don't work missing persons. If these patients were just driven to town and dumped, they could be anywhere."

Phillips looked at his watch. "Why don't you and Sam take Renee and Ryan and go home. We've got a handle on this now. Thanks for everything you've done."

Wayne nodded. "I'm not going to complain about leaving. There's probably somewhere you can take a nap. This has been a long couple of days for you, too."

Phillips grinned, "The Bureau likes to keep us up for long periods of time. They think it builds character." He lowered his voice, "The one you need to worry about is Stryker. He has to be running on empty."

Wayne laughed, "Don't you know? Nick has two tanks. He just flips over to the second one. The man is a machine."

* * *

Nick waited in the emergency parking lot of the hospital for Jen. He was glad to have this moment to himself. His heart was still pounding from seeing Lacey wounded. He could have lost her tonight. Billow had raised the stakes. Nick wondered if he could control himself when he finally caught him.

Jen opened the passenger door and climbed in. "I half expected you to forget to wait for me. I've arranged for two patrols to take Lacey, Kamber and Chad back to Lacey's. They're going to stay until you pull them off." Nick had taught Jen to read body language. She wasn't happy with what she saw in Nick right now. "You couldn't have known this was going to happen."

"What else don't we know? The campus cops said they couldn't reach Billow, AKA Dr. Bates. The phone number he provided was phony." Nick started talking faster. "They reached the fake Dr. Elmhurst though. He didn't come back to Brookfield like he had been instructed. I bet he warned Billow we were at Brookfield. If we trace Dr. Elmhurst's calls for the last couple of hours, we might get the number Billow is using."

Nick called Agent Phillips, "I have a favor. Our guys can do this, but you'll be faster. I need every call made from Dr. Elmhurst's phone tonight. Have you put a name to him yet?"

Nick listened for a few minutes and ended the call. "He said they were already working on getting the phone records. For a Fed he's not half bad. Phillips said there is nothing on our Dr. Elmhurst in any Federal or State databases. They've run fingerprints and facial recognition."

Jen said, "He had to do something to end up at Brookfield. That doesn't make sense." Jen buckled her seatbelt. "Are we going to the house Billow took Lacey to?"

Nick answered, "I am. I thought I'd drop you at home. You could use some sleep."

Jen punched his shoulder. "Think again, pretty boy. You're not getting rid of me until we get Billow. Are we going to that house?"

"Yes." Nick rubbed his arm and pretended he was injured. "Hope I can shoot now."

Jen noticed a familiar twinkle in Nick's eyes. "You're on to something. Tell me."

"I need it to cook a little more." Nick grinned. "You're getting too good."

* * *

Billow pulled the van up to a convenience store to pick up some whiskey and a newspaper. He needed to make contact with Nick soon. While at the checkout he noticed a police car pull slowly past his van and park off to the side in the dark end of the parking lot. The lights went off in the patrol car. The cop was hiding. Of course! It was that stupid registration form from Brookfield. They knew what he was driving. Every cop in the city was probably looking for his van. They knew who he was, too. The officer was waiting for backup to arrive.

Billow knew he had only minutes to form an escape. He watched a small, white Camry pull in next to his van. The Camry parked on the blind side of the van. Billow was sure it was out of the sight line of the officer. Billow had to act fast. He stepped out of the store and walked directly to the Camry's driver.

"I'm going to grab a suitcase from my van and put it in your car. We're going to trade keys and I am going to give you this $100. We got a deal? The van is better than your Camry."

Flash and Mo looked at each other and shrugged. "Fine. Title's in the car."

Billow smiled, "Title's in the van."

Billow slid open the side panel door and dragged his suitcase and rifle out. He exchanged keys, gave Mo the hundred dollar bill and climbed in the Camry. Billow slowly drove out of the lot leaving the cop and the van behind.

Flash and Mo laughed as they bought a case of beer, two handfuls of jerky and some cigarette paper to wrap their weed. Once in the van, Mo pulled out of the parking lot and told Flash to check out the rest of the van.

Flash yelled, "Title's right here where he said. This here is wicked, man. That guy must be nuts. This van's got all the whistles!"

Mo said, "Roll us some weed, dude. We be drivin' in style tonight. Maybe we can find us some chicks."

They hadn't traveled more than two blocks when police cars ascended on the van from all four directions. Sirens screamed so loud Flash put his hands over his ears. The entire block was blue flashing lights and more were coming. Officers had their patrol doors open and guns pointed at them. Spotlights blazed through the windshield blinding them. A loudspeaker demanded they exit the vehicle with their hands above their heads.

Mo looked at Flash, "Damn, them cops gettin' real serious 'bout crackin' down on weed."

CHAPTER 21

Agent Phillips called Nick. "Our mystery doctor is scheduled to board a flight to Orlando in 30 minutes. He's using the ID of the real Dr. Elmhurst. We're waiting for him. I thought I'd dump him at your station."

Nick said, "That's fine with me."

Phillips asked, "How's your girlfriend?"

"She's fine. I'm heading to the house Billow took her to now."

"I'm calling it a night. Be safe."

Nick checked his GPS. They were within a couple of blocks of the house. He had heard the radio calls that Billow had hijacked a white Camry. Nick pulled the car to the curb.

"I'm going to check the house. Watch my back from here."

Jen climbed over the console and slid to the driver's seat as Nick got out. He always teased her about being able to do that. He told her when she got old and fat it would be but a fond memory. Jen breathed a sigh of relief each she time she actually did it.

Jen would leave enough time for Nick to make entry and then would have the car crawl closer in case Billow came back. If she saw Billow, she could warn Nick; if Billow saw her and ran, she would be closer for Nick to jump in the car.

Nick walked through each room of the house, his pistol held in front of him. The house was empty. He stood in front of the large chest that blocked the closet door. He could feel the adrenaline rushing through his body. He pushed the chest to the side and opened the closet door. Torn pieces of duct tape littered the floor. Red droplets of Lacey's blood had pooled in the corner from her head wound. Nick forced his breathing to slow, shut the closet door and pushed the chest back in position.

Nick wasn't in the house more than ten minutes and came back to the car. "The house is empty. I saw where he kept Lacey." Nick's expression left no doubt about how he felt about Billow. "He's going to contact me by phone when he's ready. He thinks Lacey is here and he doesn't know we have this address. He could pull the Camry around back. If he's smart, he'll get off the street."

Nick looked around the houses on the block. The neighborhood was awful, but surprisingly quiet. The house across the street was boarded up and had a long driveway.

"Let's back into that driveway and turn off our lights. We'll give it an hour."

Jen fell asleep in ten minutes. Nick listened to the dispatcher on his radio and read his old files on Billow from his phone.

* * *

Marcus put the key in the Jeep's ignition and said, "By the way, my name is Marcus." There was a moment while crossing the street that all of his memories had come back. They weren't all pleasant. He certainly wasn't going to be able to just start a new life. Now he wished he hadn't remembered. What was he going to do?

His drunken passenger struggled with the seatbelt and answered, "I'm George. Dang things, can't ever figure them out." Marcus looked down and saw a red slot he assumed was for the seatbelt attachment. It clicked. George said thank you and Marcus looked for a belt for himself. Evidently this was something you had to do if you drove.

Marcus stepped on the accelerator and listened to the motor roar. So far, so good. He glanced in the rearview mirror a couple of times like he'd seen them do on television. He glanced over to George.

George said, "We're gonna get there faster if you put it in reverse." George pointed to the shift handle.

Marcus looked at the drive column and saw an 'R'. Easy enough. He shifted to the 'R'. The accelerator was still pressed halfway to the floor. The Jeep bolted backwards from the parking spot, made a wide screaming circle and struck the half wall cement barrier. They were three stories up.

George grabbed the dash and screamed, "Brake!"

Marcus frantically pushed buttons on the dash; surely one of them was a brake. The back of the Jeep began climbing up the four foot cement barrier. George was screaming. Marcus could smell rubber burning from the tires. Marcus took his foot off the accelerator. The back of the Jeep leveled to match the front.

Marcus screamed at George. "Sorry! Seems I don't know how to drive."

George reached over and turned off the ignition. His eyes were opened wide and he pressed himself back against the passenger door. "You could make a fortune! I am stone cold sober now. Took you less than five minutes!"

George got out and walked around to the driver's side hanging on to the Jeep for security. "Get out."

George took a couple of deep breaths, "Get in the other side. You can still stay for the night. I'm not even worried about getting stopped now."

Marcus smiled, "Thank you, George. I'm sorry I misled you about my driving skills. I guess I'm desperate."

"If you don't mind me askin', where the heck have you lived for ten years that you didn't have to drive?"

Marcus smiled, "A prison for the criminally insane."

George chuckled, "Yeah, right. No, really."

"Really."

George put the Jeep in park. He was definitely sober now. "Why were you there?"

Marcus played with the visor and dash a little and then answered, "The courts committed me to Brookfield because they think I'm delusional and dangerous. I believe I have a calling to be a doctor. I've done surgeries and everything. I even worked at a hospital for a couple of days. They understood me at Brookfield and let me help with patient care. Just no surgeries. It's really rather nice there."

George rubbed his chin. He didn't like what he was hearing. What kind of a nut job would make it up? It must be true. "Then why did you leave?"

Marcus laughed, "A nurse thought I really was a doctor being held prisoner. She smuggled me out in the trunk of her car tonight."

George started laughing so hard he was snorting. "Oh Lord, that's one of the scariest things I've ever heard. I gotta tell ya, I'm not real keen on takin' you home with me anymore."

Marcus nodded. "I understand. I'm actually not that keen to go. Would you drive me back to Brookfield Place?"

George said, "How about this: I'll take you over to the police station and you have them drive you back. I imagine if you're missing, they're already lookin' for you."

Marcus was excited to go back. The idea of trying to make it on his own, on the outside, was daunting.

"That sounds fine, George, thank you. Thank you for not treating me like a crazy."

George started laughing again as he pulled from the garage and headed toward the police station. "I'd say I'm the crazy one. I offered an escapee from an insane prison to come home with me, and drive my new Jeep. And you don't even know how to drive!" George wiped his eyes, "I've had the most honest and intelligent conversation of my week with you! What does that tell you about the people on the outside?"

George watched as Marcus walked up the steps to the police station and stopped an officer. After the officer talked into his radio a couple of minutes, he had Marcus turn around and he cuffed him. George shook his head as he realized that Marcus obviously had been telling the truth.

George put on his turn signal and checked the traffic before he pulled from the curb. Tomorrow would be a good day to quit drinking.

* * *

Billow hadn't returned to the house yet. Maybe he wasn't going to. Jen had been sleeping for two hours. Nick knew Billow would contact him. Nick nudged Jen's shoulder.

"Let's get a few hours sleep and meet at the station. I'm taking you home and I'm going to Lacey's."

Jen rubbed her eyes, "What time is it?"

"Five. Billow will call me and I'll call you. I promise."

Nick dropped Jen off at her home. Ten minutes later he tiptoed into Lacey's room. Lacey had been crying in her sleep. Nick kissed her salty cheeks and wrapped his arms around her. She snuggled close and mumbled, "I love you."

Nick said, "I love you, too." Lacey was snoring in minutes. Nick glanced at his phone on the end table, willing it to ring. In his dreams he was chasing Billow through a jungle. He had him cornered and then another, more dangerous Billow appeared behind him.

Flash and Mo were released from the police station with a citation for the marijuana, a court hearing date and a stern warning to change their lives. The cops impounded the van, the weed and their money. They had no way to get home.

Flash tried to hail a cab for the third time and watched as the driver passed them, flipping them off.

Mo said, "I heard cabbies don't pick up around cop stations. Everybody walkin' probably just left jail."

Flash took out his phone. "Think I should call Mom to come get us?"

Mo shrugged, "You want to explain to her how you lost the Camry in two days?"

Flash put his phone back in his pocket. "Lost our money and our weed, too. Not a good night."

A homeless man leaped from an alley they were passing and raised a steel rod over his head. "Give me all your money!"

Flash actually laughed, "You're too late, old man. Cops done already robbed us."

The old man started laughing, too. "You boys in big trouble if'n the cops be robbin' ya. You're gonna end up like me if'n you don't wise up. There's a free bus runs South in about ten minutes if you hurry down to that corner. Don't know that be where you want to go, but it be the only bus for hours."

Mo still had a package of jerky in his pocket and gave it to the old man. They waved goodbye as the old man tried to tear the jerky with his few teeth.

Flash cursed as it started to rain. They ran down the block to sit in the shelter until the bus arrived.

Flash said, "What'd he mean by all that?"

Mo laughed, "Beats me."

* * *

The airport parking lot was full. He glanced at his watch and decided there was enough time to watch for a while before going in. He double checked he had the ID information he was going to need for the airport check in. The pictures on the driver's license and passport looked remarkably like the real Dr. Elmhurst. There were plenty of reasons to be careful. He worried what the cops had found out at Brookfield. They may be on to him already.

He watched two men walk out of the entrance, speak to each other, and then walk separate ways down the sidewalk. Another man was casually walking through the parking lot with no obvious destination. He noticed the parking lot man's lips were moving. He obviously was talking into a transmitter. A black SUV pulled up to the front door and two men in suits walked into the airport. One of the men on the sidewalk had nodded recognition to them. Feds. Stupid, obvious Feds.

He turned on the ignition and steered the car out of the lot. They were on to his alias. No matter, he would leave tomorrow under his real identity.

Thursday 7:00 a.m.

Mitch flipped the neon 'OPEN' sign on and had the coffee machines brewing. The morning crowd would be arriving any minute and he hadn't seen Momma. Yesterday she had made the muffins for today and a large tub of sliced pastrami for the Thursday sub special.

Mitch called up to her apartment. Artie answered.

"Is Momma there? This is Mitch." Mitch was startled that Artie answered Momma's phone this time of day.

Artie answered, "Last I knew she was getting dressed. Let me check."

Mitch was beyond curious. He waited for Artie to get back on the line as Eli walked in the door.

Eli threw his hands in the air, "You're not gonna believe the story I've got for you."

Artie came back on the line, laughing. "Momma said to tell you to hold your britches. It ain't every night she has a handsome man sleep over."

Mitch hung up the phone and looked at Eli. "I think I have a story, too."

* * *

Nick looked at his watch and bolted up. He had not intended to sleep until 7 a.m. Lacey sat up quickly, "What's wrong?" Her hair was mussed and her bandage missing from her head.

Nick reached over and kissed her. "Nothing's wrong, go back to sleep. Patrol is here to guard the house, but I have to go."

Lacey held Nick's face in her palms. "Promise me you'll stay safe."

Nick kissed the end of her nose and said, "I promise."

Lacey rested her head back on her pillow. She still had a headache, but she didn't want Nick to worry. "Okay, then. I expect you for dinner."

Nick took a quick shower, changed into some clothes he had at Lacey's and tiptoed to the kitchen. Kamber and Chad were at the counter eating Cheerios.

"What happened to your homeless experiment?" Nick grinned as both their spoons froze in midair.

Kamber answered, "We flunked. Is Lacey okay?"

Kamber looked much prettier this morning. He could see the family resemblance. Chad had resumed attacking his Cheerios.

"Lacey's fine. You two are my heroes, but you should have called me."

Kamber raised her voice, "I did! Your stupid answering service made me leave a message!"

Nick laughed at Kamber's expression. He had forgotten that Control would not allow calls to go through on a level two case. "I'm sorry. Sometime today you'll need to fill out a report at the station. Can you do that?"

Chad answered with a mouthful of food, "No problem. Did you catch the bad guy?"

Nick shook his head as he called Jen. "Where are you?" After a minute he said, "I'll pick up muffins on my way in. What kind do you want?" another pause and then Nick laughed, "Yes, it's a bribe. Today is going to suck."

* * *

Billow had returned to his rental house and crashed on his bed at 5 a.m. His phone rang at seven. The caller ID said Edmund Elmhurst.

Billow checked his watch and answered, "I thought you'd be on a plane by now."

"The Feds were at the airport. We're switching to Plan B. Do you remember where to meet me?"

Billow answered, "Yes. Look, I have some business to finish first; I can be there by tonight."

There was a loud sigh. "I'm ditching my phone after this call, so there can't be any changes made. You should dump your phone, too. The Feds can track you even if it's turned off." There was a long pause. "Anything I need to know about this 'business' you have to finish?"

Billow decided to confess. "I shot three cops. I want one more before I leave the country."

There was no sound from the caller.

Billow knew he was in trouble but continued, "I'm sorry! I thought you'd already be gone and wouldn't find out. It's too late; I kidnapped Stryker's girlfriend."

There was an audible moan from the caller. "Stryker, the cop that arrested you? He was a frigging Navy SEAL. You don't stand a chance."

Billow had an idea. "I do if you'll help me. We can use his girlfriend as insurance. Tell him where she is after we're gone."

"Meet me now, not tonight. Leave the girl there. I mean it...you'd better get here within the hour."

CHAPTER 22

Eli and Mitch exchanged stories, each of them not believing the other. Mitch asked, "Are you saying there was a mutiny at that crazy prison?"

"Yes! And Renee was in the middle of it. She smuggled a doctor out of there in Momma's trunk!" Eli rubbed his chin and then winked. "Are you sayin' Momma and Artie...you know?"

Mitch nodded. "Sure looks that way!" They both started laughing.

Artie and Momma walked through the curtain door to the storefront arm in arm. Momma said, "Sorry I'm a little tardy this mornin'." She giggled and kissed Artie's cheek.

Mitch moaned, "Oh, God. Do I have to listen to this all morning?"

Artie's phone rang and he excused himself to stand over in the corner. They all tried to listen in.

Artie ended his call and motioned for Momma to go to the back of the store for a minute.

Momma asked, "What is it, dear? More bad news?"

Artie nodded, "I'm afraid so. It seems Dom survived the massacre, but the Outfit boss blamed it on Milo. There was a big meeting early this morning and now Milo's number two man is in charge of the Northside crew. A lot of Milo's men are upset. The word is they're planning to seek revenge on Dom this morning."

Momma shook her head. "Cops don't have to do a dang thing but just wait for ya to kill each other off. You just find yourself a safe apartment and then come back here. Stay away from them mobsters 'til they're done pickin' sides, ya hear? Today's Thursday if you want to help take pastrami subs to the community?"

Artie's face broke out in a big smile. "I would love that. Last time a frozen head cut my visit short, remember?" They both laughed and Artie turned to leave.

Momma said, "Tell Mitch I'll be there in a minute. I forgot something upstairs I need to bring down."

Artie said okay and waved goodbye.

Momma raced up the stairs to call Sophia. On the way she mumbled to herself, "Lordy, Lordy, got nothin' but trouble."

* * *

Wayne and Sam were in the homicide room at their desks when Nick arrived with muffins. They attacked the box like they hadn't eaten in days. Nick stood back and laughed. Jen held up a pumpkin muffin, "Thank you, pretty boy, for getting my favorite."

Nick grabbed a banana muffin, "You're welcome."

Wayne wiped his mouth and said, "Well, we all got a two hour nap. What do you think today will bring?"

Nick looked over, "Billow. Jen, I want you in both a vest and plate."

Jen said, "I will if you will."

Everyone hated to wear the iron plates because they were so heavy. It was a necessity since you couldn't trust the quality of the vests. Nor could the vests stop all ammunition types. The only safe thing to do was to wear both.

Sam asked, "How's Lacey?"

Everyone stopped to hear Nick's answer. "She seems fine. She'll probably lose it after we catch Billow."

Jen nodded, "I agree. She's strong but that had to be terrifying."

Sam said, "Breaking news. Our fake 'doctor', Marcus Newberry, turned himself back in. He said an hour on the outside was too scary."

The team laughed.

Wayne walked over to where Nick was busy cinching his vest.

Wayne said, "Sam and I are volunteering to be your backup on Billow."

"I appreciate that but I think Doll Face and I can cover it." Nick winked at Jen. "Besides I think our team is going to be stuck with the bodies from the crematorium."

Nick and Jen developed a code years ago. Jen would ask, 'You okay, pretty boy?' and Nick would answer, 'Just fine, doll face'. Any variation of those nicknames signaled trouble. Nick walked to his desk and opened the bottom drawer.

He tossed an earpiece to Jen and said, "These are better than department issue. Try it."

Jen put her earpiece on, turned away from Nick and whispered, "I want to drive."

Nick chuckled and whispered back, "You always want to drive."

Sam said, "I'm impressed. You actually heard that?"

Nick grabbed two more earpieces from the drawer and tossed them to Wayne and Sam. "I had an old buddy get these. They'll interface with each other and department issue."

Wayne and Sam played with the settings on the earpieces and then put them in their desks. Wayne said, "You've got the right kind of friends."

Sam offered, "Speaking of that, your FBI buddy Phillips called and said Dr. Elmhurst never got to the airport."

Nick raised an eyebrow and glanced at Jen. "That means we're going to fight two."

Nick grabbed a stack of ammunition boxes from his locker. He saw the extra grenade from the bank robbery on the shelf and put that in his pocket.

Wayne yelled, "I saw that! It hasn't been three days yet!"

Nick laughed.

Jen moaned.

* * *

Agent Phillips had just fallen asleep when his phone rang. His caller gave him the news about a meeting at the Outfit boss' estate, the reinstatement of Dom, the ousting of Milo and the retaliation plot for this morning.

Phillips asked the caller, "How does she get this info so fast?"

Of course he didn't get an answer, only the instruction to make sure the FBI had a presence near Bruno's Bar, Dom's meeting place, this morning to prevent a total bloodbath. The FBI would leverage the fate of survivors for more information on the mob's growing activity.

Phillips looked at his watch; there was very little time to organize. He called the Chief FBI liaison agent at the Chicago Major Crimes office and requested five agents to join him at Dom's. He took a quick five minute shower and thought about Sophia as he dressed to leave. She was certainly a remarkable woman. Her reunion with Nick was something Phillips hoped he would live to see.

* * *

Nick and Jen drove past the rental house Billow had been using. There was no sign of the Camry there. Jen asked, "Do you want to stake out this place?"

Nick answered, "No. He's going to call us when he's ready. Since we're waiting, let's drive past Dom's and make his morning meeting. I'd like to keep the pressure on."

Jen pulled within a block of the bar Dom used for his office when Nick told her to stop. "I can walk from here and surprise him. You watch the street for anything out of line." Nick tapped his earpiece to make sure it was on. "I'll only be a couple of minutes."

Jen nodded.

Nick saw Dom's big Town Car parked in front and a couple of other cars parked on either side. It was quiet in this part of town this early in the day. Chicago was a cluster of small towns and neighborhoods desperately hanging on to their heritage. The street scene here was straight out of the 60s. Six businesses stood on each side of the street with narrow alleys dividing each set. Run down residential neighborhoods butted up to the businesses. Much of the properties were owned and used by the crew for illegal activities.

No attention had ever been paid to making the area attractive to shoppers. Shoppers were not welcome. The buildings were tax write-offs or fronts for dirty business. Innocent visitors were quickly encouraged to browse elsewhere. The bar Dom used as an office had a plaque on the outside bricks that bragged 'Established 1892". Nick thought to himself that was probably the last time anything had been updated.

Nick walked in the door and saw Dom holding court with two men. His two bodyguards stiffened as Nick walked to the end of the bar, sat down and turned his stool to face Dom. Nick waved the guards to walk back toward the front. The guards looked at Dom and he nodded. They reluctantly walked to stand by the front door.

Dom leaned in and whispered something to the men sitting at the table. They quickly got up, walked past the guards and left the building. Nick heard Jen in his earpiece. "Got two getting in Mercury sedan and leaving."

Dom motioned for Nick to join him at the table. Nick took a seat across from Dom.

Dom asked, "What can I do for you this morning, Detective Stryker?" There was an emphasis on Stryker when Dom spoke.

Nick leaned back in his chair, "I heard there was trouble at your place last night. I just wanted to make sure you survived."

Dom smiled, fingered around in his shirt breast pocket and pulled out the listening device Nick had planted on his last visit. He placed it on the table and asked, "Any idea how this ended up here on your last visit?"

Nick smiled, "If you can't trust the cops, who can you trust?"

When Phillips told Nick that Frankie Mullen had killed Joey Lacastra, Nick figured that Joey had retaliated at Dom's for being set up at Travis Cummings' townhouse. Nick knew that both Dom and Joey were aware that Cummings was now in FBI custody. Now, only Dom knew. Certainly Joey had walked into a bad scene on Dom's orders. Dom was probably unaware Cummings had turned to the FBI that fast.

Nick said, "Sounded to me like you had a disgruntled employee on your hands."

Dom wondered if Nick knew about Joey Lacastra. Dom shook his head, "See? You aren't as smart as you think you are." Dom leaned closer to Nick. Nick could smell cigars on his breath. "I'll let you in on how it's done. We had an overly ambitious associate that has now been removed of his duties. That's it. Simple administrative restructuring."

Jen's voice came over Nick's earpiece. "Two cars pulling up at the end of the block. No, three. Armed…they're walking toward the door. Nick, look out, this isn't social. Wait. Two more cars just pulled up on my side of the street. I'm changing positions."

Nick said, "Take cover, Jen."

Dom asked, "What?"

Nick saw a shadow block the light at the glass front door. Dom's bodyguards were talking to each other and not paying attention.

Nick yelled, "Heads up!" just as a man pushed through the door and sprayed bullets at the first guard. Nick pushed Dom's table to stand on its edge and grabbed Dom's shoulders. He pushed Dom to the floor and said, "Stay flat."

Nick shot the first shooter squarely in the forehead. He fell as the second shooter entered the door. Dom's second guard got off two shots at close range that didn't even phase the second shooter's armor. The shooter saw Nick and used the corner of the bar for cover as he let the M4 carbine level everything that was bar height. Nick had noticed the M4 was packing a double drum, meaning it sported 100 rounds.

Jen's voice said, "Two more coming in. If I can get a shot…"

Nick heard a loud bang and Jen returning fire. Jen yelled, "More coming, Nick, get out of there!"

Nick squatted down next to Dom. "When I yell 'now', we're running out the south wall."

Dom yelled, "There's no door there!"

Nick answered, "There will be."

Nick listened as the M4 continued spitting out rounds. Wood chips flew from the table and glass shards exploded from the memorabilia hanging on the walls. He could tell from the sounds of the bullets which way the shooter's rifle was sweeping. Nick waited a moment hoping the other men would enter the building. He raised himself over the edge of the table and threw his grenade at the wall within feet of the approaching shooter.

The contact grenade exploded, rocked the old building and sent shrapnel flying. Nick had thrown himself over Dom to shield him. Nick counted two seconds from the explosion, stood and pulled Dom up by his shirt. "Follow me. Stay directly behind me."

Nick kicked two smoking studs from the opening, checked that the escape path was temporarily clear and pulled Dom through. Nick glanced both ways and saw Dom's attackers recovering from the explosion and advancing from both directions.

Jen provided cover as Nick pushed Dom down to lie between the grill of his car and the curb. Nick rolled to take cover behind a pile of debris. He saw Jen trying to keep fire pressure on the men in the street and on the sidewalk to Nick's left. Nick could see a shooter making his way behind Jen. Nick yelled, "Ten o'clock." The man fell to the pavement an instant later.

Nick caught a glimpse of a light flash from above. A shooter was on the roof of the building across the street. Nick aimed his pistol to fire. He stopped. It was a woman. She pounded her fist to her heart twice, pointed to the side and lowered herself into position.

Bullets chipped the bricks behind Nick and a man fell directly to his left. Whoever this woman was, she was on their side. Nick yelled, "Shooter on the roof is ours."

Jen answered, "Got it! Four o'clock!"

Nick shot the advancing man and looked at Dom who was bleeding from his shoulder. Nick yelled to him, "You've been hit. Stay down!"

Nick crawled over to Dom and saw a bundle taped on the undercarriage of Dom's car. Nick said, "Jen, bomb under Dom's car. Someone's got a detonator."

Dom's eyes opened wide. Nick grabbed his shirt and helped him up to a crouching position. "Run into the bar when I say 'now'. I'll cover you." Nick and Jen provided cover as Dom ran into the bar. Two more cars pulled into the scene. Feds.

Six agents jumped from the cars, rifles pointed.

The remaining three shooters in the street dropped their weapons and raised their hands. A man standing at the edge of the building opened his jacket and reached for his shirt pocket. Nick shot him in the forehead and he fell. The street was finally silent. Nick walked over and removed the detonator from the man's shirt. He held it up for the agents to see as Jen ran over.

"You okay, pretty boy?"

"Just fine, doll face."

They both leaned against the bricks and surveyed the damage. Nick looked up to the roof across the street. The woman stood, shoulder length brown hair blowing in the wind. She placed her open hand over her heart, turned, and vanished.

Nick cleared his throat, "I think I just saw my mom."

Sirens converged on the area surrounding Dom's bar. Nick walked inside to find Dom sitting in a booth. He motioned for Nick to sit.

Nick shook his head, "EMTs are here. We need to get your shoulder looked at."

Dom stared at Nick and said, "This is just a flesh wound. You saved my life. Twice. If you hadn't seen that car bomb…"

Nick said, "Just doing my job, Dom. Let's go."

"Everyone is in such a hurry. Your name will be honored by my associates."

Nick couldn't say what he wanted to. "Let's go. I just stopped by to say good morning. I've got work to do."

Dom stood and smiled, "Do you always bring grenades to your morning meetings?"

Dom clutched his wounded arm and Nick helped him stand. Dom looked through the gaping hole in the wall and moaned at the sight of his heavily damaged Town Car.

Nick grinned at Dom's expression. "That might buff out."

* * *

Renee arrived at the gate to Brookfield Place and noticed the usual guard had a uniformed Chicago police officer standing with him. She showed her ID badge and drove back to Building D. Everywhere she looked there were police cars and vans. She assumed they had worked through the night or it was a new shift. She had only gotten a few hours' sleep before her alarm went off.

She saw Ryan's car in the employee lot. Ryan was standing by the back door. Renee walked up to him and said, "I'm glad you came in today."

Ryan opened the door for her and said, "I was going to say the same thing to you."

The transformation of Building D was nothing short of miraculous. Nurses and doctors were conferring over patient charts. Housekeeping was mopping floors and Renee could hear a bustling of sounds coming from the kitchen. A loudspeaker pleasantly announced that patients were invited to resume use of the craft rooms and entertainment lounges.

Ryan must have read her mind, "Seems crazy, doesn't it?"

Renee and Ryan looked at each other and started laughing. Renee couldn't stop. It was such a relief to see Building D functioning properly. The patients deserved it. The staff deserved it. She knew it would take a lot of time before everything was fixed, but it was a strong start. The involvement of the FBI gave her hope. Certainly Brookfield Place would be under many watchful eyes now.

Renee asked Ryan, "Are you going to keep working here?"

Ryan answered, "No one has told me I can't yet. I'm a little worried about smuggling out a patient though. I'm sure there's something about that in the employee handbook."

Just then Marcus walked around the corner and headed toward them. He was holding a clipboard and wearing a white doctor's jacket. Renee's heart sank.

She whispered to Ryan, "Did you know he was back?"

Ryan shook his head.

Marcus stopped when he reached them and pointed to his ID badge that said "Pretend Doctor, Marcus". Then he turned around to show them that someone had used a black marker and wrote 'NOT a Doctor' on his jacket.

He turned back around and smiled, "I hope you both aren't mad at me for coming back. You went to so much trouble."

Ryan shook his head and Renee asked, "Why did you come back?"

Marcus rolled his eyes and sighed, "It's too crazy out there." He walked down the hall exchanging greetings with everyone he passed.

Ryan looked at Renee, "I suppose you'll be transferring back to Building A now."

Renee surprised herself when she answered, "I think I'm needed here more."

* * *

Agent Phillips stood by Nick and Jen's car. The bomb squad worked to clear the scene so the bodies could be removed.

He glanced at Nick. "These are Milo's boys. They seem to have taken issue with Milo being gone now."

"What happened?"

"A change in leadership of the Northside crew. Dom convinced the Outfit boss that Milo was behind the massacre at his estate."

Nick frowned, "Dom knows it was Joey Lacastra."

Phillips chuckled, "That's the way it works with the mob. It's all about leverage and mistrust."

Nick asked, "How did you know to come here?"

"I was just going to ask you that. I got a tip."

Nick shrugged, "We just stopped to say good morning."

Phillips threw his head back and laughed. "With a grenade? You know, it hasn't been..."

Nick interrupted him as he opened the driver's door of the car. "I know. It hasn't been three days."

Phillips looked at Nick, "I heard from the guys at your dad's place. We're never going to get them to leave. I've been told to ask your dad how long we can stay there. What do you think?"

Nick said, "I'm sure he'll work with you. I would suggest months vs. years. Dad knows how long these cases can take."

"Yes, he does. The Bureau will find something suitable if I apply pressure, which I will."

Phillips watched Nick and Jen pull away and he walked over to where Dom was being bandaged by the EMTs.

When the EMTs were done and gone, Phillips asked, "The Outfit doesn't know we have Cummings, do they?"

Dom frowned. "No, they do not."

"Sucks to be you when they find out. You were lucky this morning."

Dom rubbed his shoulder and said, "Luck had nothing to do with it. Stryker was here."

CHAPTER 23

Thursday 9:00 a.m.

Nick glanced over to Jen as they waited for the EMT van to move so they could pass through the street. "Are you sure you are okay?"

Jen grinned, "It got a little dicey for a while. Your grenade came in handy."

"That's what I keep telling the Chief! Nobody wants to listen to me." Nick and Jen both chuckled. Nick's expression turned serious, "I have a theory."

"It's cooked now?"

Nick smiled. "Billow and this Dr. Elmhurst obviously found ways to steal money from Brookfield Place both through operations and reselling drugs. Cummings said Dr. Elmhurst pulled 140 grand cash from a bottom drawer of his desk and there was more there. You get cash from selling drugs."

"Let's say that Tyler's estimate of six times the normal amount of drugs had been ordered over the last six weeks is correct. Let's also say that much of the money being sent monthly for operations was diverted to end up in their pockets. My guess is that they made close to two million just in the drugs. Who would trust Jake Billow as the number two man in a scheme that sophisticated and risky?"

Jen shrugged.

Nick said, "Not only is Dr. Elmhurst sophisticated but he's clean. No record of his prints or facial recognition on any database. No criminal record. Why pick Brookfield Place? If you're that smart, why risk everything you have pulling off a mutiny and robbery in a facility for the criminally insane? There are easier ways to start a life of crime."

Jen asked, "Why do I have the feeling you know the answer?"

"Because I do. Dr. Elmhurst is Darren Billow, Jake's older brother."

Jen stared at Nick as she processed what he had said. The EMT van had moved and Nick headed their car toward the highway.

Jen said, "I got the impression at Jake's trial that Darren didn't really like him. He threw him under the bus whenever he had the chance."

"Exactly. He wanted him to end up at Brookfield or someplace like Brookfield. I bet if the visitor logs are ever found, Darren began visiting Jake as soon as he got there. I think Darren is the brains of the two. He decided when to take over Building D and how to take it over. Jake did the dirty work. They almost succeeded without a hitch."

"I don't think Darren had any idea that the Building D administrator was in charge of sending the mob their skim every month. When they killed the real Dr. Elmhurst and stopped paying the skim, they got the mob on their backs."

"Darren knew the mob was trouble he didn't need. He paid Cummings the cash to make it go away. I think Jake followed Cummings from Brookfield and stole the cash back for himself."

Jen shook her head, "Wow, you have really given this some serious thought."

Nick grinned, "That's what we do."

Jen chuckled. "So, what do you think is happening now? It looks like both Darren and Jake are still in Chicago."

"I think they are, too. Phillips thinks that Dr. Elmhurst, Darren, got wind the FBI was at the airport. They probably were going to meet outside of the country somewhere. Darren was flying out on Dr. Elmhurst's ID and Billow was flying out on Dr. Bates's."

Jen asked, "Do you think Darren knew Jake would kidnap Lacey?"

Nick shook his head. "I don't see him wanting that complication. It doesn't fit. I think last night's 10-24's and taking Lacey was all Jake. I bet Darren is trying to figure out how to fix it. At best, they only have a few hours to escape the country. Darren could leave the country on his own ID. Jake can use

Dr. Bates' ID until his body is identified. If Darren is going to help Jake kill me before they leave it's going to have to be soon. I told Phillips to put out an APB on Darren and the ID for Dr. John Bates. We'll see."

Nick glanced to his left and then turned right, away from the city.

Jen asked, "Where are we going?"

"If I'm right, Darren has two choices: force Jake to leave now before he causes any more trouble or clean up Jake's mess and help him kill me."

Jen frowned, "Darren has been cleaning up after Jake his whole life."

Nick answered, "Yes, he has."

"You know where they are?"

"I think so."

* * *

Wayne was uneasy. He couldn't explain it. He walked over to Nick's computer and searched his recent browser history. He yelled over to Sam, "Did you know Stryker has been researching Jake Billow's brother?"

Sam answered, "Yeah. He had me do a property search on him yesterday. He asked me to look up vacant land, anything."

"Did you find anything?"

"Not much, a dumpy cabin south of town on about 80 acres. That's it. The guy must rent his primary residence."

Wayne pulled up the old newspaper articles Nick had marked on Billow's trial. "Hmm. I never knew that."

Sam stopped what he was doing, "Never knew what?"

"Billow's dad, mom and sister were killed in that theater massacre six years ago. This article says they were caught in crossfire between the two shooters and the police. The medical examiner said they had bullets from both the shooters and the police in their bodies. He couldn't determine which bullets had been the fatal shots. Billow tried to sue the state for unlawful death."

Sam said, "I heard that was why he always killed cops three at a time. One for his dad, mom and sister."

Wayne said, "It's also another reason for Jake to focus on killing Stryker. Stryker arrested him and Stryker probably seems like 'super cop' to Jake. He might be thinking he has an advantage on Nick by kidnapping Lacey."

"Except he doesn't have Lacey."

"He doesn't know that, remember?"

Wayne did a Google search on the property address Sam had given him. It turned up an article about a militia group that had been using the land for a training site. A picture of the land owner arguing with authorities was at the top of the article.

Wayne yelped. "Holy cow. Dr. Elmhurst is Darren Billow. Look at this picture."

Agent Phillips walked in the room and dropped a mangled wad of metal on Wayne's desk.

Wayne said, "I'll bite. What's that?"

Phillips chuckled, "What's left of a grenade Stryker threw this morning at Dominick Guioni's bar."

Phillips told Sam and Wayne about the morning attack of Milo's men at Dom's. "I figured he and Jen had come back here."

Wayne said, "Nick figured out that Dr. Elmhurst is Jake's brother, Darren. I think he went to hunt them down."

Wayne showed Phillips the article about the militia farm and Sam offered the address he had given Nick this morning.

Sam pointed at Wayne. "I think mother hen is worried Nick is going to get in over his head."

Phillips used the web browser on his phone and then looked up. "I'm with Wayne on this one. We've been watching this group. They're very well-funded and heavily armed. They even have a couple of helicopters. We haven't pinned anything on them yet. Darren is a member of this group. For the right price, he could easily get a few of them to help. They'd like nothing better than to kill a cop. The membership list of this bunch reads like a who's who of people kicked out of the other groups."

Phillips frowned, "I gave Nick the GPS info for the phone Darren was using. He was definitely headed toward this property. Jake's last signal was also heading south before they both went silent."

Wayne said, "That explains why Nick had me set up surveillance on Jake's house. He thinks Jake is heading to the cabin to set a trap. This militia group isn't good news."

Phillips said, "He probably figures there isn't enough time for them to organize and get to the cabin. Nick doesn't know they have copters. We found out from a tip and then confirmed it ourselves. He's not even worried about them."

Sam pulled the earpiece that Nick had given him from the drawer and so did Wayne.

Wayne looked at Sam and said, "Road trip."

* * *

Kamber left a note for Lacey that she and Chad were going to the University to talk to Professor Stryker. Kamber reminded Lacey that the police were watching her townhouse, so she was safe.

On the way to the University, Chad said, "Isn't it funny how fast we changed our mind about the documentary?"

Kamber nodded. "I'm glad we're on the same page. We'll still have a powerful documentary about the homeless, but we'll just concentrate on the homeless people that don't live in the tunnels. I don't want to even suggest that there is a community of underground homeless people. Their lives are hard enough as it is. If anyone discovers them, they'll have to move back up to the streets. I can't imagine how this system became so unfair. By the way; I Googled 'Utah homeless' like Joseph told us to do. Utah has reduced the number of homeless by 78% in the last seven years. It is a brilliant program and it's being copied by several states."

Chad said, "At least there's some good news. We have great footage from the people we interviewed that didn't live in the tunnels. Heck, the footage from people that aren't homeless is great, too. Especially those you stopped on the street and asked how long they could go without income before they lost everything."

Kamber said, "How about that lady that started crying? She was working three part time jobs so she wouldn't lose her house. That was scary. That reminds me, I want to find a cheap apartment. And maybe a roommate to help with expenses. If I can find a job, I can still take a few classes and maybe even save some money."

Chad offered, "I was looking for a roommate myself. Not a girl though."

"What's wrong with girls?"

"They can't read GPS maps for one!"

Kamber slugged his arm. "How much would it cost me to be your roommate?"

Chad looked out the window and smiled, he didn't want Kamber to see. "Four hundred bucks and we split food."

"I saw you smile in the window reflection. We're just friends, right? You're not getting all weird?"

"You're the weird one!" They bickered back and forth until they reached the campus. Kamber reached in the backseat and got their notebooks. Chad got their camera equipment.

Chad cinched the video camera strap and asked, "What do you think Professor Stryker is going to say when we tell him we want to do 'True Crime' reporting?"

Darren Billow sat in his truck and looked at the slope of the floor on the cabin's porch. The whole place had a sad, forgotten look about it. His parents had bought it for a vacation cottage decades ago. He saw the red frog watering can still sitting on the porch. Weeds grew from its opening. He glanced at his watch. The militia men were late. Why couldn't anything go as planned?

Darren hopped out of his truck, hefted an arm-load of ammunition and guns and carried them to the cabin door. It had cost him a small fortune to negotiate this morning's killing on such short notice. Jake had left him no choice.

Inside the cabin Darren stacked his pile of weapons on the table and called his militia contact.

"Where are you guys? You're late. I have a plane to catch and we need to talk before he gets here."

"I can see your property from here. We'll be landing in a minute."

Nick and Jen had parked on neighboring property, walked down a tree line and squatted in a brush patch with a sight line to the cabin's front door. They watched as Darren carried the weapons into the cabin.

Nick whispered, "Jake should be arriving soon. I'm going to make my way to the back of the cabin. Watch my back." Nick tapped his earpiece and Jen nodded that her earpiece was on. She watched Nick run across the side yard clearing and disappear around the back of the cabin.

The rhythmic sounds of a helicopter rotor could be heard in the distance. It was getting louder by the minute and was soon in sight. The helicopter lowered itself in the small clearing in front of the house. Jen watched the dirt blow and four armed men in camouflage get out. They signaled the pilot to leave. Darren greeted them on the porch.

The helicopter roared again as it lifted upward and banked to the right. Jen whispered, "Got four new buddies. One is starting to walk around to the back side of the house, Nick."

A hand rested on Jen's shoulder. She froze. It was Nick. She hadn't even heard him. There hadn't been a twig snap, nothing.

Nick whispered, "I didn't expect this. Go back to our car."

Jen looked in Nick's eyes. He meant it.

"I'm not leaving you."

Nick exhaled, "I suppose six to two isn't all that bad. Stay here. I'm going under the floor."

CHAPTER 24

Wayne and Sam sped toward the location of Darren Billow's cabin. Traffic was heavy until they were south of the city. Wayne guessed they were about ten minutes from arriving.

Sam said, "I wonder if I can call them and see what's happening?"

"Try it."

Both Nick and Jen had their phones off. Wayne got an idea, "Try the earpiece on the closed circuit setting. Nick said these were satellite boosted and could transmit 50 miles."

Sam spoke, "Nick, Jen? Do you copy?"

Wayne glanced over after a minute. Sam shrugged. Suddenly he heard Jen's voice, "Jen."

Sam asked, "Are you guys at Darren's cabin?"

"Yes." Jen was whispering and Sam could barely hear her.

"Where's Nick?"

"He's under the floor of the cabin listening to their meeting. He can't talk."

Wayne said, "Ask her how many are there."

"I heard Wayne. Darren and four that came by helicopter. Jake's not here yet."

Sam said, "We'll be there in ten. Where do we park?"

Jen answered, "Our car's at the neighbors. Glad to have you join the party."

Sam checked his gun and reached into the back-seat for more ammo. "I've got a feeling this is going to get hairy."

Wayne turned onto a side road and pushed the accelerator. "Whatever makes you think that?"

Jen, Wayne and Sam could hear the sounds of men talking, probably through Nick's transmitter.

Voice #1: "This isn't what we normally do, Darren. I think you should answer some questions before Jake gets here."

Voice #2: "All you need to know is that the club will have a million dollars wired to the account later today. Don't tell me you don't have the stomach for this. I know better."

Voice #3: "So, as soon as he gets here, you're going to leave, right?"

Voice #2: "I need to be at the airport in 45 minutes. This is the plan. When Jake gets here I'm going to tell him I need to make our travel arrangements and that you guys are here to help him kill Stryker. As soon as I leave, kill Jake. Take his body out to the pond down at the south end and leave. Make sure you kill him before he calls Stryker. You don't need that complication."

Voice #1. "Can I ask why you want your brother dead?"

Voice #2. "I have my reasons."

Jen whispered to Nick, "Jake is their target?"

Nick whispered back, "Surprise."

Wayne glanced at Sam as they sped toward the cabin. "This is a twist I didn't expect. Darren is having Jake killed, not Nick."

Sam shouted, "Stop!" Sam had seen a small, white car ahead of them clear the rise of a hill. "Jake is right in front of us!"

Jen had heard the exchange between Wayne and Sam and moved to better cover. Minutes later a white Camry pulled in the dirt drive and parked in front of the cabin. Jake Billow stepped out and stood staring at the woods, right where Jen was.

Jen froze. She hoped nothing had given her location away. Jake turned, walked up the porch steps and entered the cabin.

Voice #2. "You're late, Jake." There was the sound of a chair scraping the wood floor. "I'm going to go firm up our travel plans. I don't need to watch you guys kill a cop."

Suddenly there was a lot of background noise and the sounds of rifles clacking.

Nick's voice broke through loud and clear. "There's a flaw in your plan, Darren."

Wayne looked at Sam, "What the...?"

Nick's voice again. "You're surrounded. There is no escape from this building." There was a slight pause. "I'm arresting all of you."

Jen rolled her eyes and smacked a bug on her neck. Surrounded? Hope he has a plan.

* * *

Wayne pressed the accelerator taking the turns on the dirt road at dangerously high speeds.

Sam hung on and yelled, "Go! Go!"

Wayne yelled, "I can't believe he just walked into the room with them!"

Sam yelled back, "And told them they were surrounded!"

The sun reflected a glint on the chrome of Nick's car.

Wayne yelled, "Hang on!" He twisted the steering wheel a hard left and ended up next to Nick's car.

Wayne and Sam jumped out and rammed their way through the tree line at a dead run. They finally saw the cabin in the distance.

Nick's voice said, "Any minute officers are going to knock on that door. You boys that flew in for the party better think twice. Jake and Darren are going down on murder. So far, you guys have only committed misdemeanors."

Wayne cursed at Nick under his breath. The cabin sat on a hill, still a distance away, and Nick had said they'd be knocking any minute. He glanced back at Sam. He was holding his own.

Nick watched as the men in camouflage fingered their rifles and glanced at each other. Darren spoke, "He can't kill all of us for God's sake. We have a deal! Shoot him!"

Nick stood in the doorway between the kitchen and the main cabin room. He had a M4 carbine in his right hand and his pistol in his left. It took strength and skill to shoot them both simultaneously with accuracy. Nick could.

Nick spoke to Darren without moving his head. "Correction, Darren. I can kill all of you, easily."

Nick said, "Lower your rifles and put your hands above your head. Now."

Nick could read the indecision in the men's minds. A loud pounding at the door convinced the men to lower their rifles and put up their hands.

Nick yelled, "Come in." He had his rifle pointed at Darren and his pistol pointed at Jake.

Nick saw Jake lean toward his rifle. "Now is not the time to be stupid, Jake. These men were hired by Darren to kill you, not me."

Jake snarled at Nick. "Lying cop."

One of the cuffed men yelled over, "It's true, dude."

Darren reached in his waistband, pulled out a pistol and pointed it at Jake. Darren started backing up from the group and grabbed Jake's jacket. He pulled Jake next to him. Darren's pistol was pressed against Jake's left temple.

"Back off! You'll never see your girlfriend again! Jake has her. Now, move away from that door!"

Nick walked straight toward Darren. "Lacey is safe, just another example of little brother's screw ups. You don't have the stomach to kill, Darren. Jake always did your dirty work, didn't he?"

Darren adjusted his stance. "I mean it, back off or I'll shoot."

Nick chuckled, "With the safety on?"

Darren glanced just long enough for Nick to land a kick to his side sending him backwards into the wall. Nick lunged and grabbed Darren's pistol. Jake turned to run from the building and was stopped by Jen at the threshold. Jen's pistol was aimed directly at Jake's head.

Wayne cuffed Jake while Sam and Nick cuffed the others.

Nick ordered all of the cuffed men to lay belly down in the center of the dirt drive.

Nick called Chicago PD for transport. Jen guarded the six cuffed men at gunpoint while Wayne and Sam helped Nick secure the weapons in the cabin. Nick examined the rifle that had been brought by Jake. He had little doubt that ballistics would prove this was the rifle used to shoot at Cummings. Meaning it was also the rifle used in the killings arranged by Attorney Baxter.

Nick smiled at Wayne. "Good thing you guys showed up, thanks."

Sam asked, "Did you have a plan when you just walked in the room with them?"

Nick answered, "I figured they wouldn't expect me to show up like that. I could tell from listening to them that the new guys weren't as committed to this as Darren thought."

Nick, Wayne, and Sam waited on the porch with Jen for the transport teams to arrive.

Jen winked at Nick. "Surrounded?"

One of the handcuffed men yelled over, "That's it? You had two men and a girl?"

Jen narrowed her eyes at the man. "Nick, tell me I can shoot him."

The four militia men were loaded into a single caged transport van. Nick waited until Jake and Darren were each secured in high security transport vans. He walked over, stepped inside Jake's van and sat across from him. Jake was chained at his ankles, waist, and chest. Each wrist was cuffed to an iron ring bolt.

Jake's expression was hard to read.

Nick really wanted to understand Jake. "You kidnapped Lacey to make this personal between you and me. Was your plan to get me angry and then confront me? That doesn't make sense Jake. You've always chosen weak victims or an unfair advantage with sniper shots. I bet it was Darren's idea to have his militia buddies help you when he heard what you had done. He knew you would lose in a fight with me. "

Jake was listening but making no comment.

Nick asked, "Did Darren tell you not to contact me until you got here?"

Jake remained silent.

Nick removed his earpiece from his ear. "This thing records. Let me play you a conversation."

Jake listened to Darren clarify that the real plan was to kill Jake. He heard Darren tell them to kill Jake before he called Stryker.

Nick shut off the transmitter. "Darren wanted to be sure you lost today. No more Jake, no more problems. You need help, Jake, and it won't be coming from Darren."

Jake raised one eyebrow and leaned forward as far as his chains would allow. "Lacey was my insurance policy. I'll get out again, you watch. You're right about Darren. He doesn't have the guts to kill. I do."

Nick could see the sickness in Jake's eyes. Sometime over the last five years he really had lost touch with reality. Darren saw it and used it.

Nick shook his head. "Maybe someday someone can help you get well again, Jake."

Jake spat at Nick as he left the van.

Nick walked over to the van Darren was in and entered. Darren was seething. "You don't have anything on me! I'll be out on bond before you have dinner tonight."

Nick leaned back, "Let me tell you a story, Darren. You started visiting Jake at Brookfield and figured out fairly quick what the weaknesses were of the facility. You saw a chance to come into some big money fast. Your business had failed, you lost your house, and having Jake made it easy. You could tell that Jake was losing what little sanity he had left in that place."

Nick continued, "You picked a night, had Jake kill everyone at Brookfield that could stop you and had Jake dispose of them in the crematorium. One by one, as people got in your way, you had Jake take them out. You used Dr. Elmhurst's credibility to steal from Brookfield and even sent Jake into the hood to find a buyer for the drugs. You never risked your own safety. Jake did all of the dirty work."

"Once your scheme was discovered, you decided Jake was a liability. You set it up so Jake would take the fall for everything and you would just disappear into the sunset. When did you decide to kill him?"

Darren leaned back and smiled. "You can't have all of the answers, Stryker. I'm going to be sure my defense team calls you to the stand. You make a good case for my insanity defense." Darren winked.

Nick got up and left.

Outside the van Nick walked over to Jen. "He's going for an insanity plea. He might get it."

Jen shook her head. "Watch them send him to Brookfield Place."

Nick looked at Jen. "Talk to Darren. Somewhere on this property there is a bunker or a root cellar. Something."

Jen asked, "What are you looking for?"

Nick answered, "Jake can't hurt women. He didn't rape or kill Lacey; he never even looked at her after he put her in the closet. He's never shot a woman cop." Nick whispered, "Where's Nancy Logan?"

Jen was stunned. "You don't think she was one of the bodies in the crematorium?"

Nick pointed in the dirt drive. "Those tire tracks are fresh and not from today. Look how many there are especially over by the tree line. He's been coming here a lot. She's here."

Jen watched as Nick said something to Wayne and Sam. They all turned and quickly disappeared into the heavily wooded property. Jen entered the transport van that Darren was in and asked him about bunkers or root cellars. Darren refused to answer any of her questions.

Jen went back outside. The minutes seemed like hours. How was Nick going to find a bunker in 80 acres?

Nick's voice came over her earpiece, "We've found something."

Jen yelled at the transport officers to stay put until she came back. She ran into the woods to find Nick. The spring thaw had left the underbrush thick with budding briars and swamp like puddles. The tree canopy was so thick that the sunlight could only peek through. Jen could only see a few feet in front of her.

She spoke into the transmitter, "Where are you?"

An arm reached out and grabbed her jacket sleeve. Jen's heart stopped.

It was Wayne, "Over this way."

Jen followed Wayne up a small incline where Sam stood next to a huge hinged metal lid. The lid had been camouflaged with brush. A hollow tree trunk camouflaged a large ventilation pipe.

Sam said, "I've never seen anyone track like Stryker. He was practically running. He's down there."

Jen leaned over the four foot diameter opening and saw the metal rungs of a ladder that led far below the ground. A dim light could be seen at the bottom coming in from an angle.

Jen looked at Sam, "Is there a tunnel?"

Sam shrugged.

Nick's voice came through their earpieces. "Yes. There's a tunnel, we've got three women down here. We need EMTs now!"

Jen was calling Control Central for the EMTs when the sounds of gunfire erupted from the direction of the cabin.

Wayne said, "Nick, we've got gunfire."

Nick answered, "Wait for me."

Seconds later Nick joined them. "Jen, help the women." Nick motioned back toward the cabin. "Militia guys had a recon crew. I should have expected that. They planned to be picked up. There are probably at least two vehicles, heavily armed."

Wayne said, "There're only four transport cops there now."

Nick, Wayne and Sam ran for the cabin. Jen lowered herself into the slimy cavity.

Sam and Wayne fanned out to provide the transport cops additional cover while Nick worked his way behind the militia attackers. Since the militia men had made the decision to attack officers, the rule now was to use deadly force.

Nick got a vantage point behind the shooters; he was almost back at the street. There were two SUVs blocking the drive with shooters using the driver doors as cover. Nick saw flashes coming from the tree line from at least two more shooters. He shot the two men at the SUVs and ran into the brush for the others.

Into his transmitter he said, "I shot two at the street, now approaching shooter in west hedge. Take out shooter making his way down the east tree line."

Wayne looked over to the east tree line. He didn't see anyone there. Soon a slight movement of brush revealed a shooter poised to fire. Wayne shot him. Sam saw the back door of the first transport van opening. One of the militia men must have gained entry through the front and passed the keys to the men in the back. Sam fired as soon as the back of the van was completely open. One man fell to the dirt drive, motionless. The remaining militia men shouted "Don't shoot," and raised their hands in surrender.

Wayne saw Nick walking into the clearing, a man in camouflage walking in front of him with his hands in the air. The shooting had stopped. Nick called

Control Central and asked for additional EMTs, patrol and a few coroner wagons.

Nick, Wayne and Sam helped the transport officers secure the militia men that had almost been set free. The transport officers had held their own considering they were outgunned. The only officer badly wounded had been driving the first transport van.

Nick had the first EMT unit that arrived divide their staff to help the wounded officer and head into the woods with Sam to get the women. Wayne and Nick moved the SUVs from the driveway entrance to allow for the additional traffic that would soon be arriving. Wayne took pictures of the fallen militia men before Nick dragged their bodies to the edge of the driveway.

The first EMT van left with the injured officer. Nick directed the staff of the second EMT van to run into the woods to help Jen with the women. The wails of approaching sirens screamed from all directions.

The coroner stepped out of his van and walked up to Nick. "Good morning."

Nick replied, "Good morning."

The coroner smiled, "You run out of grenades?"

Jen and Sam helped a woman walk out from the woods. Four EMT men carried two transport cots with the other two women. Nick and Sam ran over to help.

One EMT looked at Nick and said, "They wouldn't have made it much longer down there."

The woman standing next to Jen looked frail and sickly, but her eyes were alert.

Jen said, "All three women are nurses from Building D. Nick, meet Nancy Logan."

❊ ❊ ❊

Thursday noon

Frankie pulled his car into the storage unit and closed the overhead door. He opened his trunk, took out a folding chair and sat next to the freezer. He read the morning paper, did half of the crossword puzzle, and sighed. "I do miss you."

Frankie stretched out his legs in front of him. That head had been with him for decades. To him, it was more than just a trophy. It was almost a friend.

"You know, things have really heated up lately. I've decided to buy a little house I found in New Buffalo, Michigan. You'll like it. I gotta do something with all of that cash in my mattress anyway."

Frankie stared at the freezer. "I'll buy it this weekend and get a guy I know to build you your own little room. I'll tell him it's a wine cellar." Frankie laughed at his own joke. "Wait a minute, if I get arrested, they'll find you if you're above ground. Maybe I should bury you before he pours the cement floor. Yeah, I'll bury you before he pours the floor."

Frankie stood and left the chair next to the freezer that happily hummed away. "That's what I'm gonna do. New Buffalo has a new casino, did you know that? I can go play table games, eat at the buffet and go to shows." Frankie took a deep breath. "Time the two of us got out of Chicago."

Frankie raised the overhead door, pulled his car out, locked the door again and drove away.

Sophia watched him from her parking spot across the street and then pointed her car to drive back to the city.

* * *

After the transport team arrived, Nick, Jen, Wayne and Sam all met at Cubby's for lunch. There was going to be a mountain of reports to fill out on the day's activities. They all agreed that tomorrow would be soon enough to start them.

An alert from Control Central posted to their phones: the 10-24's murderer had been caught by the homicide team of the 107th.

Wayne said, "Jeff Turner's funeral will be in a few days."

Jeff had been Billow's last victim. A bright, young cop with the 107th, fresh out of the academy, his life ended with a sniper bullet. There was silence as each of them thought about his widow and two young children.

Nick looked at Jen. "You're the one that broke this whole case. You did all the research and follow

up on Billow. I was busy with Phillips and the mob."
Nick smiled at Wayne and Sam. "You guys put the
twisted pieces together somehow and showed up as
the cavalry. I'd say we make a good team."

Sam stood to leave. "Good team or not, when the
coroner finishes identifying the bodies in the crematorium, there will be more funerals. The safeguards
don't work anymore."

Nick said, "The safeguards are gone. They've
been sold. Our elected officials think they're too
expensive."

Jen stood to leave. "But they can spend billions
to get elected to office. I don't get it."

Agent Phillips walked in just as they were leaving.

Nick smiled, "You just missed lunch."

Phillips asked, "You got time to sit while I eat a
burger?"

Jen volunteered to ride with Wayne and Sam.
She looked at Phillips, "I'm going home to sleep.
Please don't give him any more hot leads today."

Phillips laughed and he and Nick took stools at
the end of the bar. Phillips asked how it went with
Jake and Darren. Nick gave him a blow by blow
account of the arrest. Nick asked Phillips what was
happening between the Northside and Westside
mob crews.

Phillips finished his burger and smiled. "These
guys are job security for me. There's always something going on."

Nick said, "I thought the mob had mostly died
out except for some of the old timers."

"That's what they want everyone to think. Since 9/11 the Bureau has raped our budget of personnel and funds to work on mob business. Terrorism is the flavor of the month. The truth is, the mob is growing stronger every day filling that void. We just don't have the manpower to keep up."

"It doesn't sound like Mom's coming home too soon."

"She's working a short list. She might surprise you." He grinned and Nick nearly asked him if he knew more than he was saying.

Nick said, "I think I have a case on Frankie Mullen, the old mob hit man. I can tie him to the hits that were arranged by Attorney Baxter and to my dogwood blossom."

"Let's let that sit a while. Those victims aren't getting any more dead. Mullen is on my list, too."

Nick chuckled. "Speaking of your list, now you have to find Milo Spulane's body? Good luck with that. He's going to be another Hoffa."

Phillips twisted his stool to scan the room. Satisfied it was empty of curious ears he said, "We've had Hoffa since 1975 when he went missing. Well, most of him. Someone kept a trophy. We find the trophy, we find his killer."

List of Characters for Twisted:

Cops:

Nick Stryker	Chicago Homicide Detective, 107th Precinct
Jen Taylor	Chicago Homicide Detective, Nick's partner
Wayne Dunfee	Chicago Homicide Detective, 107th Precinct
Sam Flores	Chicago Homicide Detective, 107th Precinct
Steven Phillips	FBI Agent, assigned Chicago Special Cases
Agent Miller	FBI Agent assigned to track down rumor about Artie and blue cooler

Secondary characters:

Martin Stryker	Nick's dad
Lacey Star	Nick's girlfriend
Kamber Fry	Lacey's niece
Chad Wilson	Film student that befriends Kamber
Momma	Owns sandwich/ news shop
Mitch Jordan	Momma's son, half owner of sandwich shop
Eli Johnson	Mitch's friend, engineer for the City
Renee Johnson	Eli's sister, RN works at Brookfield Place

Tyler Goodman	Administrator at Brookfield, Building A
Nancy Logan	R.N. at Brookfield Place (missing)
Ryan	Works at Brookfield Place
Marcus Newberry	Patient at Brookfield Place
Sirus Corn	Homeless man
Dr. Edmund Elmhurst	Administrator of Building D at Brookfield Place
Dr. John Bates	Physician at Brookfield Place
Joseph	Self-appointed mayor of underground community
Jake Billow	Confined patient at Brookfield Place
Darren Billow	Jake Billow's brother

Mobsters (Crew):

Dominick Guioni	Westside Crew boss, (nickname Dom)
Milo Spulane	Northside Crew boss
Frankie Mullen	Semi-Retired mob hit man
Artie Corsone	Retired mob 'document' man, friend of Momma
Travis Cummings	Investment banker for Mob
Atty. James Baxter	Attorney for the mob
Joey Lacastra	New York mob hit man borrowed by Westside crew
Tommy Albergo	Old mobster just out of prison
Anthony Jarrett	Old mobster just out of prison

Other books by the Shallow End Gals:
Alcohol Was Not Involved, book one of trilogy
Extreme Heat Warning, book two of trilogy
Silent Crickets, book three of trilogy
Catahoula

Nick Stryker Series
Cusp of Crazy
Twisted

41143676R00199

Made in the USA
Lexington, KY
05 June 2019